SINGAPORE IS a good house in a bad neighborhood.

Three hundred million Muslims live in Indonesia and Malaysia completely surrounding the barely five million people living in the secular city-state. Islamic terrorism in Asia may not get much attention in America or Europe, but it gets plenty in Singapore.

They've been hit once already. Not long ago, coordinated truck bombs laid waste to three American hotels in Singapore. Thousands were killed and injured. And everyone knows it's just a matter of time before Singapore gets hit again.

Abu Suparman is the messianic leader of a radical group of Indonesian Muslims fighting for ISIS in Southeast Asia. Most people think Suparman was personally responsible for the Singapore hotel bombings. When Singapore receives a tip that Suparman is slipping into the country to meet a sister having cancer surgery, Inspector Samuel Tay gets the job of finding him before something nasty happens.

It seems at first to be a straightforward assignment. Tay is given two officers to work with him: his own sergeant, Robbie Kang, and Sergeant Linda Lee, a capable officer with whom Tay once had a disastrous and blessedly brief personal relationship. All they have to do is keep the sister under surveillance until she leads them to Suparman, right?

But things go bad. Really bad.

The surveillance turns into a shambles, people die, and Suparman vanishes. Tay's only clue to what really happened that rainy night on Serangoon Road is a girl he briefly glimpsed watching it all from a window in the building next door.

Tay's quest for the girl in the window takes him on a terrifying journey into a no man's land where there are secrets so big governments will kill to protect them. With the help of John August, a shadowy American who has murky connections with international intelligence agencies, Tay battles governments determined to bury the truth and unmasks politicians who are using their power and position to hide their own crimes.

Tay is going to get a little justice for Singapore.

If he can just stay alive long enough to do it.

WHAT THE PRESS SAYS ABOUT JAKE NEEDHAM

"Jake Needham is Asia's most stylish and atmospheric writer of crime fiction." – **The Singapore Straits Times**

"In his power to bring the street-level flavor of contemporary Asian cities to life, Jake Needham is Michael Connelly with steamed rice." – **The Bangkok Post**

"Jake Needham's books have been successful in seriously irritating the powers that be in Singapore to the point where his newest books are no longer available there. In general, if a government openly or surreptitiously bans a book or a writer it means that they are worth reading. It really is a very strong *BUY THIS* signal." – **Libris Reviews**

"Jake Needham is a man who knows Asia like the back of his hand." – **The Malaysia Star**

"Needham certainly knows where a few bodies are buried." – **Asia Inc.**

"Jake Needham has a knack for bringing intricate plots to life. His stories blur the line between fact and fiction and have a 'ripped from the headlines' feel. Buckle up and enjoy the ride." – **CNNgo**

"Mr. Needham seems to know rather more than one ought about these things." – **The Wall Street Journal**

"What you will not get is pseudo-intellectual new-wave Asian literature, sappy relationship writing, or Bangkok bargirl sensationalism. This is top class fiction that happens to be set in an Asian context." – **Singapore Airline SilverKris Magazine**

"For Mr. Needham, fiction is not just a good story, but an insight into a country's soul."– **The New Paper (Singapore)**

THE GIRL
IN THE WINDOW

BOOKS BY JAKE NEEDHAM

THE INSPECTOR TAY SERIES

THE GIRL IN THE WINDOW
THE DEAD AMERICAN
THE UMBRELLA MAN
THE AMBASSADOR'S WIFE

THE JACK SHEPHERD SERIES

THE KING OF MACAU
A WORLD OF TROUBLE
KILLING PLATO
LAUNDRY MAN

OTHER NOVELS

THE BIG MANGO

THE GIRL
IN THE WINDOW

An Inspector Samuel Tay Novel

Jake Needham

Half Penny Ltd
Hong Kong

Ebook edition ISBN 978-616-7611-28-0
Trade paper edition ISBN 978-616-7611-27-3

English-language publication history

First edition, ebook: Half Penny Ltd, Hong Kong, 2016, ISBN 978-616-7611-28-0
Second edition, trade paper: Half Penny Ltd, Hong Kong, 2016, ISBN 978-616-7611-27-3

For Aey.

Always, for Aey.

No matter how paranoid or conspiracy-minded you are,
what the government is actually doing
is worse than you can possibly imagine.

—William Blum, US State Department, retired

This ain't the Garden of Eden
There ain't no angels above
And things ain't what they used to be
And this ain't the summer of love

— Blue Öyster Cult

1

THE APARTMENT WASN'T very big and it wasn't very appealing. Just once she would like to walk into a suite at a Four Seasons rather than one of these shabby, ramshackle places with decades of unhappiness and despair soaked right into the walls.

The front door opened into a living room that was slightly longer than it was wide. She turned on the air-conditioner and listened to it wheeze and rattle until it finally caught and began slowly filling the room with tepid air. Then she took stock of her surroundings.

The living room was furnished with a brown tweed sofa, a rectangular coffee table, and a faded, threadbare rug that might once have been green. The couch sagged in the middle and the table was made of some nasty-looking synthetic material trying without the slightest success to imitate mahogany. A small dining table with a glass top and a couple of straight-backed wooden chairs occupied one corner and a tiny Pullman kitchen occupied the other. Across the room a tattered shade bleached white by the sun covered a double-hung window.

She closed the door behind her and threw the dead bolt. Dropping the two small bags she was carrying on the sofa, she went straight to the window, and lifted one side of the shade. It wasn't a view anyone was likely to put on a postcard, but the view was the reason she was there.

The apartment was on the third floor at the southeast corner of the building and it looked straight down into Serangoon Road. She had an unobstructed view along the road for at least a quarter of a mile. That might be useful later, but what mattered now was off to her left.

The Fortuna Hotel was just on the other side of a small cross street called Owen Road. It was a modest tourist hotel with fewer than sixty rooms on its five floors and from the window she had a clear view of the entrance to the lobby. She smiled. This might be the easiest job she had ever done.

She dropped the shade and went to check out the rest of the apartment. It didn't take her very long.

The small bedroom was dingy, and a lumpy-looking double bed stripped of linens almost filled it. She didn't bother to go in. She could see the crusty-looking stains on the mattress from the doorway.

She put her head in the bathroom and was relieved to see it appeared to be reasonably clean, at least it did if she didn't look too closely and she certainly wasn't going to do that. The bedroom didn't matter. She had brought a sleeping bag and had no intention of going near the bedroom. The bathroom was another thing altogether.

She might be here for two or three days. A clean bathroom was a big deal.

She went back to the living room and began unpacking her two small leather valises. The first held her sleeping bag, a half dozen bottles of water, a box of peanut butter PowerBars, and a few apples and bananas. On the bottom were three pairs of clean underwear and two shirts. She left the clothes in the valise and tossed the sleeping bag on the sofa, but she carried the food and water over to the round table in the corner and spread it around so she could tell at a glance what she had left.

The second valise contained her equipment: a pair of Steiner tactical binoculars with a built-in rangefinder; a Sig-Sauer nine millimeter with two extra magazines; two burner phones; a plastic jug of bleach and a wad of rags; and of course her Remington Defense CSR bolt-action sniper rifle which was frequently called the rucksack rifle because of the ease with which it could be broken down and concealed. She loved the rucksack rifle. It was rugged and accurate and it fired the 7.62mm NATO sniper round. She thought of it as nine pounds of pure ballistic badassery.

It took her less than forty-five seconds to put together the rifle's five components, check the action, and slide the Leupold & Stevens scope onto its mount. She snapped the AAC quick release suppressor to the muzzle and laid the rifle on the couch.

The only part of setting up that turned out to be difficult was getting the window open. It would really have been something to have to call off the whole operation because she couldn't open the damned window. Christ, they would never have let her live that one down. But she pushed and struggled and slammed the frame with the heel of her hand and eventually it opened.

She moved the window up and down a couple of times to make certain it would open again when she needed it to, but then she quickly closed it again. Singapore's air was thick, heavy, and wet. Breathing it was like trying to inhale warm Jell-O. Every single time she was in Singapore she wondered exactly the same thing: why did human beings choose to live in a place with such a crappy climate?

She pushed the sofa table against the wall near the window and stood back to examine its position with a critical eye. She nudged it a foot to the left, then a few inches back to the right. After she had it positioned exactly the way she wanted it, she laid out phones, the binoculars, and the Sig so that all three were within easy reach. After that, she dragged two of the straight chairs over in front of the window, raised the shade, and pushed the two chairs around until she had them lined up correctly. Then she sat down in one and put her feet in the other.

Whoever picked the apartment had done a good job. From where she sat, she could see both the main entrance to the Fortuna Hotel and an emergency exit next to a Western Union office on Serangoon Road. She hardly even had to move her head.

When she was satisfied with everything, she picked up the Steiner binoculars, leaned back from the window to prevent the lenses from flaring with a burst of sunlight, and took a closer look at the entry to the hotel lobby. There was just a single pair of glass doors level with the sidewalk. No steps, no ramps. A piece of white paper was taped to the door on the left. Somebody had handwritten on it *Use other door.*

She hadn't seen anyone at all go in or out of the lobby in the fifteen minutes or so she had been in the apartment. Maybe the hotel didn't even have enough traffic to make it worthwhile to unlock both doors. All the better for her.

She touched the binocular's rangefinder button and the red LCD lit up. The lobby doors were ninety-seven meters away.

Ninety-seven meters.

She could make that shot with the nine. Well, probably she could make it with the nine, but downhill shots were tricky with a handgun. Although the distance wasn't too bad, the firing angle from the third-story window would alter the bullet drop and that would make her change her normal hold for the distance. The shot wouldn't exactly be automatic, not even for her. Which really didn't matter, she supposed, since she wasn't going to try it that way.

That was why she had the Remington and why the Remington had a box magazine loaded with ten rounds of long-range MK 316 frangible cartridges, a 175-grain round designed for long-range sniping.

She wouldn't need ten rounds. She wouldn't even need two. One round was all that would be necessary.

Ninety-seven meters amounted to point blank range with the Remington. With the Remington, the shot would be automatic. With the Remington, she could make the shot with her eyes closed. But she wasn't going to try it that way either.

2

LESS THAN TWO miles away from the apartment overlooking Serangoon Road, a white Toyota idled in a *No Standing* zone on Orchard Boulevard.

Inspector Samuel Tay had been passing a pleasant afternoon browsing the stacks of the Kinokuniya bookstore that occupied a large part of the top floor of the massive Ngee Ann City shopping mall when his telephone rang. The Toyota was waiting for him. He had to go back to work.

Tay opened the Toyota's passenger door and got in. Sergeant Robbie Kang handed him a large Styrofoam cup with a Coffee Bean and Tea Leaf logo printed on the side.

Kang had long black hair and a fair complexion. He was tall and gangly for a Singaporean, and he wore his usual short-sleeved white shirt, the button-down collar open at the neck, with a pair of dark chinos. The heavy black frames of his glasses were slightly crooked on his narrow face.

Neither man spoke. For his part, Tay had nothing to say. Kang simply knew what was good for him.

Kang waited for a break in traffic, signaled, and eased the car slowly out into Orchard Boulevard. Several years back, he had taken a speed bump a little fast when Tay was in the passenger seat with a cup of coffee. The necessity of driving cautiously when coffee was present had been indelibly imprinted on Kang's memory ever since.

As Tay watched Singapore sliding by outside the passenger window, he thought about how much he had once loved the city. He wanted to love it like that again, but he doubted he ever would.

When he had been a young man, Singapore was a magical place. The streets were wide and uncrowded, the people warm and unhurried, and the hot tropical winds riffled the palm trees with a whispering sound that infused the very air he breathed with almost intoxicating feelings of romance and allure.

Sam Tay had loved his city then with a sentimentality so unrestrained it now embarrassed him to think about it. But somewhere that love had quietly stolen away and left him all alone. Ever since, he had been asking himself the same two questions nearly every day.

What the hell had happened to his city?

And what the hell had happened to *him*?

He had as yet found no satisfactory answer to either question.

Tay suddenly realized Kang was driving in the direction of the Singapore River.

"Please don't tell me the body's in the river," he said.

"Yes, sir. It is."

Tay groaned.

"They say it's probably been in there for two or three days," Kang added.

Tay groaned louder.

A corpse that had been fished out of the Singapore River after two or three days in the water?

Dear God.

Having not much liked the answer to the only question he had asked so far, Tay asked Kang nothing else. He went back to sipping his coffee and staring out the window, and he tried very hard not to think about what he was thinking about.

7

Kang crossed the river on Saiboo Street, turned right into Mohamed Sultan Road, and almost at once pulled into a driveway leading to the loading bays of two of the nearly identical-looking buildings which lined that part of the river.

Tay eyed the buildings as Kang drove toward them. They were all seven or eight stories high and constructed mostly of gray-brown granite and glass. He had always thought of this as a particularly featureless and depressing part of the city, but he never remembered it looking more featureless and depressing than it did right at that moment.

Kang stopped in the driveway behind two fast response cars, shut off the engine, and looked at Tay.

"Do you want to hear about this now, sir?"

Tay said nothing. He tilted his coffee cup up to his mouth and was disappointed to discover it was empty.

What he really wanted was a cigarette. He hadn't taken his cigarettes when he went to Kinokuniya because he knew he couldn't smoke there. There was hardly anywhere in Singapore they did let you smoke anymore, of course, other than at home. The people who ran the city, the bastards, had long ago banned smoking in public. Tay figured it was only a matter of time before the little pricks tried to ban it in private as well.

Kang cleared his throat. "I'll take that as a yes, sir. They didn't tell me very much when they called us out. Nothing at all about the cause of death, not even whether the deceased is a man or a woman. They just said a body had been found hung up on a drain outlet underneath the Alkaff Bridge."

Of course it had. Tay had always hated the Alkaff Bridge and he could already see this wasn't going to do anything to change his mind about it.

The Alkaff Bridge wasn't even much of a bridge. It was only a narrow pedestrian walkway that would have been ignored by everyone if he hadn't been for one thing. In what had apparently been a desperate effort to brighten up the neighborhood, some urban planning genius had decreed that it be painted in bright pink, iridescent blue, and puke green with scribbles all over it which looked like drawings done by a kid who had flunked out of kindergarten.

The whole undertaking had been a disaster. Not only did the bridge look hideous, but the neighborhood was so bleak almost no one ever walked across it anyway. What Singapore got for all the money it had poured into the project was a pedestrian bridge that was both ugly and useless. Chalk up another one for the boneheaded bureaucrats who dictated nearly every detail about the appearance of his city.

They got out of the car and Tay looked around for a place to dump his empty coffee cup. There was a trash barrel not more than ten feet away. Of course there was. That was one thing for which you could always count on the bureaucrats of Singapore: trash barrels.

After tossing his cup away and wiping his hands on a handkerchief, Tay turned slowly in a full circle and examined the area where they were parked.

"The river is this way, sir," Kang said, pointing helpfully between two buildings.

"I know where the river is, Sergeant. I was looking for somewhere you could get me more coffee."

"Ah."

Ah, indeed.

"There might be a place up at Robertson Quay, sir, but that's about ten minutes away."

"A nice afternoon stroll along the river will be most invigorating for you, Sergeant. Off you go now."

Tay wasn't in any hurry. Whoever he had come to see wasn't going anywhere. He shifted his weight from one foot to the other and reflexively patted his pockets for cigarettes. When he remembered he had just checked and he didn't have any, he sighed heavily, leaned back against the car with his arms folded, and idly followed Robbie Kang with his eyes as he walked toward Robertson Quay.

When he was being entirely honest with himself, Tay sometimes wondered why Kang had stuck with him so loyally all these years. He could be a shit and he knew it, but that never seemed to bother Kang, at least not in any way he could see. They had worked together for nearly five years now, and Tay had to admit that Robbie Kang's unswerving loyalty was probably more than he deserved.

A lot of people underestimated Kang, Tay knew, but he was not one of them. People looked at Kang and saw a vanilla man living a vanilla life, but Tay knew Kang had a madness hidden deep within him. There were days on which Tay wished he could find the same kind of madness somewhere in his own soul.

Kang disappeared behind a building and Tay gave his pockets another delusory pat in the hope he might have overlooked some cigarettes, but of course he hadn't. He was always promising himself he would quit smoking some day so maybe this was a sign. Maybe this was the day for him to deliver on that promise.

Who was he kidding? He was about to examine a dead body that had been in the river for several days and he was wondering if this might be a good time to quit smoking?

He was plainly becoming delusional. Doubtless driven out of his mind by a nicotine deficiency.

3

THE SINGAPORE RIVER isn't much of a river. It certainly doesn't bear any resemblance to the Thames, or the Seine, or the Hudson. It's narrow and shallow and except for the occasional sightseeing boat it doesn't even carry maritime traffic now.

Years ago, caught up in one of the fits of governmental sprucing up that periodically sweeps over Singapore, the entire channel of river was cemented and the banks closed off with railings. Tay thought all that tidying had left the Singapore River looking more like a big drainage ditch than a river, and he was pretty sure that's what most visitors thought it was anyway. Maybe instead of the Singapore River they should just call it the Singapore Ditch and be done with it.

A hundred years ago, the river had run through a tough and gritty dock area. Fleets of lighters called bumboats shuttled back and forth from there to the sailing ships anchored offshore loading cargoes of rubber, rice, and jute bound for Europe. When containerized cargo put an end to the bumboats, the government decided to turn the river into a tourist attraction. They claimed they wanted to protect its historical charm, but of course Tay knew full well they wanted to do no such thing. What they really wanted was to create a cleaned up, idealized version of Singapore's history, one that might cause future generations to forget about what the reality of it had been.

After a resolute scrubbing, the whole area around the river had been turned into an attraction that might have been constructed by Walt Disney. The crumbling warehouses were rebuilt and repainted in bright, cheerful colors, and the pathways between them were tiled and edged with perfectly matched palm trees. Stylish restaurants and bars now filled the old buildings, their tables spilling out under groves of palm trees that were crisscrossed with strings of white fairy lights. Most of the places were crowded almost every night, clogged with local yuppies, Australian tourists, and Caucasian expats.

Sometimes Tay felt like he wasn't living in a real city now at all, but a Potemkin village populated with Potemkin people. No, that wasn't really fair. Tay knew there were some real people in Singapore. Robbie Kang, of course, and…well, he was sure there were others, too, even if no names came readily to mind.

When he figured he had stalled as long as decency allowed, Tay sighed heavily, pushed himself away from the car, and set off walking in the direction of the Alkaff Bridge. He eyed the dark clouds gathering on the horizon. Maybe it would rain later, or maybe it wouldn't. Either way Tay knew the humidity would leave him so drenched in sweat that it wouldn't make any difference. When you were outdoors in Singapore, you got soaking wet whether it rained or it didn't.

There was an appropriately ominous silence all around until he got close to the river and heard the cackle and crack of a radio in the distance. His colleagues had as usual been almost frighteningly efficient. They had already erected a small shelter about ten feet square at the near end of the bridge that was made out of a scaffolding of metal poles covered by blue plastic sheeting.

Uniformed patrolmen had sealed off the scene both on the bridge and along the promenade. They were there to keep spectators away, of course, but they didn't have much to do. There weren't any spectators.

This wasn't a neighborhood in which people hung around outside, chatted with their neighbors, and congregated at the site of distasteful events. There was another reason no spectators were around, too, one which applied almost everywhere in Singapore, particularly in places where there was police activity. Singaporeans minded their own business when authority was present. They had a gift for not seeing unpleasantness, or at least pretending not to see it, even when it was right there in front of them.

Tay couldn't see what was in the blue plastic tent from the direction he was approaching it, which he supposed was the whole reason for having it there in the first place. But he knew full well what was waiting for him.

Soon enough he would have a fine, close-up view.

When Tay approached the tent, the patrolman in front of it snapped off a salute.

"Good afternoon, Inspector," he said. "It's nice to see you again, sir."

Tay didn't remember ever encountering the young patrolman before and he had decidedly mixed feelings about being recognized by someone he didn't know. While everyone's ego twitched a little at discovering a stranger knew who he was, anonymity had its advantages, too. And given a choice between a twitching ego and those advantages, Tay would choose anonymity without the slightest hesitation. If it were left up to him. Which, of course, it wasn't.

"Better watch your footing, sir."

The young patrolman pointed at the paving stones covered by a thin film of water, probably from dragging the body out of the river. Yes, Tay thought, he would be careful. Falling on his ass before he even got to the body would only extend his fame within the department. As far as he was concerned, he was more than famous enough already.

"Do you have any cigarettes, patrolman?"

When Tay saw the alarmed look on the young man's face, he had to smile. Clearly a senior officer had never before asked the kid for a cigarette. Now that one had, he had no idea what to do.

"Uh…what do you mean, sir?" the patrolman stammered.

Tay lifted a hand to his mouth and mimed himself smoking a cigarette. "You know."

The kid cleared his throat and shifted his eyes nervously from side to side.

"I don't smoke, sir."

"No, of course you don't."

The patrolman hesitated. He looked away as if he was suddenly engrossed in studying a building on the other side of the river, but he leaned his whole body back toward Tay.

"If you want, sir," he murmured out of the corner of his mouth, "I'm sure I could find—"

"That's all right," Tay interrupted. "Let's just get on with whatever we've got here."

Clearly relieved to be back on more comfortable ground, the patrolman reached for the flap covering the front of the tent, but he didn't open it.

"This one's a bit of a mess, sir," he said. "They figure it was hit by one of those tourist boats that work this part of the river. Not much left below the waist."

Wonderful, Tay thought to himself, *just wonderful. Where's my damn coffee?*

He glanced down the promenade in the direction of Robertson Quay, but Kang was nowhere in sight.

As subtly as he could, Tay took a couple of deep breaths as a precaution against nausea and nodded to the patrolman. The man pulled open the flap and Tay walked inside.

4

"GOOD AFTERNOON, INSPECTOR. I had no idea I was going to see you today or I would have worn something a little more fetching."

Dr. Susan Hoi was a pathologist at the Centre for Forensic Medicine and Tay had first met her a couple of years back when he was trying to identify the body of a western woman murdered in a room at the Singapore Marriott. It had never occurred to Tay he would see Dr. Hoi today either. If it had, he would probably have broken into a trot in the opposite direction. Their last encounter had been a source of acute embarrassment for him and he had been doing his best ever since to avoid having another one.

Dr. Hoi began making her personal interest in Tay unmistakable almost as soon as they met. She even went so far as to tell him she had off-the-record information to pass along to him from the autopsy of the woman found at the Marriott and asked him to meet her for a drink at Harry's Bar in Boat Quay. When he got there, she confessed she didn't have any information at all. She had only said she did, she admitted, to get Tay to meet her at Harry's Bar.

Tay had been avoiding the woman ever since, but now in spite of his very best efforts here he was alone with her inside a little blue tent. At least they were alone if you didn't count the dead body at their feet. Turning and fleeing wasn't really a practical response to those circumstances no matter how unhappy Tay might be about them, although he did give the possibility one brief moment of consideration. So Tay stayed where he was. Sometimes life just screwed with you and there was nothing you could do about it.

"I've never seen you out in the field before," Tay said, looking for safe ground.

"They're starting to send me out quite a lot. Do you think it's a promotion?"

Tay wasn't sure so he merely bobbed his head and tried to appear as if he were considering the question thoughtfully.

Susan Hoi was a looker, no doubt about that, and a stylish one. The first time Tay met her was on a day she was cutting up dead bodies and she was wearing a little black dress and pearls. Her hair was black with highlights that appeared almost red, and she kept it cut short and shaped tightly to her head, which gave her an air of professional crispness Tay had to admit he rather liked. Eye color was something Tay seldom remembered, but the celadon green of Dr. Hoi's eyes was impossible to forget. He could recall the first time they had met how her eyes seemed to gleam as if they were illuminated from within.

Tay just wished she hadn't been so forward. It had made him jumpy as hell and he had reflexively taken off in the opposite direction. Then again, he knew he usually found a reason to take off in the opposite direction whenever he met a woman who showed interest in him, didn't he? He supposed that explained why, at fifty, he still lived alone. Sometimes he asked himself if he was going to live alone for the rest of his life, but he didn't spend a lot of time thinking about it anymore. He was pretty sure he knew what the answer to that question was.

This afternoon Susan Hoi wore a tight pair of low-slung jeans and a man's white shirt with the sleeves rolled above her elbows.

Tay thought her face looked drawn and tired, and at a glance she appeared older than her thirty-five or so years. For once Tay's brain worked faster than his mouth and he very sensibly kept that thought to himself.

Tay made a throat-clearing noise to underscore that the personal part of the conversation was over, brief as it might have been, and the time had come to get on with business.

"So what have we got here?" he asked.

For the first time he glanced down at the corpse and he instinctively recoiled.

It was the body of a man dressed in khaki shorts and a white t-shirt, but below the bottom of his shorts most of the man's left leg and part of his right leg were gone. Shreds of flesh hung from each stump like clumps of dangling vines. The corpse's arms were intact, but the fingers were shredded away to the bone. His chest was dented and misshapen and his face had been cut off. The man's shoulders were broad and well developed and Tay could tell he appeared to be in pretty good shape. Apart from being dead and having his legs ripped off, of course.

"Yes," Dr. Hoi said when she saw Tay's reaction. "He's a real mess. It looks like a boat propeller tore him up. And of course the crabs have gotten to him."

Tay involuntarily glanced over his shoulder in the direction of the river.

"Don't worry, Inspector," Dr. Hoi laughed. "Nothing you eat in Singapore came out of *that* water."

Tay's nodded slowly.

"You look a little green, Sam."

Tay took a deep breath and nodded again. He kept his eyes well away from the corpse laid out on the plastic sheeting at their feet.

"Maybe we should talk outside," Dr. Hoi suggested.

Tay didn't even bother to nod. He just turned and pushed out through the flap of the tent.

They stood together at the concrete wall that ran along the river. Tay leaned on his forearms against the top of the wall and contemplated the dirty brown water creeping past. It looked sticky, and it flowed like maple syrup.

Susan Hoi reached into a back pocket of her jeans and produced a crumpled pack of Marlboros with a book of matches tucked inside the cellophane wrapper. She shook out a cigarette and offered it to Tay. He could have thrown his arms around her and hugged her, but he had the presence of mind to know that was probably a terrible idea. So he just accepted the cigarette with a small nod.

"I didn't know you smoked," he said.

Dr. Hoi shook a cigarette out for herself and struck a match, touching it first to Tay's cigarette and then to her own.

"That's exactly what you said the last time you saw me with a pack of cigarettes, Sam. You do remember *something* about me, don't you?"

This can go nowhere good, Tay thought, so he drew on his cigarette and said nothing.

"How much do you smoke, Sam?"

"I don't know. A few a day. Maybe half a pack."

"Nonsense. I'll bet you're a pack a day man. Sometimes probably two."

Tay raised and lowed his shoulders in a small shrug.

"Has anyone ever told you that smoking is a symptom of a self-destructive personality, Sam? Do you have a self-destructive personality? Is that who you really are?"

"Thanks for the cigarette," Tay said, ignoring Dr. Hoi's personal question. "You have officially saved my life. Now all I need is coffee and the world will be right again."

"Right behind you, sir," Sergeant Kang responded exactly on cue.

Tay turned to find Kang holding two large Starbucks cups.

"What is that?"

"It's coffee, sir. I found a Starbucks down in Shell House."

"You know I don't like Starbucks."

"Drink it, sir," Kang said, holding out one of the cups. "You can pretend Starbucks isn't American."

Tay hesitated, and then he abruptly reached out and took both cups from Kang.

"Sir, one of those was for—"

"Thank you, Sergeant. Dr. Hoi and I are very appreciative."

Tay turned his back on Kang and handed one of the Starbucks cups to Dr. Hoi. Then he took her by the elbow and tugged her along the promenade until they were more or less alone again. He popped the top off his coffee, laid it on the wall, and drank deeply.

Dr. Hoi laughed. "That wasn't very nice."

"I'm the inspector and he's the sergeant. That's how it works."

"Jesus, Sam, I'm glad *I* don't work for you."

Tay shrugged. He drew on his cigarette and drank more coffee. He could feel the caffeine and the nicotine building up nicely in his bloodstream. In another minute or two he would be back to normal.

"Okay," Tay said, trying to assume his most professional tone of voice, "tell me what you've found so far."

"A badly mangled body without a face and not a lot more."

"Any guess yet as to how long it's been in the river?"

"A while. Three days? Maybe longer."

Tay waved a hand at the river. "You're telling me a body floated around out there for at least three days and nobody noticed it?"

"Shit happens," Dr. Hoi shrugged. "Life goes on. Nobody cares."

"Jesus," Tay muttered, "aren't you cheerful today?"

"It's the wrong time of the month. You want cheerful? Call me next week."

Tay cleared his throat and looked away. He admired honesty in a woman, he really did, but only to a point. This was past that point.

19

"Anything about the body that would help us with an ID?" he asked, keeping his eyes on the river. "Tattoos? Birthmarks?"

"Nothing."

"I suppose an ID card would be out of the question."

"If he had a wallet, it's in the river now."

Tay peered at the dark water and shook his head. "We can forget about finding it down there."

"And since we can't get any prints for you, doing an identification isn't going to be easy."

"What do you mean you can't—"

Suddenly Tay remembered and he stopped talking. You needed fingers to get fingerprints, and the corpse's fingers had been eaten away by crabs. He sucked up some more nicotine and took another hit on his coffee. It helped. A little.

"Anything on the cause of death?" Tay asked.

"It's early days."

Tay gestured at the river. "Do you at least know if he was dead before he went in, or did all the shit in that water poison him?"

"He was probably dead before he went in."

Tay nodded.

"I'm reasonably certain the gunshot wound in the back of his head would have been fatal."

Tay was just taking a puff on his Marlboro and he choked on the smoke.

"Gunshot wound?" he coughed.

"Nine millimeter, I think. I can't be certain until I get him back to Block Nine and open him up, but I don't think there's much doubt about it."

"You can't be serious."

"You said that the last time I brought you a gunshot wound," Dr. Hoi smiled. "I feel like we just keep having the same conversations over and over again, Sam."

Tay and Dr. Hoi had a case together once before that involved a gunshot wound. At first, Tay hadn't believed her then either because firearms were rarely used in homicides in Singapore. He had seen hundreds of stabbings and beatings, but in his entire career he had seen less than two dozen gunshot deaths. Guns simply were not part of the culture in Singapore.

"I didn't expect that," Tay said.

"Neither did I. Somebody shot and dumped in the Singapore River? That's one for the books."

Tay's eyes drifted away to the young patrolman who had recognized him when he arrived. The boy looked so young and eager, and Tay couldn't help but wonder how many misshapen lumps of flesh he would have to encounter before all the freshness was gone from his eyes. With his thumb and forefinger, Tay flicked his cigarette butt into the river.

"Shame on you, Inspector Tay," Dr. Hoi said. "That's exactly why the river is so dirty."

"With all the crap that's already in there, one more cigarette isn't going to make any difference."

"I expected you to be a big supporter of improving Singapore's environment, Sam, knowing your strong social consciousness."

Tay sneaked a look at Dr. Hoi's face. Surely she was joking, but he couldn't tell for sure so he said nothing.

Dr. Hoi dumped her own cigarette butt into what was left of her coffee and Tay listened to it sizzle as it hit the liquid. He stared at the surface of the river, struggling to wipe from his mind the image of that mangled lump of flesh inside the blue plastic tent not twenty feet away.

5

THEY CLEARED THE crime scene quickly since it wasn't really a crime scene. Nothing had really happened there. Somebody dragged the man's body out of the river by the Alkaff Bridge, but he hadn't been killed there. It seemed unlikely the body even went into the river there. Almost certainly it had drifted for a distance before it became wedged underneath the bridge, but they had no idea yet how far.

The location to which they had been called was only a place where a lump of flesh almost unrecognizable as a human being lay on a patch of straggly grass underneath a blue plastic tent. Tay hated looking at it like that, but that was simply the way it was.

When they got back in the car, Kang took Mohamed Sultan Road out to River Valley Road

"Where to, sir?" he asked as they pulled up to the corner.

The hard white light of Singapore was beginning its daily metamorphosis into the gentle twilight that was Tay's favorite time of day to sit in his garden and smoke a Marlboro or two. His desk was reasonably clear, and what could he do about the body in the river with whatever was left of today anyway? Until they knew who their corpse was, or at least who their corpse used to be, he couldn't do much of anything. Would the autopsy turn up something to help with the identification? It seemed doubtful, at least not without a major stroke of luck. Tay pictured the corpse's fingertips gnawed away by crabs and shuddered slightly. Without fingerprints, it was going to be a struggle, and he doubted Dr. Hoi would produce an autopsy report for a day or two anyway.

The more he thought about it, the more obvious the answer to Kang's question became. Shuffling papers back at the Cantonment Complex would be even more pointless today than it usually was. And it was almost always completely pointless.

"Drop me at home, Robbie. Then go home yourself. I don't see what else we can do today."

Kang nodded and turned left.

They drove in silence for a while, but then Kang shot a glance at Tay and cleared his throat.

"There's something I want to talk to you about, sir. It's…uh, personal."

Tay shifted his eyes toward Kang. This didn't sound like anything he wanted to hear. It really didn't.

"You see, sir…well, it's like this. Lar and I are having a baby."

For a moment, Tay had absolutely no idea what Kang was talking about. He heard all the words Kang said, of course, but he couldn't immediately arrange them in any way that made sense. Then he suddenly remembered: Lar was what Kang sometimes called his wife whose real name was Laura.

They were having a baby? Why was Kang telling him about it?

Kang had been Tay's sergeant for eight or nine years now, but Tay knew next to nothing about Kang's personal life. He had only met Laura once, or was it twice? How long had she and Kang been married? Tay had no idea. Did they have children already? He was pretty sure they didn't, but he wasn't absolutely certain.

Tay liked Robbie Kang, and he relied on him and trusted him, but he couldn't honestly say they were close friends. Well…he supposed the truth was that he didn't have any close friends. He attached no significance to that. He certainly didn't feel like it was a personal failing. It was just the way his life had worked out.

"And here's the thing, sir," Kang rushed on before Tay could decide how he was expected to respond to Kang's announcement. "Lar thinks our baby should have a godfather and…well, I was wondering, sir, if you would do that."

"Do what?" Tay asked, baffled once again as to what Kang was talking about.

"We'd like you to be the baby's godfather, sir. That is…if you're willing."

"*Me?*"

"Yes, sir."

"You can't be serious, Robbie."

Tay flinched at how clumsy he had been to put it like that and was immediately embarrassed. He shot a quick look at Kang.

"What I meant, Robbie, is I can't think of anybody on earth less suited to being a godfather than I am. It's very nice of you to ask me, but surely you can find someone who would be a much better choice."

"I don't think so, sir. We think you'd be great."

"Robbie, you're forgetting I don't like children. And children don't like me."

"I think you're exaggerating a little there, sir. And besides, you don't ask someone to become a godfather to play with your kid. A godfather is someone a child can rely on as it grows up, someone you know your child can count on no matter what happens to you. And there isn't anyone we would trust more with our child than you, sir. Lar and I both feel that way."

Tay was speechless. He had always been awkward in dealing with praise, not that he'd really had all that much practice at it, and Kang's sudden declaration that he wanted to entrust his child to him left Tay totally flummoxed.

He just stared out the window and said nothing. He really didn't know what to say.

"Sir?" Kang prompted after the silence had stretched out to a point at which it became awkward. "Will you do it?"

"No one has ever asked me to do anything like this before, Robbie, and I just don't know what to say." Tay cleared his throat. "Let me have a day or two to think about it, will you?"

"Take all the time you want, sir. I just want to say Lar and I would be honored if you would accept."

They rode in silence after that. Tay couldn't imagine what Kang was thinking, but he hoped his hesitation hadn't caused any offense. Tay simply didn't know what to make of any of this.

When they were out on the street going about their business as police officers, Tay trusted Kang absolutely, but beyond that how well did they really know each other? They had certainly never reached the point where they confided in each other in a personal sense, and Tay knew they never would. That wasn't Robbie's fault; it was his. He simply wasn't someone who felt comfortable confiding in other people.

What's more, he really couldn't picture himself as the godfather to some little kid. What if he didn't even *like* the kid? Or the kid didn't like *him*? What would he do then?

He would think about it for a couple of days, but he really couldn't see it. He just couldn't. He didn't want to hurt Kang's feelings when he turned him down so he would have to come up with an excuse of some kind. Maybe he could tell Kang he was dying of some horrible disease. No, that was clearly a stupid idea. Still, it was a step in the right direction.

Tay looked around to see where they were. From here, Kang would have to take the long way around to get into the part of Emerald Hill Road where he lived. Tay loved his neighborhood, but sometimes the warren of one-way and dead-end streets that protected it from the rest of the city was a real nuisance. The only way in to Emerald Hill Road from the south was either to drive far to the north and circle back or to walk in from Orchard Road.

When Tay was coming from this direction in a taxi he usually told the driver to drop him off on Orchard Road. It was less than a hundred yard walk from there through Peranakan Place, up into the bottom of Emerald Hill Road, and straight to his front gate.

"No need to go the long way, Robbie. Just drop me on Orchard Road."

"It's no bother, sir."

"I have to go to the Cold Storage anyway. I'll only need to walk back later."

Tay had tossed out the business of going to his local market as an excuse so he wouldn't have to argue with Kang about where to drop him off, but the moment the words were out of his mouth he remembered he had nothing at home for dinner and he certainly didn't feel like going out to a restaurant. He was still carrying around in his head the image of that mangled mass of tissue and bone lying in the little blue tent, and now he needed to figure out how to extricate himself gracefully from this godfather business.

With those two things banging together in his head, he would far rather be at home eating alone in his garden than out at some restaurant surrounded by people he didn't know and probably wouldn't like if he did.

6

IT WAS TOO late for the housewives and too early for the after work crowd so the Cold Storage Market wasn't very crowded.

Tay squatted down to reach the bottom shelf in aisle four and picked up a jar of Skippy Creamy Peanut Butter in one hand and a jar of P28 High Protein Peanut Spread in the other. He had barely begun pondering their respective merits when images of the corpse hauled out of the Singapore River began coming back to him again.

Most people who lived in Singapore had no idea what went on in this city. Singapore was clean; Singapore was orderly; Singapore was safe; Singapore was a nice place to live. At least that's what you said if you didn't know what the cops knew. If you did know what the cops knew, you would have to take a shower about three times a day.

Tay supposed the truth was that most people didn't *want* to know what the cops knew. They complained about all the things people who lived in most cities complained about, but they didn't want to think about what lived under the rocks. Under the rocks was where the maggots were, and the maggots were every working cop's life, day in and day out.

Why would Kang and his wife want to bring a child into this sort of world? It was none of his business, Tay knew, but he couldn't help but wonder.

Tay sometimes thought that was why he had never married. Never even had a real girlfriend, not really. He would go out to dinner with a woman and try to find a way to tell her he had almost been stabbed that afternoon, and she would be talking about all the trouble she was having getting her apartment repainted. A guy tries to sink a six-inch knife into your chest, and in the evening his dinner date wants to talk about how difficult it is to get exactly the right shade of green.

Tay gave up thinking about it and went back to contemplating the two jars of peanut butter he was holding.

The P28 High Protein Peanut Spread looked as if it were something he ought to try. Protein was good for him, wasn't it? So surely *high* protein would be even better for him. He had regular conversations with himself about the benefits of exercise. Maybe that extra protein would be just what he needed to spur himself on to do something other than have those conversations.

He did ride a bicycle for a few months. Well, to be entirely truthful he had ridden it two or three times and those two or three times were spread out over several months. Even that had been a while ago now and the only exercise he got these days was carrying his shopping home from the Cold Storage. He should be exercising a lot more, he told himself, but every time he thought about exercise he got a mysterious urge for a cigarette. And after he sat for a while and smoked his cigarette, the idea of engaging in vigorous exercise inevitably struck him as entirely inappropriate.

Tay shifted his gaze to the Skippy Creamy Peanut Butter in his other hand. He had bought Skippy for years and never noticed it to be lacking in protein. A peanut was a peanut, wasn't it? All that stuff about high protein on the P28 label was probably just bullshit. These days every food product was high-something or low-something. He didn't understand half of it and was sure nobody else did either.

Tay glanced at the prices on the two jars, saw that Skippy was half the price of the P28, and that settled it. He shoved the P28

High Protein Peanut Spread back on the shelf, lurched to his feet, and heard his knees crack. He had turned fifty not long ago and sometimes he felt every year of it. Getting old was shit.

He selected a loaf of bread, a quart of vanilla ice cream, a couple of steaks, and packages of frozen carrots and peas. Then, overcome by guilt, he went to the produce section and picked out a head of iceberg lettuce, a few tomatoes, and a cucumber. Having a salad with his steak would be good for him, wouldn't it? Of course it would, he told himself, so he grabbed the first bottle of dressing he saw and headed for the checkout counter. He didn't even bother to read the label.

Walking home with his groceries, Tay passed a bar called Number Five that was just down the road from him. It had a scattering of tables out front and as the last of the day drained into twilight it looked like such a pleasant place to sit and have a drink that he considered stopping.

Before he had made up his mind, two women and a man, all of whom appeared to be in their twenties, swept past him and took over the last empty table. The women wore shorts and sandals with skimpy tops and they laughed loudly and talked with her hands and tossed their manes of long, shiny black hair while the guy nodded and smiled, no doubt amazed at his luck in being the object of both women's attention.

Enjoy it while it lasts, kid, Tay thought to himself. *Because I'll bet you it doesn't last very long.*

Tay lived on Emerald Hill Road, a quiet dead-end street in a sleepy neighborhood of classic row houses. It was an area steeped in dignity and tranquility, yet it was barely a hundred yards from busy Orchard Road. Tay's house was a three-story structure with a tiny front garden surrounded by a high wall of white-painted brick. In the back, through French doors from his living room, was another garden, this one surrounded by an even higher brick wall.

When Tay got home, he dumped his groceries in the kitchen

and got a bottle of John Powers Irish whiskey out of his small liquor cabinet. He had developed a taste for Irish whiskey a year or so back at the same time he developed a taste for a Dublin-born woman he met while standing in line at a bank. He no longer had a taste for the woman, but he still had a taste for the whiskey.

He poured a couple of fingers into a heavy glass tumbler, added a little water from a pitcher in the refrigerator, and went looking for his cigarettes. When he found them, he kicked off his loafers, walked out through the French doors in his stocking feet, and settled down at the teak table where he ate when the weather wasn't too hot.

Tay took a slow pull on his whiskey. When he shook a Marlboro out of the pack and lit it, he tilted his head back and watched the smoke rise in the air. The evening was still and the smoke lingered around him like the breath of banished ghosts.

Tay had always loved dusk. It enveloped him in a calm as velvety as the nuzzle of a cat's nose. Out over his garden wall, just above the roof of his neighbor's house, he watched the green lights winking from the top of the Orchard Gateway Building to the south. After he reread *The Great Gatsby* a few years back, those green lights took on new meaning for a while, but it hadn't lasted. It was simply too difficult to coax the same romance out of aircraft warnings lights on the roof of an office building that Scott Fitzgerald had coaxed out of that green light at the end of Daisy's dock.

Perhaps, Tay thought, that was why he was such a misfit in the modern world. He treasured stillness; he sought tranquility; he glimpsed eternity in the mundane. Yet he lived in an age that had little regard for any of those things. Perhaps he should have become a Buddhist monk instead of a policeman, but what could he do about that now?

One thing he could do was sit and enjoy his cigarette and his whiskey in the twilight without fretting over the sorry state of mankind.

And that was exactly what he was doing some fifteen minutes later when the bell at his front gate rang.

7

SHE MADE TWO trips to the bathroom and once she got up to get herself another bottle of water and a PowerBar, but other than that she had been sitting almost immobile in the same straight chair for nearly eight hours now. She had been shifting her eyes continually back and forth between the entrance to the lobby of the Fortuna Hotel and the emergency exit on Serangoon Road, but she had seen nothing of any value to them.

They hadn't given her any photographs of the target, only a sketch that could have been almost anyone, but she did have pictures of the woman the target was meeting and they were a lot more useful. She had been counting on someone calling and narrowing down the time frame a little to limit the chance of misidentification, but now she realized there weren't enough people going and coming from the hotel for that to be an issue.

If it hadn't been for one bald, middle-aged guy, the hotel wouldn't have had any business at all the whole time she had been sitting there. She spotted him the first time about three hours ago when he entered the lobby towing a Chinese-looking girl in a very short skirt who couldn't have been a day over twenty. An hour or so later, they left. A couple of hours passed and then, to her complete disgust, the same man returned with another girl. She thought this one looked Thai and was even younger, but she wasn't certain about that.

For some reason, she started thinking of the guy as the German. It wasn't that he looked German; she didn't even really know what that meant. Maybe this guy was American or South African or maybe he was from Iceland, but she still kept thinking of him as the German. She supposed whether the guy was a German or not didn't really matter. Either way, watching an overweight, sweaty foreigner going and coming from a hot sheet hotel with a succession of hookers who looked like children got on her nerves.

The second time the German left with his hooker, she picked up the Remington and followed him through the scope. She kept the crosshairs on his head until he flagged a taxi on Serangoon Road and got into the back seat. She told herself she was only checking the sight lines and the lighting and gauging the downward angle of the shot she might eventually be called on to make, but she knew that was only part of the reason she followed the German through the Remington's scope.

She had half decided. If nothing else happened and the fat bastard came back again with another of his kiddie hookers, she might shoot *him* just for the fun of it.

One of the burner phones suddenly erupted with the sound of a rooster crowing. She wished someone would check the default ringtone on these things before they put them into service. She really did. A simple trill or even, well, a *ring* would have been fine. The sound of a crowing rooster, on the other hand, was completely obnoxious.

Reflexively, she noted the time when she answered: 6:17pm.

"We have nothing for you yet," said a male voice she didn't recognize. "We have no additional information on either the fox or the rabbit."

The target had been designated as the fox and the target's sister, who was supposed to be coming to meet him at the Fortuna Hotel, had been designated as the rabbit. She thought these childish code names were downright silly, but she guessed it was all part of being one of the fellows so she let them play their little-boy spy games without arguing about it.

"Have you seen any indication that the fox is in the area?" the man asked.

"Negative. Not unless he's disguised as a fat German who likes young hookers."

There was a pause, as she expected.

"Say again?" the man asked.

"Never mind. Forget it. What was your question? Oh wait, I remember. Uh...negative. No sighting of the fox."

"Is it possible you missed him?"

"You do know I'm here by myself, don't you? I eat a little. I even pee occasionally, and I did take one dump. So, sure, I guess I could have missed him. If you wanted to be absolutely certain I didn't miss him, maybe you shouldn't have tried to run this deal on the cheap and come up with the budget for a full team."

"This is a closely held operation, hunter."

That was how they had designated her: hunter.

Fox. Rabbit. Hunter. These were sharp guys. Tough, hard-nosed professionals. The best she had ever known at what they did. But their creativity was for shit.

"We have eyes on the rabbit," the man continued, "and she has made no move toward your location."

That wasn't a problem for her. She was used to this kind of thing. She could sit for days on a surveillance, almost unmoving, waiting for a target to appear. She had trained herself to sleep in ten and fifteen minute bursts. She had once gone for four days waiting for a target, lying on wet leaves under a Ghillie blanket and peeing on the ground. In comparison to that, this apartment was heaven. She was dry and comfortable; she had an actual bathroom; she was sitting in a real chair; the air-conditioner worked. She could wait indefinitely.

"I understand," she said.

"What is your plan, hunter?"

"To sit very still and not pee any more than I have to."

Sometimes the target appeared; sometimes the target didn't appear. It didn't really matter to her. Her job was to take the target if he did appear, not worry about whether or not he would.

"Maybe the rabbit will flush him," the man added.

These ridiculous codes always somehow ended up weaving themselves into narrative absurdities, but for some reason nobody ever laughed. *Maybe the rabbit will flush the fox.* What a stupid thing to say. Perhaps she ought to laugh this time just for the hell of it. No, this humorless prick wouldn't understand and then she would have to explain why she was laughing. She couldn't be bothered.

"So what do you want me to do?" she asked instead. "If she doesn't flush him, I mean."

"It's your call, hunter. I have no instructions for you on that."

"I could always shoot the sister. I mean, why not? Otherwise all this was just a waste of time."

Another pause. She listened to the man breathing and said nothing.

"Are you trying to be funny, hunter?" he eventually asked when the silence had stretched almost to the breaking point.

"If I am, I gather it's not working."

She listened to the man clear his throat. It was not a pleasant sound.

"Stay alert, hunter. We don't think the fox will appear until the rabbit moves, but you can never be certain."

She said nothing.

"Did you hear me, hunter?"

"Of course I heard you. I just thought your comment was too dumb to be worth a reply."

"You'll be notified if the rabbit moves or if I have further instructions for you. And one more thing…"

"Yeah?"

"Don't fucking shoot the sister."

8

TAY THOUGHT OF the Senior Assistant Commissioner in charge of the Criminal Investigation Department as a politician and a paper shuffler rather than a real policeman. The SAC certainly didn't make a habit of getting out in the field. In fact, Tay was fairly sure he had *never* seen the SAC anywhere other than inside the Cantonment Complex.

Tan Kim Leng wasn't even Tay's direct boss. Tay worked for the Deputy Assistant Commissioner who ran the Special Investigations Section of CID. The SAC was his boss's boss. The Singapore Police had a lot of ranks. A lot of ranks gave the bureaucrats more opportunities to keep people happy.

All of which was why, when Tay opened his front door, he was surprised to see the SAC ringing the bell at his gate. And why he went out to open the gate enveloped by an overwhelming sense of foreboding.

The body in the Singapore River wasn't just another floater or the SAC himself wouldn't be ringing his doorbell a few hours after he got home from the scene. It had to be somebody awfully important to bring the SAC out in person rather than simply delivering whatever message he had to deliver over the telephone. But how could the SAC even know whose body they had when no one else seemed to have any idea?

This couldn't be good, Tay thought to himself. It really couldn't.

"Good evening, sir. This is quite a surprise."

"Yes, Inspector, I suppose it must be."

To Tay the SAC looked more like a professor at a not very prosperous college than he did a policeman. He was small and slim and altogether unremarkable in appearance. This evening he wore the only thing Tay had ever seen him wear: a white, short-sleeved, wash-and-wear shirt open at the neck that was tucked into dark wash-and-wear slacks. His glasses were rimless and inexpensive looking and they sat high on his long, thin face.

Tay led the SAC up the walk and into his house. Neither of them spoke until they were inside.

"Can I get you something?" Tay asked when he closed the door. "Coffee?"

"Do you have any whiskey?"

In spite of his best efforts, Tay was fairly certain he gaped in surprise. Could this be merely a social call? Surely not. He and the SAC were always professional, even cordial, but he would never describe their relationship as friendly. Tay had certainly never socialized with the SAC. Of course Tay never socialized with anyone at all, not really, but the point was he had never had any relationship with the SAC other than a strictly professional one entirely confined to the interior of the Cantonment Complex.

"Certainly, sir. Is Irish whiskey all right?"

"That's fine, Sam. Neat, please, if you don't mind."

Tay pointed to the French doors. "I was just having a drink in the garden myself. Why don't you go on out and make yourself comfortable and I'll get that whiskey for you."

The SAC glanced around Tay's living room and through the paned windows of the French doors into the garden.

"You have a nice house, Sam."

"Thank you, sir."

"A very nice house."

Tay gathered he was being nudged into explaining how a policeman could afford such an expensive house in a neighborhood like Emerald Hill. Everyone wondered, but most people were too polite to ask straight out.

"Did I hear somewhere that you inherited money?" the SAC asked while Tay was still making up his mind exactly what he ought to tell him.

"Yes, sir. From my father."

"He was American, wasn't he?"

"Ah...yes, sir. He was."

Tay couldn't see where this was going, and that made him a little edgy. What was the SAC going to ask him next? But the SAC didn't ask him anything next. He just nodded once, walked to the French doors, and let himself out into the garden.

In the kitchen, Tay poured a couple of fingers of John Powers into another heavy tumbler, hesitated, then added a little more whiskey to the glass. He made himself another drink, too. Something told him he was going to need it.

Tay served the drinks and sat down opposite the SAC. "I only left the scene a couple of hours ago, sir. I'm afraid there's not much I can tell you yet about—"

"I'm not here about your floater, Sam."

For moment Tay felt a great sense of relief, and then suddenly he didn't. The SAC had shown up at his house unannounced and now he was sitting here drinking Tay's whiskey and looking grave. Whatever he had to say, it was serious, probably more serious than anything to do with the body they fished out of the river would have been.

The SAC hesitated and looked off into the distance over Tay's garden wall to the lights in the hotels and shopping malls that lined Orchard Road. He sipped at his whiskey, then he took a deep breath and let it out.

"I received a telephone call this morning from a friend who is a high-ranking officer in the Indonesian National Police," the SAC said. "He runs their intelligence division."

Tay nodded.

"I trust him, Sam."

Tay nodded again.

"He told me they have information Abu Suparman is either already in Singapore or soon will be."

Tay stopped nodding.

Singapore is a good house in a bad neighborhood. Three hundred million Muslims lived in Indonesia and Malaysia completely surrounding the barely five million residents in the tiny secular city-state. Islamic terrorism in Asia may not get much attention in America or Europe, but it gets plenty in Singapore.

Abu Suparman called himself a Muslim cleric, but nearly everyone else thought of him as a violent, remorseless murderer. Suparman was Indonesian and he had been linked with nearly every outbreak of sectarian violence in Southeast Asia for over a decade. He was the messianic leader of a radical band of misfits who styled themselves as jihadists and took credit for every outrage perpetrated against non-Muslims in Indonesia or Malaysia or anywhere else in Southeast Asia.

Sometimes Jemaah Islamiah claimed the credit. Sometimes it was Abu Sayyaf or Mujahidin Indonesia or even occasionally Lashkar Jundullah or the Moro Islamic Liberation Front or the Legion of the Fighters of God. But regardless of the name they used, you could bet Abu Suparman was somewhere in the mix. He had vowed years before to bring about the destruction of all the governments in Southeast Asia and the establishment of a regional Islamic caliphate governed by Sharia law. And exactly how did he intend to do that? Simple. By killing as many non-Muslims as he could as well as any Muslims unlucky enough to get in his way.

Singapore had avoided the worst of it for a long while. In the rest of Southeast Asia, the outrages were as regular as clockwork.

Suicide bombings in Bali; attacks on the Marriott and the Ritz Carlton in Jakarta; the kidnapping of foreigners in the Philippines; and a succession of beheadings in Southern Thailand. But in Singapore, all people knew of those things was what they read in the *Straits Times*. Asia's gleaming city-state was untouched by the terrible brutality and violence that plagued its neighbors.

Until it wasn't.

Tay had been in his garden when terrorists launched simultaneous bomb attacks on three American hotels on Singapore's most famous and most expensive thoroughfare. He heard the explosions at the Hilton, the Hyatt, and the Marriott. He felt the concussions as they rolled through the earth.

When Tay ran out of his house to do whatever he could to help, he was caught in the secondary explosion the terrorists had set to kill as many of the rescuers as they could. If he hadn't stopped next to an abandoned bus to stare at the thirty-story tower of the Singapore Marriott, cleaved exactly in half as if it had been sliced straight through by a giant ax; if he had not taken a couple of steps backward in an involuntary retreat from the horror in front of him and stumbled over a tattered mattress blown down into the road; if he had not fallen across the mattress and up against a disabled bus, Tay would have died there and then.

He would never forget the powerful pressure wave that blew a rolling wall of flames across what was left of Orchard Road. The very oxygen in the air ignited. The sudden release of gas, heat, and light made Tay feel as if the world were ending.

For many, it did.

This fourth bomb collected the thousands of shards of broken glass the first three explosions had created and hurled them back through the air like a cloud of razor-edged knives. Rescue workers caught out in the open were shredded. Most of them had to be identified through DNA tests since nothing was left of their bodies large enough for anyone to recognize. The heavy rubber tire behind which Tay had fallen had protected him. It was all that had saved his life.

Tay had wondered about that a lot since then. He had been spared by his own clumsiness while those less bumbling were sliced into pieces by flying glass and bled to death on the debris-littered pavement of Orchard Road. Each time he thought about it, he became angry all over again at the whimsy and fickleness of the uncaring, unjust universe in which such injustices were permitted.

The ruins were still smoking when Abu Suparman issued a statement through Jemaah Islamiah taking credit for the attack. There was, of course, no way to tell for certain if Suparman was involved or not. Tay had heard whispers the explosions were strictly a domestic matter, an attack on the rigid establishment that had governed Singapore from its very beginnings as an independent country, but no one wanted to say that right out loud so putting the blame on Suparman at least made conversation easier. When the security establishment laid the bombings at Abu Suparman's extremely convenient doorstep, everyone nodded and that was that.

Terrorist attacks in Singapore? Had to be foreigners, didn't it? No Singaporean could possibly be responsible. Singaporeans all loved their country and their government, didn't they?

Ever since the day the savagery had finally come to Singapore, regardless of who was really responsible for bringing it, the police and the Internal Security Department had been on high alert. Lunatics tried to blow up Singapore once and everyone knew they would try again, and then again, until they were hunted down and killed. Abu Suparman was number one on everyone's list of most wanted men, but as far as Tay knew no one even had any idea where he was.

Not until now.

"Most of these Asian whack jobs used to claim an affiliation with al Qaida, but al Qaida has gone out of style." The SAC looked at

Tay as if he wanted to make sure Tay was paying attention, and Tay went back to nodding. "These days Abu Suparman says he's connected to the Islamic State, ISIS. Maybe he thinks ISIS sounds more sinister, more threatening, more violent. Maybe it really is. We're not sure, but we do know ISIS has rekindled terrorism in Southeast Asia after years of decline. There have been at least two thousand Southeast Asians in Iraq and Syria fighting for ISIS and some of these people are back now. They are well trained, battle hardened, and ready to fight."

"But, sir, what does this—"

"The threat of ISIS in Southeast Asia is real, and the threat to Singapore is real," the SAC said. "We've got to cut the head off this snake before it bites us again, and Abu Suparman is the head of the snake."

The SAC tossed back the rest of the whiskey and put the glass down.

"I'd just tell you to get out there, find the bastard, and arrest him, but it's not going to be as easy as that. The Internal Security Department got the same intelligence I did, but they got it a week or two ago. That's why my friend called me. He knew ISD wasn't going to tell us a damn thing about all this and he thought I should know."

Tay doubted that was the real story, but he nodded anyway. Perhaps the SAC's source in Indonesian intelligence really *was* a friend doing him a favor. In Tay's experience, however, few things about relationships between international law enforcement agencies were that simple. Could Indonesia have another motive for leaking information that would push Singapore's police force into a tug of war against its Internal Security Department? Of course it could.

"Here's what I know, Sam. Suparman has a sister who has been diagnosed with cancer. She is coming to Singapore for an operation this week and there is intelligence that Suparman will try to meet her somewhere here in Singapore before her operation since there is a risk she will not come through it. ISD is putting her under surveillance while she is in the country in the hope she will lead them to Suparman. I spoke to the Minister of Home Affairs this morning. I told him I know about what ISD is planning and I demanded CID be included in it. He agreed."

The SAC looked at Tay. Tay wasn't certain how he was supposed to react to that so he just nodded again. That must have satisfied the SAC because he started talking again.

"The Minister made it clear ISD is in charge of this operation. I think that's a mistake. If ISD gets their hands on Suparman, they'll tuck him away somewhere under the Internal Security Act and we'll never see him again. This bastard is a criminal, Sam. I want him hanged."

All at once Tay understood exactly why the SAC was sitting in his garden drinking his whiskey instead of talking to him on the telephone. There were some things you didn't talk about on the telephone in Singapore. There were a great many such things if you knew what was good for you, but without a doubt the first topic on nearly anyone's list of things not to talk about on the telephone in Singapore would be exactly the same.

The Internal Security Department.

9

THE SECURITY ESTABLISHMENT in Singapore is ferociously efficient. The police are the visible part of that establishment, but the Internal Security Department is the part of it that really scares the crap out of most Singaporeans.

Officially, ISD is an intelligence agency that collects whatever intelligence is required to protect Singapore against threats to its internal security such as espionage, terrorism, and subversion. Unofficially, ISD is a sort of Singaporean secret police.

ISD is officially acknowledged to exist, but that's all most of the public really knows about it. It doesn't appear in the Singapore Government Directory and it cultivates an air of mystery Tay always thought downright laughable. Even the name of the Director of ISD is an official secret. Tay was willing to bet he could find out who the current director was easily enough, but he didn't care enough to try.

Under Singapore's Internal Security Act, ISD has extraordinary powers to detain people more or less indefinitely without charges, and it is not reluctant to use those powers. In real democracies, people are justifiably horrified when they hear about security agencies that can arrest anyone they like and hold them without charges for however long they want. Singaporeans seemed to accept ISD secret detentions as an everyday part of government.

Maybe that meant Singapore wasn't much of a democracy. Funny, Tay thought, how few people seemed to notice that.

Tay didn't much like either the Internal Security Department or the people he knew there. He had been forced to work with them a few times in the past and it wasn't an experience he wanted to repeat. The little pricks just rubbed him the wrong way. They were smug, they were arrogant, and they treated the police like cops were good for nothing but manual labor.

Tay picked up the pack of Marlboros he had left on the table and put it down again.

It was his garden, of course, and even in Singapore he didn't need to ask anyone's permission to smoke in his own home—not yet, at least—but the whole idea of lighting a cigarette in front of a senior officer seemed so peculiar he couldn't quite bring himself to do it.

"If the Minister told you ISD is in charge of this operation," Tay asked, clasping his hands together in front of him to prevent them from making another grab for the Marlboros, "what part is CID supposed to play?"

"The Minister said he was concerned the operation could touch on domestic issues like people who might be sheltering Suparman, and he thought CID ought to be available in case issues not related to the Internal Security Act come up. He also said the first order of business was locating Suparman, and he thought a better chance of doing that existed if ISD and CID worked together."

"And what happens if we do find him, sir?"

"That's a good question. I just don't know what the answer to it is. I suppose we'll cross that bridge when we come to it."

Tay didn't much like the sound of that. A public tug of war between ISD and CID over taking control of Abu Suparman, assuming they could even cooperate enough to find him, would be unseemly at best, humiliating at worst. Especially if it ended badly for CID.

"I'll keep pushing the Minister, Sam, but he's not a man who likes to make difficult decisions. You'll probably be on your own if you do find Suparman. You'll just have to figure it out then."

Tay didn't mind being on his own. The truth was he rather preferred it. Better to ask for forgiveness, as the saying went, than to ask for permission.

On the other hand, he couldn't exactly see how the SAC imagined this would play out. Say they spotted Suparman in this joint surveillance operation. What then? Did ISD and CID race each other to see who got to him first? Did ISD and CID shoot it out over who would control the prisoner? Tay didn't see any way this would end well unless the Minister made a firm decision before they found Suparman.

"I could always just shoot the bastard, sir."

The SAC pursed his lips and looked thoughtful.

"I was only kidding, sir."

"Were you? Too bad."

Before Tay could decide what to say to that, the SAC pointed to his empty glass. "Another one would be very welcome, Sam. We have more to talk about."

Did they? Tay wondered what that could be. The SAC had already deputized him to fight a war against ISD for control of a notorious international terrorist. What came after that? Taking on the Prime Minister, too? But he didn't say any of that, of course.

What he said was, "Yes, sir. Coming right up."

When Tay returned with the SAC's drink, he brought another one for himself as well. They sat in silence for a few moments, each man sipping his drink and sorting through his own thoughts. Tay gave up worrying about what the SAC might think and shook out a Marlboro from the pack on the table. He lit up without apologizing, but the SAC didn't seem to care. He didn't even appear to notice.

"I want you at New Phoenix Park at nine o'clock tomorrow

morning, Sam. There is a briefing at ISD then about the surveillance operation. The Minister has agreed to include you and your officers in that briefing and ISD will be expecting you."

New Phoenix Park was the heavily secured compound of the Ministry of Home Affairs located on the north side of the city. The compound housed the general headquarters of the Singapore Police as well as the headquarters of ISD and some other law enforcement agencies supervised by the Minister of Home Affairs such as the Immigration and Checkpoint Authority and the Civil Defense Authority. The Cantonment Complex where Tay had his office housed only CID and the Central Narcotics Bureau.

A group of buildings off to itself in the back of the compound was ISD's operating base. All glass and concrete, the buildings were structures so humorless and overblown Tay always believed they would have embarrassed Albert Speer. It was inside those imperious looking buildings that ISD did whatever it was it did, and Tay wasn't at all sure he even wanted to know what that really was.

"ISD is expecting me specifically, sir?"

"Yes, you specifically. That's what I told the Minister."

"And the Minister was fine with that?"

The SAC hesitated. "He accepted my decision to assign you to the operation."

Which apparently meant, no, he was not fine with that, but I shoved you down his throat anyway.

This just kept getting better and better.

"You're in charge of this operation, Sam, or at least in charge of whatever CID's part in it turns out to be, and you will report only to me. I'm assigning two other CID detectives to work with you. The three of you and myself will be the only people at CID I want involved in this."

"Two other detectives, sir?"

"Sergeant Kang, of course. And since Inspector Aw is on annual leave, Sergeant Lee has very little to do so she'll be your third detective."

Tay hesitated. "Sergeant Linda Lee?"

"Yes. You know her, don't you, Sam?"

Tay did indeed know her.

A couple of years back he and Linda Lee had gone out a couple of times and the result had been so disastrous neither of them ever mentioned it to anyone. Even now, Tay didn't really understand exactly what had happened.

Linda was attractive. Tay would be the first to say that. And he would even concede she was intelligent and articulate, too. Tay thought the problem might have been that he and Linda were too much alike. He had never believed opposites attracted and he was certain that cliché had been responsible for more divorces than infidelity, but he didn't think being too much alike was exactly the road to heaven either. You had to find a balance of some kind; although God only knew he didn't have the first idea how to do that. And that explained as well as anything why he had never married.

Tay drew on his cigarette and exhaled slowly. Could this get any worse? He really didn't see how.

"What about the floater, sir? If Kang and I are looking for Suparman, I don't see how we can work that case the way it needs to be worked. We don't even have an ID on the corpse yet."

"I'll put somebody else on it."

"It was a gunshot death, sir."

The SAC's mouth dropped open. "What?"

"That's what Dr. Hoi says."

"Who?"

"The pathologist who examined the body at the scene, sir. She said there was a gunshot wound in the back of the head. Probably nine millimeter."

For a moment the SAC appeared to Tay to be too astonished to speak, then he sighed and shook his head so slowly he seemed concerned it might fall off.

"That's all we need," he said. "I'll put somebody on getting an ID tomorrow and then we'll see where we are."

In other words, Tay thought, *if it turns out to be somebody important, or God forbid a foreigner, I'll keep the case regardless of having to battle ISD over Suparman at the same time. If it's nobody, they'll give the case to the first guy who walks by.*

That was what he thought, but what he said was nothing at all.

"One other thing, Sam. The Minister didn't argue nearly as hard as I expected him to when I demanded he force ISD to include us." The SAC hesitated. "You see what I'm getting at, don't you?"

"Not really, sir."

"They made it too easy. So it's occurred to me that they might be setting us up."

"Setting us up? For what?"

"To take the fall if everything turns to shit. ISD would like nothing better than to dump all the blame for anything that goes wrong right on CID."

"You mean like—"

"Like a very public fuck up. The kind that leaves bodies behind."

Tay didn't like the sound of that so he said nothing.

"Watch your butt out there, Sam. Watch *our* butt. Those sons of bitches are going to try to blame CID if this goes bad. I can feel it."

Tay nodded, but he stayed silent.

The SAC tossed back the rest of his Irish whiskey and put the glass down on the table.

"That's it, Sam. I'm going home. I'll arrange for Sergeant Lee to meet you at New Phoenix Park tomorrow morning, but I'll leave it to you to talk with Sergeant Kang. After the briefing call me and tell me what you think."

Tay already knew what he would think. He would think this whole mess had the makings of a major cluster fuck and he was standing right on the bull's eye.

At the front door, the SAC stopped and put a hand on Tay's shoulder.

"Be damn careful, Sam. And look out for Kang and Lee, but don't tell them any of this came from me. Just treat this as a routine assignment through normal channels."

"I'll do that, sir."

Tay watched as the SAC walked to the front gate and let himself out. Tay raised his hand prepared to wave when the SAC looked back at him, but he never did. He just closed the gate and walked toward Orchard Road without turning around.

10

AT A LITTLE before nine the next morning Kang pulled up to the main gate of the Ministry of Home Affairs compound. He and Tay held up their warrant cards and the guard at the security post leaned down and flicked his eyes back and forth between their faces and the pictures on the cards until he was satisfied.

"Yes, sir." The guard straightened up and saluted crisply. "You are to go to room 3271 in Block B. Do you know where that is?"

"No idea," Kang said, since he was doing the driving.

"Follow the road until you come to a fork." The guard stepped out of his hut and pointed toward the center of the compound. "Go to the right and continue straight ahead all the way to the end. You'll be in a parking lot and you can park anywhere there you can find a space. Block B is the building right in front of you and room 3271 is—"

"On the third floor," Kang cut in. "Got it."

"Yes, sir," the guard said.

He stepped back, tossed out another snappy salute, and pushed a large red button on the side of the guardhouse. The yellow and black striped anti-terrorism barrier sticking out of the road slowly lowered.

"Christ," Kang muttered as they drove through the gate. "Is

everyone around here like that?"

"Every single one of them," Tay said.

When they got to the third floor of Block B, they saw that room 3271 was all the way down at the end of the corridor. It was as far from the elevators as you could walk and still be inside the building. Tay briefly wondered if ISD was holding the meeting there so they would have more time to examine people over CCTV as they walked the length of the corridor. That was probably silly, but anything to do with ISD just naturally kicked his paranoid instincts into high gear.

Tay opened the door to room 3271 without knocking and was surprised to discover it wasn't an office or even a conference room, but what looked like a reception area of some kind. Two beefy Malaysian-looking men with military-style haircuts stood in an approximation of parade rest on opposite sides of a door directly opposite them and to their left a third man sat behind a mahogany desk. He looked so much like the other two they might all have been brothers.

"ID's," the man at the desk said, holding out his hand. "Please."

He did say please at least, but Tay was pretty sure he didn't mean it.

Tay and Kang handed over their warrant cards and stood quietly while the man scrutinized first one and then the other as if he suspected they might be forgeries. When he was apparently satisfied their warrant cards were genuine, the deskman turned and tossed them into separate compartments in a wooden rack mounted on the wall behind him. About six inches deep and divided into five rows of small compartments, it made Tay think of the key racks that were always behind hotel reception desks in old black and white crime movies from the forties.

"No phones, cameras, recording devices, or firearms permitted inside," the deskman announced, holding out his hand again. "You can pick up your stuff when you come out."

Tay and Kang surrendered their telephones, and the man put them into the compartments with their warrant cards.

"Any other electronic devices of any kind? Cameras, recorders? Anything like that?"

They both shook their heads.

"Are you armed?"

"No," Tay said.

Kang nodded his head.

"Seriously?" Tay asked him.

Kang looked at Tay and shrugged. He reached under his shirt and unclipped an inside-the-waistband holster from which peeped the butt of what looked like a big semi-automatic and handed it over. The deskman reached back and plopped Kang's holster and pistol into the same compartment as his mobile phone.

Tay didn't much like carrying a gun and he seldom did. It wasn't that he harbored high-minded scruples that prevented him from shooting people. He had a long list of people in mind he thought could *use* shooting. It was more a matter of not wanting to be tempted.

Most of the time, Tay left his service revolver at home in the top drawer of his bedside table. It was an old-fashioned wheel gun, a Smith & Wesson .38, five shots with a two-inch barrel, and it marked him as even more of an old fart than most people already thought he was, which was really saying something. The Smith & Wesson .38 hadn't been issued to CID detectives in nearly fifteen years. It was practically an antique. Carrying it now was like making telephone calls with a rotary dial phone.

These days most CID cops carried Heckler & Koch forty calibre semi-automatics, but Tay had never bothered to qualify with one and just stuck to his old-fashioned .38. He knew his colleagues snickered about it. It's a great weapon if you ever get into a gunfight in an elevator, they had joked so often Tay had decided to smack the next guy who said it, but he almost never carried a gun anyway so it didn't matter much to him what it was.

To tell the truth, he was such a lousy shot he figured one gun was pretty much as useless to him as another.

The deskman pointed to one of the heavies flanking the door and the man stepped forward and held out a black plastic paddle Tay recognized as a handheld metal detector. He didn't speak, but he gestured to Tay and Kang to hold their arms out from their sides.

"You don't trust us?" Tay asked.

"Standard procedure," the man muttered.

"Standard procedure for everybody or just for CID people?"

"Look, pal," the deskman said, "We only work here. We just do what we're told. I suggest you do the same thing."

Tay and Kang stood silently while the security man ran the wand over them with what Tay thought was grossly exaggerated care under the circumstances. Each time it beeped, they were forced to pull out whatever they had in their pockets for examination.

"Okay," the deskman said when the procedure finally finished. "Go straight in. You're the last. They're waiting for you."

"And you've made them wait longer," Tay said.

When he walked through the door, Tay didn't find himself in a conference room as he had been expecting, but rather in what seemed to be a small lecture hall. He was looking down on it from behind the top row and saw about two dozen people scattered over four rows of theater seats arranged in tiers that rose up from a small platform. On the platform was a long wooden table with four chairs behind it, three of which were occupied.

Tay was surprised to see he knew one of the men on the platform although he tried not to show it. He had encountered Philip Goh several times in cases he was working. Goh did something or another at ISD, but Tay wasn't sure what it was and he had never gotten Goh to give him a straight answer to the questions he had asked him about that subject.

If Tay were feeling generous, he could probably say he and Goh had worked together, but saying they had worked together would be stretching it a bit. It would be more accurate to say they hadn't worked against each other. At least, not that anyone would notice.

Goh was a man of average height and weight and mostly forgettable appearance. He could have been the manager of a grocery store or a guy who worked at an insurance company. Perhaps it was that very anonymity which qualified him for ISD. He had a square Chinese face and black, badly cut hair. His most prominent feature was a scar that started somewhere inside his hairline above his left ear, meandered more or less diagonally across his cheek, and then disappeared below his jaw. It looked like a dueling scar on the face of some nineteenth-century German aristocrat and seemed completely out of place on a man like Goh who was otherwise so ordinary.

"Inspector Tay," Goh called up from the front of the room. "So glad you could join us. We've been waiting for you."

Tay said nothing. He merely nodded and sat in the first empty seat he saw. Kang glanced around, spotted Sergeant Lee one row further down, and slid in next to her.

"Not back there, Inspector," Goh called out. "You're down here." He pointed to the empty chair on the platform right next to him.

Kang glanced over his shoulder at Tay, who gave a half shrug. Tay stood up and walked down to the platform and sat in the chair Goh had indicated.

"What am I doing up here, Goh?" Tay asked in a low voice.

"You're in charge of the CID people. I figured you should be down front with me."

"And why are you down front?"

"I'm running ISD's operation."

"You mean you and I are jointly in charge of this?"

"I guess we'd better get this straight right now, Tay. ISD and CID aren't partners and CID isn't here to help me. If I had my way, you wouldn't be here at all. But to get the snatch approved, we had to agree to have you here. If it becomes necessary to make arrests under Singapore law, that's your department. Everything else is my department."

"Snatch?"

Goh looked annoyed. "What?"

"You used the world *snatch*. I just thought that was an odd way to characterize an operation to arrest a man."

"I should have guessed having you here was going to be a joy, Tay. I ought to have my head examined for not refusing to let them stick me with you."

"And yet here I am."

"Look, ISD is taking down Suparman and holding him under the Internal Security Act. That has nothing at all to do with CID. But if anyone interferes with us, you might actually be useful. Something like that wouldn't fall under the Internal Security Act. That would be a breach of civil law and CID will be responsible for making an arrest, if one is necessary."

"In other words, you're saying—"

"Can I conduct my briefing now, Tay? Would that be okay with you? If you have any questions, I'll try to answer them when I'm done."

Goh flashed a grin he probably thought looked nasty. Tay just thought it made Goh appear constipated.

"Who are they?" Tay asked, jerking his head at the other two men sitting on the platform.

"Everything in this operation is on a need to know basis. And you don't need to know that."

"Oh, for Pete's sake, Goh, give it a rest. Where do you guys get all this spy crap?"

"How much do you know about this operation, Tay?"

"Nothing at all."

"Then, for once in your life, keep your mouth shut and listen. You'll find out everything you need to know, and nothing you don't." And then Goh winked at him, actually *winked*. "That's what need to know means."

Tay gave a little wave with one hand that could have meant almost anything. Then he leaned back, folded his arms, and waited.

11

"AS ALL OF you already know," Goh told the room, "we have intelligence Abu Suparman has either already slipped into Singapore or soon will. We're going to take him down the moment he shows his face, and you're the people who are going to do it."

No one said anything or offered any obvious reaction to Goh's announcement. There was no applause, certainly no pumping fists. These people were all far too professional for that. But there was electricity in the air, and Tay could feel it.

"We're setting a trap for him," Goh continued. "His sister has been diagnosed with third-stage breast cancer. Her doctor in Indonesia recommended a radical mastectomy and the surgery is scheduled here in Singapore on Saturday. Even with the procedure, she has only been given a fifty-fifty chance of survival. We are therefore certain that Suparman will try to see her sometime before the surgery."

Suparman was a dangerous terrorist and taking him out of circulation was absolutely necessary, Tay knew, but going about it this way gave him a moment of pause. Using a man's sister who was dying of cancer to lure him into a trap? Somehow that didn't seem decent.

The lights in the room abruptly lowered and a large screen on the wall behind Goh came alive. A photograph of a pleasant but unremarkable looking middle-aged woman appeared on the screen. Tay thought she looked Malaysian or Indonesian.

"This is Atin Hasan," Goh said. "She is Abu Suparman's sister."

The woman was of medium height and slightly plump with the chubby red cheeks of a healthy baby. She had on a dark red hijab with strands of black hair peeking from beneath it and was wearing jeans and what looked like a man's shirt with the tails hanging down over her waist. The woman had a white plastic carrier bag in her left hand and on it Tay could just make out the Cold Storage Market logo. The photograph had the oddly flattened look of one taken through a long telephoto lens.

"Atin Hasan will be arriving at Changi Airport from Jakarta around eleven-thirty this morning. We will have eyes on her from the moment she leaves the airplane. The intelligence we have now is that she will be staying at the Temple Street Inn in Chinatown until Friday, when she will check into Mount Elizabeth Hospital for her surgery on Saturday morning. Because of her condition, we assume she will go straight to the hotel on arrival, but if she goes anywhere else we are prepared for that, too."

"Do we know who she is traveling with?" The question came from a Caucasian man on the left side of the room and Tay thought he detected traces of an Australian accent.

"Our information is that she will be alone," Goh said.

Tay raised an eyebrow. That didn't feel right. Who traveled by himself to another country for medical treatment when you had only a fifty-fifty chance of survival? Surely the woman must have family who could give her help and support at such a time. Why would she be in Singapore alone unless...well, unless *what*? Tay couldn't come up with anything at all.

"How solid is this intelligence?"

The question came from a tall man with a Chinese face sitting in the second row. Tay assumed he was probably ISD. The man looked to Tay to be no more than twenty-five or thirty years old. People around him seemed to get younger and younger every year.

"This intelligence is as solid as intelligence gets," Goh answered.

Tay snorted, but he did it quietly. If that was the best Goh could do, he figured they were in trouble.

Tay worked on the basis of facts; things he either knew to be true or had good reason to believe were likely to be true. When people told him they worked on the basis of intelligence, it usually meant they didn't have very many facts. They had collected what some people told them or what other people told them other people had told *them* and were trying hard to make it all sound like facts. In Tay's view, relying on so-called intelligence to make decisions was nearly always a sure way to get your ass handed to you.

"What can you tell us about the source of your intelligence?" Tay asked.

He noticed everyone else in the room turned to look at him, and he didn't detect a lot of warmth in their looks.

"Nothing," Goh said.

"So you want us to take all this on faith."

"ISD has vetted the intelligence and views it as actionable. That's all you need to know."

"It seems to me—"

"Look, Tay, I don't really care how anything seems to you. ISD is taking down Suparman on the basis of this intelligence and holding him under the Internal Security Act. If anyone interferes with us, or if we discover citizens of Singapore involved in sheltering or protecting Suparman, CID might be needed since that wouldn't fall under the Internal Security Act. Otherwise, the details of this operation are of no concern to you."

"Then you're saying—"

"Can I go on with my briefing now, Tay? If you have any questions, I'll try to answer them when I'm done."

The screen behind Goh began to flash as it displayed a

succession of images of the woman Goh had identified as Abu Suparman's sister. In most of them she was wearing the same jeans, shirt, and dark red hijab she had been wearing in the first picture, which suggested most of them were made at the same time.

The screen stopped flashing and held on a picture of a row of shophouses that looked vaguely familiar to Tay.

"This is the Temple Street Inn. As most of you probably know already, it's on Temple Street just east of New Bridge Road in Chinatown. The hotel consists of four shophouses, each three stories high, joined together into a single structure."

Tay always thought it was a little strange that Singapore, which was as a practical matter a Chinese city, had a neighborhood called Chinatown. The narrow streets lined with small shophouses and filled with restaurants and souvenir shops were a big draw for tourists, particularly western ones, but the area bore more resemblance to an amusement park than it did to any real Chinese city Tay had ever seen.

"If Suparman does try to see his sister as we expect, we are certain it will be at this hotel, not at a public place like the hospital. That's why we're going to put a net over the Temple Street Inn from the moment Atin Hasan arrives until she leaves for the hospital. We have every confidence we will snare Suparman in that net."

"Let me lay out the operational plan for you," Goh went on. "Three teams of six men will work eight-hour shifts to keep the Temple Street Inn under constant surveillance. We have taken over two apartments on Temple Street, one about fifty yards to the east of the hotel and one about thirty yards to the west, and we have access to the back of a restaurant on Pagoda Street which overlooks the loading dock at the rear of the hotel. One team will man each of those positions twenty-four hours a day. Nobody will be able to get in or out of the hotel without us knowing it."

"What about putting somebody inside, sir?" a man two rows up asked. Tay assumed he had to be ISD since he addressed Goh as *sir*. Tay couldn't imagine anyone else would be willing to do that.

"We can't put surveillance inside the hotel since it's small and there's no way we can do it covertly. We considered approaching management and getting their cooperation, but we decided not to. We are simply not certain we can trust either the management or the staff and we don't want to take a chance of tipping off Suparman if he has sympathizers there. If we scare him off, we might not get another chance at him."

"How about cameras?" the same man asked.

"Again, we can't access the hotel's own CCTV system with somebody there knowing about it. We looked at putting our own cameras inside the hotel, but we don't think we could do that either without at least some of the staff finding out. We simply don't want to take a chance on this operation being blown by gossip or even by an informer."

"Anything else?" Goh asked, looking around the room. When nobody said anything, he went on.

"Now, as most of you are already aware, the biggest problem we're going to have is that Suparman has never been photographed. There are no authenticated pictures of him we can use for identification."

Well, yes, I see how that might be a problem, Tay thought. *When you're peering down out of a window into the street looking for somebody, it's reasonably important to know what he looks like.*

Tay settled back to see how the geniuses at ISD were going to deal with that one.

A black and white pencil drawing flashed onto the screen behind Goh. It was of a man who appeared to be about fifty years old with a generically Asian face. He could have been Indonesian or Malaysian or, for that matter, Singaporean. The man had a prominent nose, widely set eyes, bushy eyebrows, and long, dark, slightly stringy hair that hung straight down almost to his shoulders.

"This is a composite sketch based on the description of Suparman given to us by two of the men involved in the Bali bombings," Goh said. "They had contact with him on several occasions while the bombings were being planned, so their descriptions should be reasonably accurate."

"Wait," Tay interrupted. "That was…what? Ten or twelve years ago?"

Goh turned his head slowly and looked at Tay. "We're not completely stupid, regardless of what you might believe. This drawing has been aged to compensate for the timeframe. Now, do you have any other helpful observations?"

Tay wiggled one hand in what he thought was a suitably ambiguous gesture and folded his arms.

"We also know," Goh said, shifting his eyes back to the room, "that Suparman is tall for an Indonesian, perhaps six feet. But he walks with a stoop and may appear shorter."

That's just wonderful, Tay thought. *They're going to try to pick out a guy in the street who's tall but appears shorter, has a face that looks like any one of about ten million other men, and had long hair ten years ago. Piece of bloody cake.*

Goh started talking again before Tay could say any of that out loud, which even Tay understood was probably for the best.

"Each surveillance post will have a copy of this sketch plus copies of the photographs of Suparman's sister I showed you earlier. You will also have field glasses equipped for night vision and an encrypted radio tuned to the operations channel."

A few heads around the room bobbed, but nobody said anything.

"When we pick up Suparman entering the hotel, an army Special Operations Force will be standing by to seal off Temple Street from both ends. After that, ISD will move in on Suparman. We don't expect him to be armed and we think the possibility of him resisting is remote, but you should all be armed and fully prepared if he tries to leave the hotel before the army seals off the street or if he does resist. Now…any questions about all that?"

Sergeant Kang raised his hand in the back of the room. "What is CID supposed to be doing while these three ISD teams watch the hotel?"

"We've organized a room for CID at the Santa Grande Hotel across the street from the Temple Street Inn."

The screen behind Goh flashed through several more pictures of the Temple Street Inn and stopped on one Tay saw had been taken looking toward South Bridge Road. Along one side of the hotel there was a tiny alleyway too narrow for cars that ran all the way from Temple Street through to Pagoda Street and which was lined end to end with vendors' carts selling tourist junk. Opposite the alleyway on the other side of Temple Street, Tay saw the entrance to the small hotel called the Santa Grande.

"Whichever CID officer is on duty," Goh continued, "will remain at the Santa Grande until we need you. If something arises which requires the exercise of civil police authority, I'll call for you on the operations channel and give you instructions. If I don't call for you, you'll wait in the room and stay out of the way."

"Wait a minute," Tay cut in. "You want CID to sit in a hotel room twenty-four hours a day waiting for you to call us?"

Goh tossed out another of his obnoxious grins. "I thought I'd find something for CID to do that you could handle, Tay."

"That's ridiculous," Tay snapped.

"I'm sorry you think so, but I'm running this operation and that's what you'll be doing." Goh turned back to the room. "There will be no one on the operations channel except for the three surveillance posts, the CID post at the Santa Grande, and my supervisory post. I want you to stay off the radio until you have located and identified Suparman. Is that clear?"

A few people nodded.

"Okay," Goh concluded, "any final questions?"

For his part, Tay had *lots* of questions, but he knew it would be prudent to save them for a private conversation with Goh. Starting an argument in front of everyone else would do nothing but piss

Goh off and create even more ill will between CID and ISD, if such a thing were even possible.

Nobody else spoke up either.

Welcome to Singapore, Tay thought. *Where we obey orders and don't ask any questions.*

"I want everybody in place before the sister arrives so the first shift will begin immediately and run until six tonight," Goh said. "The second shift will run from six until two in the morning, and the third shift from two until ten tomorrow morning. We will maintain that schedule until we have Suparman or until his sister leaves the hotel and checks into the hospital."

"ISD personnel already have their assignments and will be covering the two surveillance posts on Temple Street plus the post in the restaurant overlooking the loading dock. Tay, you can assign your people however you see fit as long as one person from CID is always on standby at the Santa Grande Hotel. Everybody got all that?"

There were a few more nods, but nobody spoke up.

"Okay," Goh said as the screen behind him went dark and the lights in the room came up. "Get out there and nail this bastard for me."

12

PEOPLE GOT TO their feet and began shuffling up the steps toward the exit. The other two men sitting at the table stood up and, without even a nod to Tay and Goh, began climbing the steps, too. Tay stayed where he was and watched them go.

So who the hell were those guys?

After the room was largely cleared, Tay pushed his chair back up and stood there waiting for Goh to acknowledge him.

Goh looked the other way and said nothing. It was a childish power play and Tay knew it so he just stood there and waited Goh out. Eventually Goh gave up, as Tay knew he would.

"You have a question, Tay?"

"Yeah. Who were those two guys sitting up here with us?"

Goh's eyes flicked automatically toward the last backs at the top of the stairs. Tay thought he saw a frisson of anxiety, but perhaps he was mistaken. Goh wasn't a guy to be anxious about much of anything.

"We have several observers attached to the operation," Goh muttered as the last of the men left the room.

"Observers?"

"You want me to define the word for you, Tay? Observers are people who observe."

Tay just looked at Goh as if he knew there was more and waited.

"Besides," Goh shrugged after a few moments, "I'm glad to have the support if we need it."

"Support from who?"

"The UK, Australia." Goh paused. "The US."

"In other words, you telling me there were people from MI6, ASIS, and the CIA in this room today?"

Goh gave a very small nod, but he didn't say anything else.

"Didn't you tell me this was your operation?"

"It is my operation, Tay. And don't you forget it."

"Either you're dumber than I think, Goh, or you're lying both to me and yourself. You can't possibly believe MI6, the Australian Intelligence Service, and the CIA are here to hang around watching ISD. They're here because they want something."

"They want us to grab Suparman. He's not just our problem. He's everybody's problem."

"And if you do grab him—"

"Not if, Tay, when."

"And if you do grab him, what do you figure happens then? All those guys congratulate you on a job well done, have a little chili crab, and head home? Rubbish. They're going to want a piece of Suparman, too."

"I'm calling the shots here, Tay. Simple as that."

"Look, Goh, you can't really—"

"And another thing. Be careful who you talk to. You can't be certain where their loyalties lie."

That pulled Tay up short.

"What are you talking about?" he asked.

"We have reason to believe that ISIS has supporters in Singapore, possibly even on the police force."

"But not in ISD."

"Don't be ridiculous, Tay. I know our people."

"And I know ours."

Tay and Goh focused their most macho glares on each other,

but after a few seconds Tay shook his head and looked away. He was wasting his time. Without another word, he turned around and started up the steps to the little auditorium's exit where Kang was waiting for him with Sergeant Lee.

As he climbed, Tay found himself looking at Sergeant Lee and realizing he had forgotten how attractive she was. Her Malaysian-Chinese ancestry had provided her smooth, golden skin to set off her striking Chinese features. She had straight, lustrous black hair that fell several inches below her shoulders, a wide face, high cheekbones, and deep brown eyes.

Tay tried to remember exactly how their brief personal relationship had veered so disastrously off the rails. Had he broken it off, or had she? Maybe neither of them had really broken it off. Maybe they had just allowed the relationship to slink off somewhere and die a quiet death. Although he couldn't remember exactly what had happened or how it had happened, the closer he got to where Sergeant Lee was standing with Robbie Kang the more certain he was he must have been out of his damned mind to *let* it happen.

"Morning, Inspector," Sergeant Lee smiled when he got to the top of the steps.

Tay nodded, but he said nothing.

"Bloody hell, sir," Kang said, "what in the world—"

"Not here, Sergeant," Tay interrupted. "Let's keep the conversation for outside."

Out in the anteroom the same guy who was manning the desk when they came in was waiting for them. He handed over their ID's, telephones, and weapons. Tay was surprised to see Sergeant Lee was carrying, too, and even more surprised she was carrying a revolver. Patrolmen in Singapore were still being issued revolvers, but all the CID personnel he knew now carried the H&K forty calibre semi-automatics. Tay would have bet he was the last detective in CID with a wheel gun.

He tried to see what kind of a revolver Sergeant Lee had without being too obvious about it, but he couldn't be certain. It was big and he thought it might be something chambered in .357 magnum. His first thought was that a .357 magnum was a lot of gun for a woman, but his second thought was that he was glad he hadn't spoken his first thought out loud. He was reasonably certain Linda Lee already thought he was a misogynistic old fart. No point in handing her solid proof she was absolutely right.

Still, he couldn't help but wonder a little about Sergeant Lee's choice of sidearm. Why wasn't she carrying the H&K semi-automatic like everybody else? Why an old fashioned revolver? Maybe she was just an old fashioned kind of girl after all.

Sergeant Lee's revolver was in a brown leather paddle holster. With a graceful flip of her right hand, she tossed back the bone-colored cotton blazer she wore over her jeans, used her left hand to snap the paddle over her belt at about the four o'clock position, and let the blazer swing forward to cover it. It was such an elegant move that Tay caught himself staring.

The security man pulled a black cloth backpack from under the desk and held it out to Sergeant Kang.

"Here you go," he said. "Your ID materials and an encrypted radio. There's a key card for your post in there, too."

Kang took the backpack with a nod and turned away, but the security man grabbed his elbow.

"Not so fast, buddy."

He scooped a clipboard and pen off the desk and held them out to Kang.

"You've got to sign for everything. If it's not all returned in good condition when this operation is over, you're responsible."

Kang started to say something, but thought better of it. He accepted the pen and the clipboard without protest, signed the form, and handed it back.

"Aren't you going to check the stuff?" the security man asked.

"I trust you," Kang said.

"Huh," the security man snorted. "I sure as hell wouldn't."

Out in the hall, Tay looked at Kang and Lee and gave a very small shake of his head. None of them said a word as they took the elevator to the ground floor, crossed the parking lot, and got into Kang's car.

Kang slid behind the wheel and Tay got into the passenger seat. Sergeant Lee got in back and slid forward until she could lean against Tay's seat on her folded arms.

"They're not serious about us sitting in a hotel room waiting for them to call, are they, sir?" she asked.

Tay had always thought Linda had a wonderful voice, throaty with a slight rasp like a smoker, although as far as he knew she didn't smoke. Whatever the reason, Tay thought it was downright sexy.

"They sounded serious to me, Sergeant."

"Are you going to let them get away with that?"

"What would you have me do, Sergeant? Wrestle Mr. Goh to the floor and slap him around until he relents and gives us a more important role?"

"No, sir, but…well, there must be something we can do. This sucks."

Tay considered trying to find a way to convey to them the SAC's suspicions CID was being set up to take the fall if the operation went sour, but he had promised the SAC not to bring him into the discussion, and voicing that concern without mentioning the SAC would probably make him sound like a paranoid old fool. He might have said something anyway if he had been alone with Sergeant Kang, but having Sergeant Lee in the conversation changed things for Tay. Her being there made him more reluctant to say something that might make him look silly. That was the major drawback to being around a beautiful woman, he supposed. It made you self-conscious.

"We're going to do what ISD has asked us to do, Sergeant. Not one bit more or one bit less. And we're going to keep our eyes open and be very careful."

"Eyes open for what, sir?" Kang asked.

Tay hesitated. He wasn't quite sure how to put it.

"I think I understand, sir," Sergeant Lee broke in.

Maybe she did, it occurred to Tay. Kang still looked puzzled, but Tay rushed on before he could say anything else.

"I'll take the first shift," he said as he glanced at his watch. "You relieve me at six, Robbie, and then Sergeant Lee can relieve you at two. I'll come back at ten tomorrow morning and relieve her. We'll keep up that rotation until we're told to stand down."

"I'll take the two o'clock shift, sir," Sergeant Kang said. "It doesn't seem right to ask a woman to take an overnight shift."

"What?" Sergeant Lee asked from the backseat.

Kang turned his head and looked at her. "I was only trying to—"

"You figure the two o'clock shift is a man's shift? Maybe it's too risky for a woman to work after midnight? Are you for real, Kang?"

"I've given you your assignments," Tay cut in. "This is not a negotiation. Any questions?"

Tay paused a second or two at most.

"Good," he continued before anyone could say anything. "Take me down to the beautiful Santa Grande Hotel, Sergeant Kang, then drop Sergeant Lee wherever she wants to go. Both of you need to get some rest. Overnight surveillances suck."

"But we're just going to be sitting around waiting for a call, aren't we, sir?" Kang asked. "We're not really going to have anyone under surveillance, are we?"

"Let's pretend we are, Sergeant. Let's simply pretend we are and maybe that will make us feel like we're at the table with the grown-ups."

13

THE SANTA GRANDE Hotel was nothing to write home about but, since Tay didn't intend to write home or anywhere else for that matter, he didn't much care.

The room allocated to CID was on the third floor at the front and it was furnished like any other room in any other tourist hotel: a double bed with a dark maroon bedspread matched to the drapes, a mahogany-veneer chest with four drawers, an old cathode-ray television set, a narrow desk with a lamp, and a straight wooden chair. The room had only one window, but at least the window overlooked Temple Street and provided a fine, unobstructed view of the Temple Street Inn.

Tay dumped the backpack with the encrypted radio and the photographs on the bed, walked straight to the window, and pulled the drapes all the way back. He was directly across Temple Street from the pedestrian alleyway he had seen in the photograph during the briefing. It was a space designed for tourists and was lined with vendors' carts selling souvenirs, soft drinks, and food, but it ran all the way down the east side of the hotel and could be used to walk all the way from Temple Street to Pagoda Street.

Was there another door to the Temple Street Inn somewhere down there, Tay wondered? He didn't recall it being mentioned in the briefing so he decided there probably wasn't. He might not think much of ISD, but they weren't *that* stupid.

Tay had always hated the tedium of surveillance operations and he always found a way to push them off on somebody else. He couldn't remember the last time he had been stuck with one himself, but here he was. And this wasn't even a CID operation.

He hadn't brought anything to read and he only had one pack of Marlboros, and he knew unless he fixed both of those problems right away he would lose his mind well before Kang came to relieve him at six o'clock. A quick run for supplies was an absolute necessity. He needed cigarettes and a couple of paperbacks as well as something to eat and drink. He would take the radio with him. How would Goh know he wasn't dutifully waiting in the room?

Reaching into the backpack Tay pulled out a black plastic box about the size of a paperback book. It had a slide switch on one side and a button and two dials mounted on the front below a perforated grill that appeared to cover a loudspeaker. Did the loudspeaker also work as a microphone? He supposed it must since he didn't see any other possibility.

Tay flipped the switch back and forth a couple of times, but nothing seemed to happen so he began fiddling with the two dials. All at once a loud burst of static erupted from the grill. He was so startled he dropped the radio on the bed, but he retrieved it in time to hear Goh's voice above the static.

"Testing. Radio check. All posts please acknowledge."

"One here," said a man whose voice Tay didn't recognize.

"Two here," another man said.

"Three acknowledging," a third voice chimed in.

There was a brief silence, then, "Are you there, Tay? Or haven't you figured out how to turn on the radio yet?"

Fuck him, Tay thought. He twisted both dials counterclockwise as far as they would go and dumped the radio on the bed.

Then he headed out in search of supplies leaving it behind.

Less than fifty yards up Temple Street, Tay found a 7-Eleven with a rotating metal rack right inside the front door crammed with at least a hundred paperbacks.

He was happy to see a couple of titles in the rack that looked like they might hold his attention for a while: a Don Winslow novel he hadn't read yet, and something called *Bali Dreaming* by a travel writer named Vanya Vetto. He didn't know who Vetto was, but a blurb on the cover compared him favorably to Hunter Thompson which was a pretty good recommendation in Tay's book so he took both Vetto's book and the Winslow novel. He also picked up a bag of pretzels, a package of Japanese rice crackers, a six-pack of Coke Zeros, and a package of cookies.

He took everything over and piled it on the counter in front of the cash register and asked the clerk for two packs of Marlboros and some matches. The clerk stacked the Marlboros and matches with the rest of Tay's shopping.

"That all?"

Tay contemplated the pile of books, cigarettes, and junk food and was suddenly overcome with embarrassment. He had the judgment of a twelve-year-old boy when it came to taking care of himself. He really did. He was going to have to do better. After a moment's thought, he pushed the package of cookies to one side.

"Forget those and give me two more packs of Marlboros instead," he told the clerk.

Almost at once he felt better. Nothing beat healthy living, did it?

Walking back to the Santa Grande Hotel with his provisions, Tay impulsively took a quick detour down the alleyway he could see from the room. It was jammed with what looked like the usual batch of tourists roaming Chinatown, and the crowds gathered around the vendors' carts made walking difficult. Tay was nearly halfway to Pagoda Street and about to turn around when he spotted what looked like an emergency exit from the hotel. It was a metal door that had on some long-ago day been painted green. Tay stood for a moment and contemplated the scarred metal door.

Why wouldn't Goh have mentioned the emergency exit in the briefing? Tay tugged at the handle, but the metal door didn't move. Either it was sealed completely or it opened only from the inside. Still, it was a door. Unless ISD had somehow established it couldn't be opened at all, someone ought to be covering it. Was there a surveillance team back here that Goh hadn't told them about for some reason?

Tay looked up and down the alleyway. Unless ISD had people disguised as food vendors or tourists, and he didn't for a moment think they would do anything so pedestrian, the only location from which the emergency exit could be observed was a building directly across the alleyway from the hotel. The space, now empty, had once been something called the Mango Travel Service, but now nothing was left of that doomed enterprise other than a sun-faded sign in the front window and the few pieces of abandoned furniture Tay saw beyond the plate glass window. He also saw a staircase at the rear of the room, and he leaned back and spotted another Mango Travel Service sign in a second floor window. An abandoned two-story shophouse straight across from the emergency exit? That was almost too good to be true. Was ISD upstairs right now?

When Tay tried the door to what had once been the Mango Travel Service, he discovered it was unlocked. Surely that settled it. ISD must be upstairs right now watching the emergency exit, but why hadn't Goh told them he had another observation post?

When Tay started up the stairs, he called out, "This is Inspector Tay of CID. I'm coming up. For Christ's sake don't shoot me."

No one shot him. And when he got to the second floor, he saw why.

The place was dusty and deserted. No ISD surveillance team. No one at all. It looked like no one had been there in months. It was odd the front door had been left unlocked, but in real life odd things occasionally did happen.

Tay looked around and an idea occurred to him.

Wait in a hotel room until ISD felt like calling, huh? Fat chance of that now. Finding this place gave him an opportunity to get back in the game and he wasn't going to lose out on that. Goh would shit himself if he found out, but how would he?

Tay dumped his bags of junk food and cigarettes on an old desk that had been left pushed up against one wall, and then he headed to the Santa Grande to collect the rest of their stuff.

He had only been back at the Santa Grande for a few minutes and had just finished stuffing everything into the black backpack when he heard a soft knock at the door. He opened it expecting to see a maid or perhaps a room service waiter who had the wrong room, but Sergeant Kang and Sergeant Lee were standing there.

"We thought you might want some company, sir," Kang said. "Sitting around a hotel room waiting for ISD to call can't be much fun."

Tay smiled in spite of himself.

"It isn't, Sergeant, so that's not what we're going to do."

Tay's joy at stumbling over a place from which they might be able to cut themselves in on the action had worn off quickly. All they could see from their vantage point in the abandoned travel agency was the hotel's emergency exit into the alley and not much was happening there.

The highlight so far came an hour or so back when a woman opened the emergency exit and stepped outside for a cigarette. While she smoked she walked down the alleyway for a few yards and then turned around and walked back again. Once she lifted her head and seemed to look straight at Tay while he was watching her through the field glasses and Tay had been so startled he jerked the glasses down and leaned away from the window. By the time he peered cautiously back outside again, the woman was knocking on the green door. It opened almost immediately and she went into the hotel.

She couldn't have been looking at him, Tay knew, not really, no matter how much it seemed like she was. Besides, the woman obviously wasn't Suparman's sister. The photographs they had of the sister showed a middle-aged but pleasant-looking Indonesian, perhaps a bit on the plump side, with a coy smile and sparkling eyes. The woman he had been watching as she smoked outside the green door was probably a hotel maid on her break. She looked bent and tired, and she was elderly, likely in her sixties.

Tay winced even as that thought crossed his mind. The woman was probably no more than ten years older than he was and he was thinking of her as elderly? That was too sad to contemplate.

The radio crackled and all three of them glanced automatically at where Kang had left it on the desk next to the black backpack.

"Sit-rep, please, position one." Goh's voice emerged from the static.

"Position one?" Kang asked. "Is that us?"

"I think we're four," Tay said.

Tay hated the kind of military talk that men of a certain sort seemed to use whenever they got near a radio, and Goh was apparently a man of that certain sort.

Sit-rep? Why not just ask in plain English what was going on? Asking for a *situation report* would have been dumb enough, but asking for a *sit-rep* reached for a whole new level of dumbness. If only he could figure out how to send a smiley face back through the radio, Tay thought, that's what he would do.

"All clear, sir," a voice said. "No sign of him."

"Position two?"

"Nothing, sir."

"Position three?"

"Clear here."

"Position four?"

Kang looked at Tay. "You must be right sir. There's nobody else left."

Tay stood up, walked over to the desk, and picked up the radio. Having no better idea what he was supposed to do, he pushed a button on the front.

"I'm watching reruns of *Law and Order*," Tay announced into the grill. "Try not to disturb me unless it's important."

Kang looked away to keep from laughing, but Lee giggled in spite of herself. After a moment the radio crackled again.

"Very amusing, Tay. I should have expected something like that from you. At least now I know you're awake."

"Roger wilco, over and out," Tay said and dropped the radio back on the desk.

14

SERGEANT LEE TOOK over watching the emergency exit and Kang sat and fiddled with his telephone.

Tay pulled out his Marlboros, settled himself in a chair against the wall, and lit a cigarette. He wasn't sure he wanted a cigarette, but he had nothing else to do so he lit one anyway. At least here no one would start screeching at him to put it out. Nobody was around but Kang and Lee and they knew better than to complain. Tay thought it was ridiculous there was almost nowhere anymore you could smoke in peace. He blamed the Americans for that, he really did. One more way the do-gooders of the western world had fucked up the universe.

Tay understood he would have to stop smoking someday. He had resolved to do it a hundred times already, but making resolutions was as far as he had gotten so far. He had never taken even a single concrete step toward really stopping. Maybe tomorrow he would. Or maybe not.

Clouds slid over the sun, the world darkened, and it started to rain. At first, the rain fell softly, tiny drops that barely dimpled the oily sheen of the alleyway. It was almost as if the whole city were being sprinkled with heavenly absolution. But at the very moment the notion crossed his mind, the rain abruptly changed into big, fat drops that thudded against the alleyway like globs of spit. So much for poetic musings, Tay thought. Back to the real world.

The vendors hurriedly threw plastic covers over their carts and the swarms of pedestrians clogging the alleyway vanished as completely as if they had never been there at all. If there was one thing Singapore knew how to cope with it was rain. There was hardly a day when it wasn't either raining or the humidity was so high it felt like it was raining. Tay had lived all of his life in Singapore and he had never for a moment understood what possessed human beings to build a city in a place with such lousy weather. Hot and raining, humid and hot, humid and raining and hot. Thus had it been for all of Tay's fifty years in Singapore, and thus no doubt would it always be.

As the world outside the window darkened, Tay caught a sudden glimpse of his reflection in the glass. It was a dim, wavering image superimposed over the building across the alleyway and it looked almost spectral. For a moment Tay saw himself with a terrible objectivity, helpless to dissemble as most people do when they look at their own reflection. In that moment all his sense of personal loyalty to himself vanished, and he stared at his reflection with cruel clarity.

He thought he looked a hundred years old. Bags under his eyes, fleshiness under his chin, flecks of gray scattered through his hair like a sprinkling of salt. He didn't remember being that gray. Had it just happened, or had it happened so slowly he had never noticed? Maybe he should get his hair dyed. How much did something like that cost?

He contemplated his reflection for a moment as if he were observing a stranger.

You're getting old, son. Getting old.

He almost said it out loud, but he stopped himself just in time. He had heard that senility began with talking to yourself and at least he damn well didn't do that yet. Well, hardly ever.

Tay pulled his shoulders back, sucked in his stomach, and looked himself in the eye, but it didn't do any good. He just didn't much like what he saw.

Even if he dyed his hair or lost some weight, he knew it wouldn't really matter. He was never going to like himself very much. He retained his self-respect only by doing the best work he could and striving to be someone who was valuable to the world. Even when senior officers pushed back on him, he just let them take their best shots. Up until now they had always missed. Maybe they wouldn't always miss.

He knew it didn't matter. If he stopped doing the best he could regardless of how they pushed him, he would have no self-respect left. It was as simple as that.

The radio crackled again and a voice said, "We have a subject approaching the hotel from the east who's the right height and build. He could be Suparman."

"Could be?" Goh snapped. "Does the subject resemble the drawing or doesn't he?"

"He's wearing a hoodie, sir. Because of the rain. I can't see his face."

"Is he alone?"

"Yes, sir."

"Let me know if he enters the hotel."

There was a long silence and Tay felt the tension building. He kept his eyes on the radio while he waited for more. It was stupid to look at the radio, of course, but he did it anyway.

"Ah…this is position one again," the same voice said after a minute or two had passed. "The subject is by the hotel. I don't think he's going in."

"Position two," Goh said, "do you see the subject?"

"Yes, sir. He's coming straight at us and I can see his face now. He does look like the drawing…well, a little. But it's not Suparman. He's too old. Repeat, not Suparman."

"Roger, positions one and two. Stay alert. Out."

Tay lit another cigarette and went back to staring out the window. Perhaps he would sit here until he smoked himself to death. Eventually they would find his corpse with an empty pack of Marlboros in one hand and a box of matches in the other. That had to be about as good a way to go as any.

The thought took Tay back to the barely human pile of flesh he had seen in that tent at the side of the Singapore River. Now that was a horrible way to die. Who was that man? Did anyone miss him, or had he been forgotten already? The lesson was pretty clear, Tay told himself not for the first time. Never be a victim. Make your own choices, do what you have to do, but never be a victim.

Tay smoked quietly until his cigarette was finished. When it was, he dropped it on the floor and ground it out with the toe of his shoe.

The radio clicked on again.

"This is position two. We have three males approaching from the west. There is a subject in the center of the group who might be Suparman."

Tay's eyes flicked first to the radio then to the window, but of course he couldn't see the three men from where they were.

"The whole group is stopping about twenty feet from the entrance. Subject is still in the center. Stand by."

The silence stretched on so long after that Kang got up and walked over to check the radio. The moment Kang put his hand on it, Goh's voice boomed out of the speaker and he jumped slightly.

"What's happening, position one?"

"Ah...nothing, sir. They're just standing there."

"Are they checking for surveillance?"

"I don't think so, sir, but their backs are to us so I can't be sure. Subject is wearing a light jacket with the collar up and a baseball cap. I can't really see him very clearly."

"Do you have them, position two?"

"Yes, sir. The subject in the center has very short hair and pale skin. I don't see how he could be Suparman."

"Can you see his face clearly?"

"Uh…not really, sir."

"All three men are moving again," the first voice interrupted. "They're past the hotel entrance now and proceeding west."

"This is position two. They're coming toward us now and I can confirm the subject is not Suparman. Repeat. Not Suparman."

"Okay, positions one and two," Goh said. "Stay on it. Out."

As suddenly as the clouds had appeared they vanished, the rain stopped, and the sun came out. Tay's reflection vanished from the window and he stood up and looked down at the green door across the alleyway. It looked exactly the way it had looked an hour ago, two hours ago, four hours ago.

"This is bullshit," Tay said.

He yawned and stretched.

"This is complete bullshit," he repeated. "We're stuck in a damned alley while all the action is out front."

"It doesn't sound to me like we're missing much, sir."

Tay shrugged. He supposed Kang was right.

"Want me to take over?" Kang asked Lee.

She nodded. "Thanks."

Kang took the field glasses from Lee, nudged around the chair where she had been sitting until he was happy with its position, and then put the glasses up to his eyes. "We've only got another forty hours until this woman is supposed to check into the hospital," he observed cheerfully.

Tay shot Kang a look and saw he was grinning behind the field glasses.

Forty more hours, Tay thought. *Or until I have a complete mental breakdown. Whichever comes first.*

Instead of lighting another cigarette, Tay opened one of the books he bought at the 7-Eleven. He had recently discovered the

American novelist Don Winslow and was methodically working his way through his books. Finding one he hadn't read in a rack at the 7-Eleven was a stroke of luck.

Winslow wrote mostly about Southern California, a place Tay had never been and never wanted to go, but he had still found himself drawn into the almost apocryphal way Winslow described it. California was the future, Tay had heard for most of his life. Maybe it was. But that was only one of the many reasons Tay figured the past had so much to recommend it.

Tay read while Kang watched the green door and Lee sat in a chair and looked at something on her phone. The silence they shared had a quality to it that Tay rather liked.

After a while Tay closed the book and yawned. He walked over to the window and looked over Kang's shoulder. A fat, yellow cat had appeared from somewhere and Tay followed it as it stopped next to the green door, rubbed its back against something, and then slowly meandered away.

No more than a dozen feet down the alley the cat abruptly turned around, strolled back to the green door, and rubbed up against it again. Did the cat have an itch it couldn't scratch, or was it just wandering aimlessly, doing the first thing that came to mind? Either way, Tay knew how that cat felt. The story of his career in CID was exactly like that: half unscratched itch, and half pure aimlessness.

Despite collecting more than his share of commendations over the years, Tay had never really fit in. He knew a lot of his colleagues attributed that to the fact that his father was American. Tay was too independent, too individualistic, too…well, American. A good Singaporean kept his mouth shut, followed orders, and never stepped out of line. By that standard, Tay was not a good Singaporean.

Somehow, though, he had survived. His senior officers seemed as surprised as Tay was to find that, year after year, he was still around. He had put down roots in CID, he supposed, at least roots of a sort. He was like a tree growing out of a concrete parking lot. Stable, but not thriving.

Tay went back to his chair and picked up his book, but he didn't open it.

Three days was a long time to hang around an abandoned travel agency doing very little but watching a door through which almost no one either came or went, listening to false alarms over the radio. You ending up thinking about a lot of things at times like that, and Tay didn't really want to.

Surveillance was simply mind-numbing. Gloom and boredom were your unremitting companions because nothing happened.

Until it did.

"I may have something here, sir."

15

KANG'S VOICE WAS a merciful interruption to the plummeting spiral of Tay's increasingly dreary meditations. He got up and stood behind Kang who was bent forward bracing his elbows on his knees to steady the field glasses.

"I think it's her. The sister."

Kang handed the glasses back over his shoulder. Tay lifted them and studied the woman leaning on the wall next to the green door. Her arms were folded and she was looking up and down the alleyway.

"She just came outside," Kang said. "Maybe she's there for a smoke like that old woman we saw before."

Old woman? Tay lowered the glasses and looked at the back of Kang's head. He thought about telling Kang the *old woman* was only about ten years older than he was, but he knew he would sound ridiculous saying that so he didn't.

"What do you think, sir? It's her, isn't it?"

Tay swallowed his annoyance and went back to studying the woman.

Was it the same woman ISD identified as Suparman's sister? He wasn't sure.

Sergeant Lee came over to have a look and Tay handed her the glasses. "What do you think?" he asked.

Lee studied the woman. "She looks better than she does in the photographs," Lee said. "But I think Sergeant Kang is right. It's her."

"At least we know now that she's really here, sir," Kang said. "Do you want me to put it on the radio?"

"Not yet," Tay said. "Let's see what she does."

The woman hadn't taken out a cigarette so she hadn't come outside for a smoke. Besides, she was a guest at the hotel, not an employee, and in four hours of watching they hadn't seen a single guest use the emergency exit for any reason. What was this woman doing? She was just standing there looking up and down the alleyway.

Like she was waiting for someone.

Tay took the glasses back from Lee and trained them on the woman. She was wearing a light gray golf shirt, long black shorts which came to the center of her knee, and white athletic shoes. In her left hand she held a straw purse large enough to park a Volkswagen. She looked a little heavier than in photographs ISD gave them. Her skin was more sun-browned, and she even appeared a little younger. The longer Tay studied the woman, the more it seemed to him something here was not right.

Goh told them Suparman was slipping into Singapore to visit his sister because she was dying from cancer. Tay knew he ought to be cautious about offering a medical diagnosis from fifty yards away after watching the woman through field glasses for a few minutes, but there simply was no doubt in his mind.

This woman leaning against the wall outside the emergency exit wasn't dying from cancer or from anything else. At least not anytime soon. From what Tay could see, he was willing to bet she would outlive him.

Tay handed the glasses to Lee.

"Does she look sick to you?" he asked.

Lee studied the woman again and Tay waited, curious as to what she thought.

"I don't know, sir. She looks okay to me, but what do I know?"

Kang glanced back over his shoulder at Tay. "Why would they lie to us about that, sir?"

"Because it's what they do."

Kang looked puzzled. He didn't understand exactly what Tay meant by that. Tay didn't blame him. He wasn't absolutely sure what he meant either.

"What do you want to do, sir?" Kang asked.

"We are supposed to be watching for Suparman, not for her, so I suppose we do nothing."

"Maybe she came outside to wait for Suparman."

Tay nodded. That was exactly what he was thinking.

For a long while after that nothing at all happened. Tay, Kang, and Lee passed the glasses back and forth and watched the woman, but she only leaned against the wall next to the door, glancing up and down the alleyway.

The sun had reappeared and the alley was again filled with swirling hordes of people, which meant they occasionally lost sight of the woman. Singapore was usually a quiet, uncrowded city, except in tourist areas like Chinatown. Tay had observed that western tourists in particular had a way of walking that commandeered a lot of space in a crowd. He didn't know why that was, but it was clearly true.

"She's talking to someone, sir."

Tay took the glasses from Kang. The woman was still leaning against the wall next to the door, but now a man was standing directly in front of her. They looked as if they were carrying on a conversation.

"Where did he come from?"

"I'm not sure, sir. Just out of the crowd."

"Not from the hotel?"

"No, sir. I'm certain of that."

The man's back was to them and Tay couldn't see his face. He looked to be of average height with short black hair, and he was wearing dark slacks and a white, short-sleeved shirt with the tail out. He could have been anybody. Every man in Singapore was of average height with short black hair, and an untucked, short-sleeved white shirt over dark slacks was the standard male uniform.

"Do you think it's Suparman, sir?"

Tay said nothing. He simply had no idea.

"I don't think so," Lee offered. "He's not tall enough, is he?"

Tay said nothing. He just stared at the man's back through the glasses, willing him to turn around.

"Shouldn't we put it on the radio, sir?"

"And how is it we see what we're seeing, Sergeant Kang? Had you forgotten we're actually back at the Santa Grande Hotel watching television and waiting for our pals in ISD to give us a call?"

"Yes, sir, but—"

"Forget it. We say nothing unless we're absolutely sure we're looking at Suparman."

The problem was that Tay had no idea how they were going to do that unless the man cooperated by turning around and giving them a look at his face. If the conversation finished and the man walked away without them seeing his face, Tay knew he would feel like a real idiot.

"Go downstairs, Robbie. See if you can walk past them at an angle that will give you a good look at him without being obvious about it."

Kang picked up the radio. "If it's Suparman, sir, should I—"

"Just telephone me. But be absolutely sure *before* you telephone me. I don't want to be responsible for another false alarm."

Kang nodded, put the radio back on the desk, and headed downstairs.

16

THE WOMAN ABRUPTLY pushed herself away from the wall. It looked to Tay like the conversation was over. He also thought the man might have handed the woman something, but his view was blocked and he had no idea what it was, if it was anything at all. The woman and the man started walking slowly away together and for one tantalizing moment the man turned his head slightly. Tay was sure he was about to get a look at his face, but he didn't turn it quite far enough and all Tay saw was a flash of his profile. It wasn't nearly enough.

When Kang stepped out into the alleyway, he saw what was happening and called Tay.

"They're moving so slowly I think I can walk past them and come back. I ought to be able to see his face that way."

But before Tay could say anything, everything changed.

All at once the woman turned around and came directly toward Kang. The man speeded up and walked away in the opposite direction.

"Sergeant Lee and I are coming down, Robbie. You and Lee stay with her. I'll take him."

Tay and Lee left the radio, the backpack, Tay's books, and everything else, and ran for the stairs. When they stepped into the alleyway, Tay saw Kang's back disappearing into the crowd. He gathered Kang had eyes on the woman and she was somewhere in front of him. Back to his left, the news was not so good. The crowd had already swallowed up the man.

"Go," he snapped at Lee. "Don't lose her."

Turning in the opposite direction, Tay weaved through the throngs of tourists trying to catch sight of the man. He dodged a pushcart from which an elderly woman was selling ice cream and stepped out of the end of the alleyway into Pagoda Street.

The crowds were a bit thinner there and he swept his eyes back and forth. Then he had a stroke of luck. A flash of red caught his eye and he glanced toward a little girl who was jerking a balloon up and down by its string. About twenty feet beyond her, walking west toward New Bridge Road, he spotted the man. Something about the posture and the body language left Tay with no doubt he was looking at the same person he had seen in the alleyway.

That part of Pagoda Street had been blocked off to vehicles and turned into a walking street for tourists. Strings of hokey red and white paper lanterns fluttered overhead and carts displaying every imaginable kind of tourist junk stood shoulder to shoulder along both sides. Tay plowed into the crowd and hustled forward to keep the man in sight.

Following someone undetected when you are working alone is an almost impossible task, even for an expert. Tay understood that, and he also understood all too well that he was no expert. About all he knew about street surveillance was what he had picked up from reading John le Carré novels. Which suddenly gave him an idea.

Scanning the vendors' stalls, Tay spotted a middle-aged man looking at baseball caps that said *Singapore!* across the front. The man appeared to be having a hard time deciding between a blue one with white lettering and a red one with blue lettering, and he had taken off his own cap to try on first one and then the other and examine each in a little mirror hanging on the side of the stall. The man was concentrating on his image in the mirror and the stall's owner was concentrating on his customer to be sure he didn't steal anything, which gave Tay an opportunity to scoop up the man's old cap from the place he had momentarily set it aside.

Sliding back into the crowd, Tay glanced at the front of the light green hat he had just stolen. *Dolphins*, it said across the front beneath a cartoon of a large fish.

Why would anyone put the name of a fish on the front of a baseball cap?

Tay had absolutely no idea. He shook his head, jammed the cap down to his ears, and kept walking.

If the man he was after checked behind him for surveillance, he would see a man in a green cap that said *Dolphins*. After that Tay could ditch the cap and his appearance would be different if the man checked behind him again. It wasn't much, Tay knew, it might not be anything really, but the trick usually worked in spy novels and it was the only idea he had.

All of a sudden Tay lost sight of the man altogether. Three large Caucasian women in bulging shorts and t-shirts were walking very slowly right down the middle of the street with their arms linked and Tay couldn't see past them. As long as he could remember, the rotund nature of the city's Caucasian tourists had been a source of wonder and amusement for the locals. Did all the thin tourists go some place else, Singaporeans asked each other, or were the Caucasian tourists everywhere that fat?

Tay cut left between two t-shirt stalls, trotted through a scattering of small metal tables surrounded by white plastic chairs, and rejoined Pagoda Street on the other side of the three bovine woman. He was certain he had lost the man, but he moved back and forth through the crowd a few times and then a space opened in front of him and he found the man again. He was about fifty feet ahead and making straight for New Bridge Road.

But was it Suparman? Tay still had couldn't tell.

"Turn around, you son of a bitch," Tay muttered. "Give me a look at your face."

The man apparently wasn't feeling cooperative. Heedless of Tay's plea, he kept walking.

When he reached New Bridge Road, he jogged up the steps of a pedestrian bridge, crossed over the busy double roadway to the northbound lanes, and took the steps back down to a taxi stand in front of the People's Park Complex. A blue Comfort taxi pulled up when Tay was still forty feet from the stand and the man got in. Tay looked around frantically and was amazed at his luck when he saw another Comfort taxi just turning in. The cab hadn't even stopped rolling when Tay jerked open the door, ripped off his stolen baseball cap, and dived into the backseat.

"Follow that taxi, the blue one right in front of you," he snapped.

The driver turned his head and stared at his passenger, his eyes wide. He was an elderly Chinese man with a heavy black glasses and a bad haircut.

"I drive taxi more than thirty year," he said. "I always dream somebody say that to me."

Tay fumbled in his pocket, pulled out his warrant card, and held it up.

"This is police business. Get moving."

"Yes, sir!"

The rear tires spun as the driver gunned the engine and shot out of the taxi stand into New Bridge Road.

"Don't get too close," Tay snapped. "Just keep that taxi in sight and don't lose it."

"I no lose," the driver said. "I see *Fast and Furious*."

Wonderful, Tay thought. *I learned about surveillance from spy novels and this guy learned about driving from car chase movies. What could possibly go wrong?*

The traffic heading north on New Bridge Road was light and they had no difficulty keeping the other taxi in sight. They crossed the Singapore River on the Coleman Bridge and passed the Old

Hill Street Police Station without slowing down.

Before they reached Raffles, the little convoy turned west on Stamford Road, passed Fort Canning Park, and headed toward the hotels and malls of Orchard Road. It seemed unlikely to Tay that Suparman had been seized by an impulse to do some shopping, and even more unlikely he was staying in one of the very public five-star hotels in the area. Tay began to feel some serious doubts creeping in. Maybe this wasn't Suparman he was following. Notorious international terrorists didn't stay at the Four Seasons, did they?

Tay's telephone began to buzz. He fished it out of his shirt pocket and looked at the screen. Kang.

"What have you got?" Tay asked.

"We're in the Raffles Place MRT station, sir. She's getting on a train."

"Can you and Lee stay with her?"

"I don't know, sir. We'll try, but she may spot us. Neither one of us has much experience at this."

"Have faith, Sergeant. Surely she doesn't have any more experience at detecting surveillance than you have at doing it. Just don't lose her."

Tay disconnected the call and shoved the phone back in his pocket. He looked up in time to see they were coming up on the glass curtain walls of the ION Orchard Complex, still not completely rebuilt from the bombings. When he glanced back at the road ahead, he saw three blue Comfort taxis at different distances in front of them.

"Which one are we following?" Tay asked the driver.

"Right lane. Maybe one hundred feet in front."

The traffic light at Paterson Hill Road changed from green to yellow and the taxi they were following accelerated through it. Then the light changed to red.

"Don't slow down," Tay snapped. "Run the light!"

The driver's head began to rotate slowly toward Tay like a radar dish trying to fix on something unfamiliar and mystifying. Willfully disobeying the law was a foreign concept to every Singaporean, and Tay could see the man struggling to comprehend an instruction to do it.

"Run the fucking light! I'm the police!"

Disobeying the police was an even more foreign concept to every Singaporean.

The man floored the accelerator, slalomed between two buses, and shot through the intersection against the light. It was probably the most thrilling moment of his life.

The taxi they were following rolled along Orchard Boulevard. At the Camden Medical Centre, it turned right and headed north on Grange Road. Now they were moving away from the commercial district and nothing was in front of them but expensive apartments, even more expensive homes, and foreign embassy compounds. Did Suparman have wealthy supporters who had loaned him a house or an apartment to lie low in? That seemed unlikely, but Tay had seen stranger things.

Still heading north, the two taxis passed Tanglin Road, merged into Napier Road, and passed the American Embassy. The low-slung building was built out of giant blocks of stone that made the whole structure seem massively oversized. It sat well back from Napier Road atop a small, doubtless artificial rise and the grassy expanses surrounding it were a jangling contrast to its harshness of uncompromising gray stone structure. The American Embassy always reminded Tay of a cross between a Japanese warlord's castle and the elephant house at a very prosperous zoo.

A minute or two later Tay saw the blue Comfort taxi slow and signal a left turn into Middlesex Road.

That's strange, Tay thought. *There's nothing up there but…*

Before Tay had even completed his thought, the taxi turned off Middlesex Road into the main entrance of the Australian High Commission and stopped at the security gate.

"Keep going, keep going!" Tay shouted at his driver. "Don't slow down!"

The driver understood exactly what Tay meant and they rolled right on by Middlesex Road at a steady rate of speed. Just one more nondescript taxi plying the streets of Singapore.

As they passed the Australian High Commission, Tay watched the man he had been following get out of the taxi. He could see his face clearly now. The man was a Caucasian. He certainly wasn't Suparman.

Tay swiveled his head as they passed and watched the man as he was quickly cleared to pass through the security gate. Obviously somebody who was well known at the Australian High Commission.

So who the hell *was* he? And, more to the point, why had he met Suparman's sister outside the Temple Street Inn?

Oh, shit, Tay thought. *What have I gotten myself into?*

17

"TURN AROUND AND go back to Chinatown," Tay told the taxi driver.

He pulled out his telephone and pushed the speed dial number for Kang. "Do you still have Suparman's sister in sight?"

"Yes, sir. She got off the MTR at Farrer Park and took the steps up to Serangoon Road. She's walking south now."

"Has she spotted you?"

"I don't think so. Linda…uh, Sergeant Lee got ahead of her on the other side of the street so I've dropped back now."

"That sounds pretty slick."

"It was Linda's idea, sir. She's really good at this."

Tay lowered the telephone and leaned forward toward the cab driver. "Forget Chinatown. Take me to Serangoon Road."

"What place on Serangoon Road?"

"I'll tell you when we get there."

"Sir? Sir? Are you still there?"

The tinny scratching of Kang's voice from the telephone caused Tay to lift it back to his ear.

"Yes, I'm here, Robbie."

"She turned off to the right on some side street and I lost sight of her, but Linda is coming back toward me now. Maybe Linda

96

saw where she went."

Tay listened to the murmur of conversation between Kang and Lee, but he couldn't make out what they were saying.

"Sir?"

"Yes, Sergeant."

"Linda says Suparman's sister went into the Fortuna Hotel. It's over—"

"I know where it is."

Tay was as familiar as he wanted to be with the neighborhood where the Fortuna Hotel was. He thought it didn't have much to recommend it. It was…well, it wasn't anything really. Block after block of old shophouses had been razed a decade or so back in a harebrained rush to modernize the city, and all that had been put in their place were new buildings of no particular design. These days that part of Serangoon Road wasn't a real neighborhood at all, just a jumbled looking collection of unrelated buildings separated by empty lots and connected by mostly empty sidewalks. Serangoon Road carried a lot of traffic, but most of it was heading somewhere else as fast as it could.

"Just a minute, sir," Kang said.

The sound of murmuring started up again and Tay waited.

"Linda says there's a vegetarian restaurant on the other side of the street where we can watch the entrance to the hotel. What do you think?"

"Do it. Does the hotel have a back door?"

"I don't know, sir. It must. Doesn't everything in the world have a back door?"

Kang's question raised a metaphysical issue Tay had no interest in pondering, at least not right then. So he kept his response simple and practical.

"One of you check the hotel for other exits."

"Right, sir. Did you ID the man you followed? Was he Suparman?"

Tay hesitated. The story about following his man to the gate of the Australian High Commission was too strange to get into over the telephone, so he decided to keep it simple for now.

"No. Turned out to be just some guy."

"Then we don't—"

"I'm coming to you," Tay interrupted. "We're only a few minutes away." He broke the connection before Kang could say anything else.

Did ISD lie to him about Suparman's sister being sick, or did someone lie to ISD about it? And who was the man she met outside the Temple Street Inn? He could only enter the Australian High Commission as quickly and easily as Tay saw him enter it if he were someone who worked there. And it was probably safe to assume he didn't handle visa applications. If he was working on the street and involved in counterterrorism operations, he had to be either a cop or a spook.

So why was some Australian who was either a cop or a spook meeting with the sister of one of the world's most wanted terrorists? And Tay thought he had seen the man give her something. If he had given her something, what in the world could it have been?

Tay was sure he could detect the unmistakable odor of a set-up. But, if it was a set-up, that raised a much harder question.

Who exactly was being set up, and by whom?

Tay remembered a poker player's maxim he had heard somewhere once. *Look at the other players at the table*, the saying went, *and figure out who the sucker is. If you can't, it's you.*

The taxi driver's voice cut into Tay's reflections. "Serangoon Road just up here."

"Do you know the Fortuna Hotel?"

"I know."

"Quickly, please."

The driver looked at Tay over his shoulder and grinned. Then he slammed the accelerator to the floor.

Tay got out of the taxi across the road from the Fortuna Hotel, paid off the driver, and strolled slowly up the sidewalk to give himself enough time to look over the area.

The Fortuna Hotel was on the upper five floors of a reasonably modern six-story building facing Serangoon Road where it met Owen Road in a T-junction. A nondescript, four-story apartment building faced the hotel from the other side of Owen Road.

The ground floor of the hotel building was painted a dazzling shade of red in a vain effort to make it look more cheerful and the street-level space was entirely occupied by local businesses. There was a travel agency, a convenience store, a Western Union money transfer office, a fruit and vegetable stand, and a restaurant with a large sign in Arabic. The hotel lobby was also on Owen Road, but there wasn't much to it. No doorman, no grand staircase, no decoration at all. Just a pair of glass doors tucked between the travel agency and the convenience store. The Fortuna Hotel looked like a respectable tourist hotel, but the Ritz-Carlton it wasn't.

Just across Serangoon Road from the hotel and the apartment building a row of old shophouses had somehow survived. Some looked to be abandoned and some housed small shops, but in the middle of the row was an open-fronted restaurant with inexpensive metal tables and plastic chairs scattered around the cool dimness of its interior. The sign read, *The Vegetarian Restaurant*. Tay smiled at the admirably economical use of language and he decided that was where Sergeants Kang and Lee had to be waiting for him.

The table Lee and Kang had claimed offered a clear view across Serangoon Road to the entrance to the Fortuna Hotel.

"Is she still inside?" Tay asked as he walked up.

The metal folding chair was an unattractive shade of brown and when Tay pulled it out it scratched noisily across the cement floor.

"Yes, sir. The only exit other than the lobby door is right there."

Tay sat down and looked where Kang was pointing across Serangoon Road.

"See that gray metal door next to the Western Union office? It's some sort of emergency exit from the hotel. There're no exits on the other side of the building at all."

Tay nodded.

"What do you want to do, sir?"

"I have absolutely no idea."

Tay picked up a menu lying on the table. It was torn and stained and altogether unappealing. He was hungry, but what did you order in a vegetarian restaurant? A plate of green beans? Kang had nothing in front of him except a bottle of Coca-Cola and Lee had only a bottle of water. Perhaps that answered his question right there.

An Indian-looking woman in a maroon sari materialized beside the table and looked hopefully at Tay. She was very short, not even five feet in height, and had the wizened, deeply lined face of someone who had lived through a great deal. Tay didn't have the heart to tell her he didn't want any food so he picked something at random on the menu and pointed to it. Then he pointed to the Coca-Cola in front of Kang. The woman remained expressionless, but she nodded and walked away.

"Shouldn't we call this in now, sir?" Kang asked.

"Call in what?"

"We should tell ISD the sister is here now." Kang pointed unnecessarily at the Fortuna Hotel to indicate what he was talking about. "They think she's at the Temple Street Inn, but she's not."

"Forget it. We're not here, remember?"

"But, sir—"

"Besides, Sergeant, have you forgotten the radio is back in that building from which we were watching the inn, the one where we weren't supposed to be? So even if I agreed with you that we should contact Mr. Goh, how would you propose we do that? Perhaps telephone ISD and leave a message for him?"

Kang didn't say anything, but he didn't look happy.

"We are on our own here, Sergeant. We either figure out what to do, or we eat some broccoli and go home."

The woman in the maroon sari returned just then and plunked down in front of Tay a bottle of Coca-Cola and a blue plastic plate. The plate had something on it that was long and flat and looked brown and slimy.

What in God's name had he ordered?

It certainly wasn't broccoli or even green beans, which were the only two vegetables that came readily to mind. Tay tried to remember which line he had pointed to on the menu so maybe Lee could explain to him what he ordered, but he couldn't remember.

At least the Coca-Cola looked safe enough. He took out a handkerchief, wiped the mouth of the bottle, and took a long pull.

It was warm.

18

THE MOMENT SHE saw the woman walking toward her on Serangoon Road, she was pretty sure it was the rabbit.

She picked up her phone, scrolled through the photographs, and glanced back and forth between the phone and the woman. She didn't have much doubt, and when the woman turned on Owen Road and pushed through the glass doors into the lobby of the Fortuna Hotel, she had no doubt at all.

But what was going on? Her people were supposed to have eyes on the woman and give her a heads up when she headed this way. Did she give them the slip somehow? Or was something else going on, something she didn't quite yet understand.

And where the hell was the target? Maybe he was already inside the hotel. She was certain she hadn't seen him go in, absolutely certain, but it was possible he got past her. She couldn't keep her eyes on those doors twenty-four hours a day. She was good, but nobody was *that* good. It would have been lousy luck for the target to walk into the hotel when she was in the toilet or napping, but was it possible? Of course it was possible. Every operation came with a little bit of lousy luck. Perhaps this was hers.

She told the cheap bastards to give her a full team, but they said it wasn't necessary. Not necessary, huh?

She took a long drink from a bottle of water and thought about it. She would give it an hour, she decided, and see what developed. If nothing developed, she would call in for instructions.

Either the target was inside the hotel now or he was coming soon. Even if he had gotten past her going in, there was no way on earth the bastard was going to get past her going out. She'd get him. One way or the other, she'd get him.

This was what she did. And there was nobody better at it than she was.

After the sister disappeared into the hotel lobby, the woman's eyes instinctively quartered the area around the hotel looking for surveillance patterns. She had no reason to believe anyone else was tracking the sister, but she checked regardless. She always checked.

And it was that checking that drew her attention to the woman walking on the opposite side of Serangoon Road. She had stopped exactly at the moment the sister went into the Fortuna Hotel, turned around, and crossed the road where she and a man who had been walking behind the sister on the same side of the road met on the sidewalk. They talked for a moment and the man made a telephone call.

The man was tall and very thin and wore heavy black glasses. The woman was young, fit looking, and attractive. Her guess was they were both locals, but of course she couldn't be sure.

Were they working surveillance on the rabbit, or were they just two people who knew each other well enough to say hello on the street? She watched as the conversation ended and the man crossed Serangoon Road and took a table in an open-fronted vegetarian restaurant which had a clear view of the entrance to the Fortuna Hotel. The woman made a circuit around the hotel, checking for other exits it looked like, and then she crossed the road and joined the man in the restaurant.

That seemed to settle it. She couldn't think of any other reasonable interpretation.

The sister was under surveillance by somebody, but who? Was it possible the couple she was watching even worked for the same people she did? Not likely, she decided, but not completely impossible.

She picked up one of the burners and hit the speed dial for the only number in its memory. When the call connected, she spoke without waiting for the man on the other end to say something because she knew he wouldn't.

"Do you have eyes on the rabbit?" she asked.

"Affirmative, hunter. She is still at the Temple Street Inn."

Really? Then those couldn't be their people sitting in that vegetarian restaurant, could they?

"Then hold onto your hat because I've got a real surprise for you. Your rabbit just walked up Serangoon Road big as life and straight into the lobby of the Fortuna Hotel."

There was a pause. She waited.

"Are you certain, hunter?"

"Absolutely certain. She's inside the hotel now."

"That's not my information." The man thought about it for a moment. "Can you get eyes on whoever you saw and reconfirm her identity?"

"No chance of that. On the other hand, I do have eyes on the man and the woman who have her under surveillance."

"Say again?"

"A man and a woman tailed her here. Now they're both sitting in a restaurant with a view of the lobby doors."

That brought another silence, as she thought it might.

"Can you identify them?"

"My first thought was they might be yours."

"Negative."

"Yeah, I've already worked that out for myself."

The man cleared his throat. "What about the fox?"

"No sign of him. Either he's not in the hotel yet or he got past me."

"It was your job to make sure he didn't get past you."

"Well, fuck you very much. I sleep a little and I even pee occasionally just like a real human being. If you had given me a full team, we would have had eyes on twenty-four hours, but you didn't give me a team and I'm doing the best I can working alone here. So shove that sanctimonious crap about me doing my job right up your ass, pal. Are we clear?"

The man chuckled. "You're a real piece of work, aren't you, little girl?"

"Call me little girl one more time, you piece of shit, and I'll shove something a lot bigger than your sanctimonious crap up your ass."

She stabbed at the off button and slammed the phone down on the table.

Prick.

She got herself another bottle of water and a PowerBar and sat back down in front of the window. While she ate and drank, she thought about what to do.

Well, what *could* she do? The target was either in the hotel or he wasn't. If he weren't inside already, he would be coming soon. If he was inside now, he had to come out again, and she wasn't going to miss him this time. Looking at it that way, she felt a lot better.

A taxi caught her eye as it pulled to the curb on Serangoon Road. She watched a man get out and walk slowly south. It wasn't the fox. Not even close.

Still, this wasn't the kind of neighborhood in which a lot of people took strolls so she followed the man with her eyes. She wasn't particularly surprised when he joined the man and woman she had made for surveillance and sat down at the table they had taken in the vegetarian restaurant. She lifted the binoculars and studied him.

He was middle-aged, of average height, and could honestly stand to lose a few pounds. He was also older than the other two, and from their body language she could see he was in charge.

Okay, she thought, they've called in some kind of supervisor, although she still didn't see what he might be a supervisor *of*.

Who the hell was she dealing with here? Cops? Not likely. Why would the local cops have the target's sister under surveillance? She certainly hadn't done anything to attract the attention of law enforcement, at least not as far as she knew.

If it wasn't law enforcement, it had to be an intelligence operation. Most likely it was the locals, which meant Singapore's Internal Security Department, but she supposed it could be almost anybody. The Brits, the Aussies, the French, the Germans, even the Israelis were active in Singapore. Could it be one of them?

Whatever it was, she wasn't real happy. Taking down the target in front of people working for an intelligence organization that was obviously looking for him just meant she was going to piss off somebody big time, and they were almost certainly going to come looking for her. She had an exit route from Singapore mapped out, of course, a damned good one, and a couple of alternatives just in case something went wrong with the primary one, but that wasn't what bothered her. She just didn't like performing in front of an audience. That was something you never did in her business unless you absolutely had to. At least not if you intended to stay in her business.

She was still thinking about that when a dirty white Toyota pulled up across Serangoon Road from the vegetarian restaurant and stopped near the hotel's emergency exit. When no one got out, she shifted her field glasses to the Toyota and examined the two men in the front seat. They were younger and thicker than any of the three at the table in the restaurant. She didn't know who they were either, but they sure weren't students of architecture admiring the local cityscape.

She swung the glasses back to the restaurant. The three at the table appeared to have noticed the Toyota, too, but it looked like they had no idea who it was either. Did that meant she had two entirely separate sources of company now, not one? It certainly looked that way.

Who the hell are all these people?

She was already considering packing up and scrubbing the whole operation when the older man sitting in the restaurant got up and walked out to the sidewalk. He lit a cigarette and stood quietly smoking in the shadows. There was something about the man she liked. She couldn't put her finger on what it was, but there it was anyway. Just something in his body language, she supposed.

The man turned and spoke over his shoulder, and the man and woman at the table got up and joined him. The three of them stood there, the older man continuing to smoke, and all of them looking at something on the other side of Serangoon Road.

She swung the binoculars to follow their eyes and saw that a silver blue Hi-Lux van, unmarked and without windows, had stopped right behind the white Toyota. While she watched, the door in the side of the van opened and three men got out. They all wore sunglasses in spite of the fading light, and they all had their shirts hanging over their belts. Guns were concealed under those flapping shirttails. She had not the slightest doubt of that.

So who were *they?*

It didn't really matter, she supposed. She knew a cluster fuck when she saw one, and this was shaping up as a doozy.

She was out of there.

It would take her no more than five minutes to pack everything, maybe another ten minutes or so to wipe down the place with a little bleach. Then she was out the door and no one would ever know she was there. Not unless she wanted them to know.

19

"MAYBE WE'RE NOT on our own after all, sir."

Kang pointed and Tay shifted his eyes to where Kang was pointing.

"Doesn't that look like CID surveillance to you?" Kang asked.

A dirty white Toyota was parked on the other side of Serangoon Road not far from the hotel's emergency exit. Two men sat in the front seat. They had short hair and wore nondescript short-sleeved white shirts. They appeared to be watching the Fortuna Hotel.

Tay studied the men for a moment. "I don't recognize either of them. Do you?"

Kang shook his head and looked at Lee, who shook her head as well.

"Might be Central Narcotics Bureau, sir," she said. "It's that sort of neighborhood."

Tay grunted. "Or it could be ISD."

"I don't think so, sir," Kang said. "If ISD had followed her from Temple Street, we would have seen them, and we didn't."

"Unless they knew where she was going and didn't have to follow her."

Kang scrunched up his face. "That doesn't make any sense, sir."

"Maybe not," Tay said, inclining his head in the direction of the

Toyota, "but then who the hell *are* they and what are they doing here?"

"Maybe it's got nothing to do with Suparman's sister," Kang suggested. "Maybe it's just a coincidence."

Tay gave Kang a look, but Kang wouldn't meet his eyes.

Tay reached for his cigarettes and the Indian-looking woman scurried over to the table before the pack was even out of his shirt pocket.

"No, no!" She waved both her arms above her head like a sports referee signaling a foul, which in a manner of speaking Tay supposed she was. "No smoking! No smoking! I call police!"

Everyone in Singapore loved enforcing the law. Sometimes Tay wondered why it was necessary for Singapore to have a police force at all. He considered telling the woman that they *were* the police, but he almost immediately abandoned the idea. This business with Suparman and his sister was getting stranger and stranger by the minute, and Tay had an unhappy feeling the end of the strangeness was still a long way off. Making a fuss about the presence of three policemen on the scene that might cause them to be remembered later seemed like a really bad idea.

Tay sighed, stood up, and walked out to the sidewalk. He shook a cigarette out of the pack and glanced back at the woman. She glared at him, still itching to order him not to smoke, but he was outside the restaurant and now there was nothing she could do about it.

He had always believed there was something deranged about the fanatics who treated smokers as if they were having public sex with goats. Didn't these people have anything better to do than scream at other people who enjoyed a cigarette now and then? No, probably not, which was no doubt the reason they put so much energy into their screaming.

Tay stood in the shadows smoking quietly. It had begun to rain again and he listened to the staccato splashing of the drops on Serangoon Road and the *plop, plop, plop* of a drip from a gutter somewhere nearby. The street was the color of steel and the rain scratched the twilight and gave it the silvery, monochrome tint of an old silent movie. The city hung in the air like a spectral projection.

The two men in the Toyota hadn't moved and Tay still couldn't work out who they were or what they were doing there. He doubted they were CID or even Central Narcotics. His gut told him they were ISD, but then how did they get there? If they had followed Suparman's sister there, surely they would have spotted Kang and Lee and they would know somebody else was around, too. But if they knew somebody else was around, would they just be sitting out there in the open? No, of course they wouldn't. That meant they didn't know, even if Tay couldn't quite see how that could be.

If they hadn't followed the sister, how did they get there? Had ISD known all along she would slip out of Chinatown and go to the Fortuna Hotel? Tay shook his head. He didn't see how that made the slightest amount of sense. All this cloak and dagger bullshit gave him indigestion so he decided to stop thinking about it, smoke his cigarette, and see what developed.

Nothing at all developed the whole time he was smoking. But then he took a final puff, dropped the butt on the sidewalk, and stood on it with the heel of his shoe, and that was exactly when something *did* develop.

A silver blue Hi-Lux van, unmarked and without windows, stopped right behind the white Toyota. The door in the side of the van slid open and three men got out. Big men, all wearing dark sunglasses and all with their shirts hanging over their belts. Tay knew the look. They had guns under those shirttails.

"You better come see this," Tay called out softly to Kang and Lee.

When they both got to the front of the restaurant, the three men were standing on the sidewalk next to the van. They weren't exactly hiding, but Tay noticed the men stayed far enough up Serangoon Road so as not to be visible from the hotel's lobby. One of them walked over to the passenger side of the Toyota and bent down to talk to the men inside. It was a short conversation. After less than a minute he straightened up and walked back to the group by the van.

"Who are those guys?" Lee asked.

Tay said nothing.

"You think they're ISD, don't you, sir?"

Tay looked at the faces of the three men. He didn't think he recognized them, but at that distance he couldn't be sure. Maybe he had seen a couple of them in the meeting at New Phoenix Park, maybe he hadn't.

So Tay said nothing. He only lifted his shoulders and let them fall in the smallest possible shrug.

"Now who the hell is *that?*"

Tay glanced at Kang to see what he was talking about and Kang pointed at the apartment building across Owen Road from the hotel.

The building was old and a little rundown. Once white with blue trim, nothing was now even close to the color it must have been on whatever long-ago day it had last been painted. Rusty air-conditioner units poked through the walls at regular intervals and long streaks of brown water striped the building beneath them. Something about the structure seemed vaguely familiar to Tay. Had he once investigated a case that had some connection to it? If he had, he couldn't put his finger on what case it might have been.

"Third floor, sir. The corner window."

Tay counted up to the third floor and his eyes found the corner of the building.

"Do you see her, sir? The girl?"

Tay did see her. She was standing close to the glass and appeared to be watching the same men he and Kang were watching.

She was European, or perhaps American or Australian. Certainly not Asian. Long blonde hair pulled back in a ponytail, suntanned face, and features so neat and regular they could have been molded from plastic. She was attractive, no doubt about that, but something in the way she held herself gave Tay the sense she carried a presence, too, although what kind of presence he had no idea.

The distance was too great to be certain, but Tay guessed the girl was in her thirties, which meant he probably shouldn't be thinking of her as a girl. At Tay's age, however, he found himself thinking of almost all the attractive woman he encountered as girls. No doubt a great many people, most of them women, would be outraged to know he was harboring such thoughts, but thankfully none of them did. And if he kept his mouth shut, maybe none of them ever would.

"If those men are ISD and they're watching Suparman's sister," Kang said, "who is that girl watching *them*? She's not one of ours, is she?"

Tay shook his head.

"Okay, we're CID and she's not ours. They're ISD and she's watching them so she's not theirs either. Who does that leave? Who the hell *is* she?"

It was a good question. Tay had no answer for it so he said nothing.

20

SERGEANT LEE HAD kept her eyes on the men in the Toyota while Tay and Kang were speculating about the girl who appeared to be observing from the apartment building.

"Look, sir," she cut in, "they're getting out."

Tay shifted his eyes from the girl in the window to the men in the Toyota. He watched them walk up Serangoon Road and turn right into Owen Road. Whoever the men were, they were going into the Fortuna Hotel.

"I'll bet Suparman is in there with his sister right now," Kang said. "And those guys really are ISD and they are going to take him down."

"Why would ISD have all those people watching the Temple Street Inn for Suparman if they knew he was really at the Fortuna Hotel?"

Kang shrugged. "You got me, sir."

Tay looked back up at the window in the rundown apartment building from which the girl had been watching. She was gone. That was strange. Had she just lost interest or had she—

"Bloody hell," Kang muttered, interrupting Tay's meditations. He looked back to see what had caught Kang's attention.

The silver van was rolling slowly down Serangoon Road. When

it got to Owen Road, it turned, crossed over to the wrong side of the street, and stopped in front of the hotel entrance. The sliding door slammed back on the sidewalk side of the vehicle and four men piled out, the three who had been standing on the sidewalk before and a tall man wearing an Indonesian-batik shirt that Tay couldn't see clearly.

"What do you want to do, sir?"

Tay said nothing.

"We can't just stand here and watch."

"Why not, Sergeant? We don't even know what the hell it is we're watching."

"But, sir—"

"Look, why do I have to keep reminding you we're not here? And if we're not here," Tay said pointing toward the lobby of the Hotel Fortuna, "we're certainly not over there either."

That was true as far as it went, Tay knew, but it didn't go very far.

Tay was certain the men they were watching were ISD. They must be at the Fortuna Hotel because they knew Suparman's sister was meeting Suparman there, and now they were going in to take Suparman down.

But if these men really were ISD and they were there to take Suparman down, what was all that bullshit Goh had shoveled over everybody about the Temple Street Inn? Was that just intentional misdirection for some reason, or had everything simply changed at the last minute and no one bothered to tell CID?

Tay wasn't a stand-and-watch kind of guy, but he didn't see what alternative they had. What were they going to do? Rush into the hotel and shout, *you're under arrest!* They had two pistols between the three of them and there were five or six armed men in the hotel. The odds were lousy.

"It's a hotel, sir."

It was the first time Sergeant Lee had spoken up since the flurry of action began and both Tay and Kang looked at her.

"A hotel is open to the public. I can just walk into the lobby and see what's going on."

"We all could, Sergeant Lee, but we're not."

"I think we should, sir, and I ought to be the one to do it. People usually think a woman is harmless. You and Sergeant Kang might spook them."

"And are you harmless?"

"Only if I want to be."

Tay smiled in spite of himself.

The three of them stood in silence and watched, but because of the silver van blocking their view of the lobby entrance there wasn't much to see. The upper floors of the hotel were all visible, of course, but no one was at any of the windows, none of the windows were open even if they could be opened, and nothing up there seemed unusual or out of place.

If there was gunfire, Tay knew, they would have to go in. Although he didn't say that out loud, he was certain Kang and Lee knew it, too. They couldn't just stand there if they heard gunfire. So he hoped to hell he *wouldn't* hear gunfire because he didn't have the faintest idea what they would do if they did have to go into the hotel.

"Did you say there are no entrances or exits other than the lobby and one emergency exit?"

"Yes, sir," Sergeant Lee said. "The emergency exit is that metal door next to the Western Union office."

Tay ran his eyes over the shops on the ground floor of the hotel until he found the Western Union office. The metal door next to it looked insignificant, more like the door to a storage room than an emergency exit from the hotel, but he knew Lee was certain or she wouldn't have said anything.

After what felt like half an hour but was really more like five minutes, one of the men came back out through the lobby entrance and walked out to Serangoon Road. He stood on the corner looking in first one direction then the other as if he were expecting someone. He took out his telephone and spoke for perhaps fifteen seconds. Then he shoved his phone back in his pocket, turned around, and went back inside the hotel.

"What was that all about?" Kang asked.

Tay shrugged. "I have absolutely no idea."

"It looks like they're expecting somebody. You think it's Suparman they're expecting?"

Tay said nothing.

"I don't get it," Lee said. "They're not making any effort to conceal themselves. Won't that frighten off Suparman if he does show up?"

"Maybe he's already inside," Kang said.

"Then why hasn't ISD grabbed him?"

"Maybe those guys aren't ISD."

"We're going around in circles," Tay said.

The rain had stopped, but the tires of the cars passing on Serangoon Road made little hissing sounds in the water spread over its surface. Tay got bored looking at nothing. He shook another Marlboro out of his pack and lit it.

"Did either of you try the emergency exit to see if it opens from the outside?" Tay asked.

"No, sir," Lee said. "I wasn't thinking about making entry, just about how people could get out of the hotel."

"I want you and Sergeant Kang over there by the emergency exit. Check and make sure you can get inside through it. If something happens and we have to go in, I'll take the front and the two of you take it."

"You're not armed, sir," Kang said.

"I'm well aware of that, Sergeant, but we aren't going to shoot it out with those guys. Our best hope is for me to get their attention and then you and Sergeant Lee come in behind them. If you can cover them before they realize you're there, perhaps we can get control of the situation before anybody gets hurt."

"And what will we do then, sir?"

Tay smoked quietly and thought about that for a moment. Finally he shrugged and said, "I have no idea."

Kang and Lee crossed Serangoon Road about a hundred feet north of the hotel and strolled casually back toward the emergency exit on the sidewalk. When they were still thirty yards away, Kang stopped walking so abruptly that Lee bumped into him.

"Did you hear that?" he asked her.

She shook her head.

"I thought I heard gunshots."

"From inside the hotel?"

Kang nodded and cocked his head, but now all he heard was the traffic on Serangoon Road.

"You really didn't hear anything?" he asked.

Sergeant Lee shook her head again.

Kang glanced across the road at Tay, but he didn't look like he had heard anything either.

"Maybe it was something else," Kang said.

But it wasn't something else, because at exactly that moment everything began to happen at once.

The gray metal door next to the Western Union office banged open from the inside and a woman ran out into Serangoon Road. She spotted a taxi moving north and jumped into the street to cut it off.

A chorus of car horns sounded and a green Mercedes veered out of his lane to avoid the woman. A bus trying to get out of the way of the Mercedes clipped the side of a flatbed truck that was loaded with automobile tires. The impact dislodged one of the truck's tie-downs and two tires slid off the back of the truck, bounced upright on the concrete road surface, and wobbled wildly off into the traffic.

"Bloody hell," Kang muttered to Lee. "Where did *she* come from?"

One of the bouncing tires crossed in front of the green Mercedes and the driver slammed on his brakes. He was immediately rear-ended by a white Audi whose driver had turned his head to look at the truck that was now skewed sideways across the road.

The woman ran into the inside lane waving her arms at the taxi and it slammed to a stop right in front of her. She stumbled and fell, catching herself on the hood.

"That's her!" Lee shouted to Kang. "That's the sister!"

Kang took half a dozen running steps and grabbed the emergency exit door just before it slammed shut.

"You grab her, Linda! I'm going in!"

Holding the door open with his hip, Kang unholstered his H&K forty calibre, racked the slide to chamber a round, and plunged into the hotel.

Kang's run toward the emergency exit had caught the eye of the woman even though she was still lying against the hood of the taxi. When she saw Kang disappear into the hotel, she pushed herself up, abandoned the taxi, and took off running up Serangoon Road.

Sergeant Lee went after the woman just as Kang had asked her to, but she was uneasy and she kept shooting glances over her shoulder at the emergency exit. She knew she shouldn't have let Kang go in by himself. Then she spotted Tay sprinting through the traffic toward the lobby of the hotel and that made up her mind for her. She let the woman go, turned around, and ran after Kang.

Inside the door, Lee found herself in what looked like a large storeroom. Several pieces of luggage sat in front of a set of open shelves filled with cleaning supplies. There were two black vinyl chairs pushed into the opposite corner and several large cardboard boxes piled on and around the chairs. In the wall next to the shelves was a door with an aluminum crash bar and a sign above it that said *EXIT*.

Behind her, the din of car horns was deafening.

The collisions had blocked Serangoon Road and drivers were frustrated and impatient. When the woman got about a hundred feet up the road, she saw nobody was chasing her and she slowed to walk and looked back over her shoulder at the havoc she had left behind her.

That was why she didn't see the white box truck.

It came out of a side street and the driver was so surprised to discover the break in what was normally heavy traffic that he gunned the truck straight out into Serangoon Road without slowing down. He hardly expected to find a woman standing in front of him.

She never had a chance.

The impact flipped her high into the air and she came down on top of the truck's cab. Her body bounced off the truck and onto the roadway twenty feet behind it. Then it rolled another ten feet until it stopped up against the curb.

21

THE LOBBY OF the Fortuna Hotel was as small, nondescript, and functional as Tay had imagined. A reception desk on the left, two low-backed black vinyl chairs on the right, and an elevator and a staircase straight ahead. Next to the staircase was a black metal door with a sign above it that said *Emergency Exit.*

An elderly Chinese man peered quizzically at Tay from behind the tiny registration desk. He wore a rumpled white shirt and rimless glasses with lenses so thick they looked as if they had been cut from the bottoms of soft drink bottles.

"How you get here so quick?" he asked Tay.

"What are you talking about?"

"I just call police," the desk clerk said. "One minute ago. But you here already." The old man's eyes narrowed. "You no police?"

Tay pulled out his warrant card and held it up. The old man leaned forward. He squinted at Tay's warrant card so intently his eyes were almost closed. He began slowly reading it, moving his lips with each word.

"Look at me," Tay snapped. "Why did you call the police?"

The man lifted his eyes from Tay's warrant card.

"Heard *BANG*, didn't I? Sound like gun, I think. Then woman run downstairs and go out there."

The clerk pointed at the black metal door next to the staircase.

"Are you sure it was a gun you heard?"

The desk clerk looked at Tay like he was an idiot.

"*BANG!*" he said again, making a little gun out of his thumb and forefinger. "*BANG, BANG.* Like that. Two times. I good citizen. I call police. I call right away."

The metal door slammed open and Sergeant Lee dived through it in a crouch, her revolver thrust out in front of her. She saw Tay talking to the clerk and she straightened up and tilted the barrel of her gun toward the ceiling, but she didn't put it away.

The clerk's face twisted in puzzlement. "What the fuck?"

Tay ignored the clerk. "Where's Kang?" he asked Lee.

"He said he heard shots and came in ahead of me."

Tay glanced back at the clerk. "Another police officer came in here right after the woman ran out?"

The clerk nodded very slowly and pointed to the staircase. "He go up."

"Call it in," Tay said to Lee.

"Yes, sir."

She pulled out her phone and Tay turned back to the desk clerk.

"The woman who ran out. Was she a guest here?"

"No. She come maybe one hour ago. Say she meeting brother in room 201."

"Who's in room 201?"

The clerk bent forward and reached below the counter top. In the silence Tay could hear the clicking of a keyboard.

"Uh...it say here Mr. Tan."

"Of course it does. What does Mr. Tan look like?"

"Not know," the clerk shrugged. "Room rented last night. I not here."

"So this woman went up to Mr. Tan's room?"

The clerk nodded.

"What happened after that?"

"Nothing happen until other men come. Two men first. Then

four more." The clerk's eyes flicked left and right and then settled. "They have guns. They say they police, but I no think they real police."

Tay wasn't sure what that meant, but he let it go.

"What happened then?" he asked.

"They say they here to see Mr. Tan, too. They go upstairs. Three on elevator. Others take stairs."

Tay figured Mr. Tan's room had to be pretty full by then.

Sergeant Lee put her telephone away. "Fast response cars on the way, sir."

BANG!

The noise came from somewhere above them and it sounded like a gunshot. All three of them reflexively looked up, but of course they saw nothing but the ceiling.

"Robbie is by himself," Lee said. "I'll lead, sir. You're not armed."

Tay pointed a finger at the desk clerk. "Stay here. When the other officers get here send them to 201 and tell them that CID is already up there."

The clerk nodded, but neither Tay nor Lee saw him nod. They were already running for the stairs.

At the first landing, Lee paused and put her ear to a metal door that had the number 1 painted on it.

Silence.

Tay felt like an idiot just standing there, but without a weapon he knew he was only in the way.

Lee turned the knob as quietly as she could and cracked the door enough to peer into the hallway. It appeared empty so she gave the door a hard shove and moved through it in a crouch, her revolver out in front of her in a two-handed grip. She swung the barrel left and right, but the hallway was deserted in both directions.

She started back to the stairs, but Tay put a hand on her arm.

He walked along the hallway and examined the numbers on the door until he found 101 all the way at the end. It was well past the elevator and at least sixty feet from the stairs.

"The rooms are probably arranged the same way on every floor," he said. "When we come out of the stairs on the second floor we should be far enough away that they won't hear us."

"If they're in room 201."

"It's all we have."

At the second landing, Lee went through the same routine again: first her ear to the door, then a tiny crack to peer through, then a push and a lunge into the hallway with her pistol in front of her while making herself as small a target as she could. But this time Tay didn't just stand there. He came through the door right behind her.

This hallway wasn't empty like the first floor hallway had been. In fact, it was so crowded that for a moment Tay couldn't process everything he saw there.

About fifty feet up the hall a man sat on the floor with his back to the wall. He was dressed in brown pants and a short-sleeved red and white Indonesian-style batik shirt with open-toed leather sandals on his feet. He was tall and thin with long black hair brushed straight back. Even from a distance, Tay could see the man's breathing was labored and he clutched his left arm awkwardly across his chest.

The two men who had been watching the hotel from the Toyota were now squatting in front of the man with the batik shirt and one of them was holding a plastic bottle of water to his lips. Behind them, the three men from the silver van stood in a knot talking. Two of them had handguns out and held them down by their legs.

Halfway between the stairway door and the group of men at the other end of the hall was another man. He was lying face down on the dirty brown carpet with a handgun next to him and he wasn't moving.

It was Robbie Kang.

22

WHEN TAY AND Lee burst out of the stairwell, the men in the hallway all swiveled toward them and an instant later they had five handguns trained at them.

"Police! Police!" Tay and Lee screamed almost together. "Put your guns down and get on the floor!"

That brought smiles all around as well as a few chuckles. Nobody put his gun down, and nobody appeared to be considering getting on the floor.

One man detached himself from the group and walked slowly toward Tay and Lee. He was older than the others, and he had a shaved head, a blocky face, a muscular body, and big, slightly pointed ears that stuck straight out from his head. Tay thought there was something familiar looking about the man. Did he know him from somewhere? No, he didn't think so. Then all at once it hit him. The man looked like Bruce Willis with Chinese eyes.

"Now who the *fuck* are you?" Bruce Willis demanded, swinging his pistol from Tay to Lee and back again.

Tay ignored him, walked straight to where Kang was lying on the floor, and dropped to his hands and knees.

"Robbie," Tay called softly, "can you hear me?"

Kang didn't reply, and he didn't move.

Tay took Kang by the shoulders and gently rolled him over. He saw the jagged hole above Kang's left eye just below his hairline. An exit wound. The entry wound must have been lost in Kang's hair. The bastards shot him in the back of his head.

"Call an ambulance, Sergeant!"

Tay tried not to look at the raw wound bubbling blood. Kang's pupils were already dilated and he knew what that meant. He reached out and rubbed a streak of blood off of Kang's face with his hand.

"Nobody is calling anybody," Bruce Willis snapped. "Stand up and put your hands on your head."

Tay never took his eyes off Robbie Kang. "I'm Inspector Tay and this is Sergeant Lee from CID."

"I don't give a shit who you are or where you say you're from. Stand up and put your hands on your head!"

Tay looked over his shoulder at Bruce Willis and slowly rose to his feet. He kept his hands away from his body, but he moved slightly to his left to block the man's line of sight to Lee.

"My warrant card is in my wallet in my right back pocket."

Behind him Tay heard Lee murmuring into her phone and he knew she hadn't backed down. *Good girl!* he thought. Maybe he was wrong. Maybe it wasn't too late for Robbie after all.

"Turn around," Bruce Willis snapped at Tay.

Tay turned very deliberately and lifted his eyes to Lee just as she pushed her phone back into one pocket.

"Ambulance is on the way, sir."

When Tay's back was to him, Bruce Willis stepped forward, placed the muzzle of his gun against Tay's neck, and shoved his free hand into the right back pocket of Tay's trousers. He pulled out Tay's wallet and flicked through it with his thumb until he found the warrant card. He plucked it out between his thumb and forefinger and let the wallet drop to the floor.

"Hey!" Lee snapped. "Show a little respect."

"Shut the fuck up."

Lee shook her head, but she shut up.

The man studied Tay's warrant card for a moment then he opened his fingers and let it fall to the floor near Tay's wallet.

"What are you doing here?" he asked.

Tay started to turn around.

"Hey, I didn't tell you to move!"

Tay turned around anyway and lowered his hands.

"I don't give a fuck what you told me. I'm an inspector in the Special Investigations Section of the Criminal Investigations Department of the Singapore Police. How dare you point a weapon at me? I demand you lower that gun and identify yourself at once."

"You demand, huh?" Bruce Willis snickered. Then he glanced around at the men jammed in the hallway behind him. Right on cue they all snickered, too.

"It looks to me, man, like we're the ones in a position to do the demanding here, not you."

Tay took a step forward and leveled his finger at the man's face. "What are you going to do? Shoot a CID inspector? Even you ISD goons aren't that stupid."

"I never said I was ISD."

"You didn't have to. You're not smart enough to be anything else."

"You've really got a mouth on you, don't you, man?" Bruce Willis looked at Tay for a long moment, and then he grinned. "You got anything else funny to say?"

"Yeah. You're under arrest."

"Under arrest?" the man snorted. "Yeah, that's a good one all right."

"I'm placing you under arrest for the attempted murder—"

"John," Bruce Willis called out, his voice rising over Tay's, "bring the van around to the side door. Henry, get up here."

There was a shuffling around of the bodies in the hallway. One man walked past Tay and Lee to the stairs and headed down, and another stepped up next to Bruce Willis.

"Just a damn minute," Tay growled. "If you think you going to—"

"Cuff the asshole," Bruce Willis snapped to the guy standing next to him, jerking his head at Tay. Then he glanced at Lee. "Her, too. Take her gun."

The man stepped forward, spun Tay around, and shoved him into the wall. With professional ease he quickly frisked Tay. Then he produced zip-ties from his pocket, slipped one around Tay's wrists, and pulled it tight. He pulled Lee's gun out of her hand, shoved it in his waistband, and did the same to her.

Tay started to turn back around, but a big hand pushed him roughly into the wall and held him there.

"Sit down, both of you. Put your backs against the wall."

Tay saw how pointless it would be to resist so he looked at Lee and nodded, and they sat down.

Bruce Willis looked back over his shoulder. "Pick up our guy and help him downstairs. Put him in the van when John gets it around."

At the other end of the hall two of the men helped red batik shirt to his feet. He looped his right arm over the shoulder of one of the men and they moved unhurriedly past Tay and Lee to the stairs and started down.

"You're not going to get away with this," Tay said.

"There's nothing to get away with," Bruce Willis said. "We were never here."

"Then who shot my sergeant?"

"No idea, man. How *could* I know?" Bruce Willis gave Tay a grin that made him want to jump up and rip the man's face off. "Since I was never here."

Tay heard car horns out in Serangoon Road where frustrated drivers were trying to get past the flurry of accidents blocking the road and from somewhere far away came the *wal-wal-wal-wal* of approaching sirens.

"Henry, secure their feet. Then strap them to each other. That will hold them until their buddies get here."

The man put his foot against Tay's shoulder and pushed him onto his side.

"What the hell do you think you're doing?" Tay yelled back at him.

The man didn't bother to answer. Instead he produced another zip-tie and whipped it around Tay's ankles, hauling it up tight before Tay could react. After securing Lee's feet the same way, he turned them both on their sides, pushed them together, and used two more zip-ties to lace their bound hands and feet to each other.

"Let's go, guys," Bruce Willis said.

Tay and Lee watched in silence as one by one the men trooped past them and into the stairwell. Bruce Willis brought up the rear.

"Why did you have to shoot Robbie?" Tay shouted just as Bruce Willis went through the door to the stairwell.

To Tay's surprise, the man stopped. He held the door open with one hand and looked back at Tay.

"We didn't shoot him."

"Now I suppose you're going to tell me that Suparman was responsible for shooting him?"

Bruce Willis took a deep breath and pursed his lips.

"So you know who that is," he said.

"Yes, I know who that is. I thought ISD was supposed to be taking him down. You look to me more like you're protecting him."

"You should have stayed out of this, Inspector."

"I don't even know what the hell *this* is."

"I'm not sure I do either, man."

Bruce Willis started to say something else, but he hesitated. He stood there in silence holding the door open and looking at Tay for several long moments. Tay just waited.

"Look," the man finally said, "we didn't shoot anybody. We brought Suparman up here to see his sister like we were supposed to, but she wasn't waiting in the room where we had been told she'd be. She was behind us when we came out of the elevator and she had a gun. We weren't ready for anything like that. Maybe we should have been, but we weren't. She shot Suparman and was down the stairs before we could react. Then that other guy came busting in here and Suparman shot him as he tried to take cover. He must have figured it was somebody who was here to finish him off."

"That is the dumbest story I've ever heard," Tay said. "You don't really expect me to believe that, do you?"

"That's what happened."

Tay shook his head and looked up at the ceiling.

Bruce Willis appeared to consider Tay's skepticism thoughtfully for a moment.

"Look," he said, "don't take this the wrong way, man, but I don't really give a fuck whether you believe me or not. I got a lot bigger problems than that to worry about right now. My boss is going to gut me for this."

"Who's your boss?"

Bruce Willis chuckled. "Nice try, but you're going to have to do better than that."

"You can count on it. I'm going to do a *lot* better than that. I'm coming for you, and I'm coming for your boss, and I'm coming for his boss's boss. I'm going to roll up the whole mess of you for this."

"Tough guy, huh? You don't look so tough lying there on the floor."

"Just be patient. You'll see me again, and when I do you'll be the one on the floor."

Bruce Willis made a little clucking sound with his tongue.

"You don't know what you're getting into, man. Take my advice. Stay out of this. Stick to giving out traffic tickets. This is big boy stuff, and the big boys will grind you up and spit you out."

Then Bruce Willis stepped through the door into the stairwell and let the door slam shut behind him. The sound was the exclamation point on his disdain.

The ambulance attendants burst out of the elevator a few minutes later pushing a gurney stacked with equipment cases. One of them grabbed the closest of the cases and went straight to Kang while the other one produced a knife and cut away the zip-ties binding Tay and Lee together.

"Either of you hurt?" he asked, looking from one to the other.

Lee rubbed at her wrists and shook her head.

Tay didn't even do that. Instead he pushed himself up on his knees and looked at the man bent over Kang. The man raised his head and caught Tay's eye. He didn't say anything. He just gave a small shake of his head. Tay sank back against the wall and closed his eyes.

The hallway quickly filled with patrolmen from the arriving fast response cars. The patrol sergeant who had command of the scene recognized both Tay and Lee and shooed the other cops away from them.

"What happened?" he asked Lee.

"Somebody shot Robbie Kang."

"Do you know who it was?"

She shook her head.

"Did you or the inspector see him shot?"

She shook her head again.

Tay said nothing.

The sergeant pointed at the handgun lying in the hallway. "Is that Kang's?"

"Yes," Lee said.

The patrol sergeant walked over to the gun, got down on his hands and knees, and smelled it without touching it.

"Sergeant Kang didn't fire?"

"If he did, I didn't hear it."

The sergeant looked at Tay as if he was going to ask him what he had heard, but Tay wouldn't meet his eyes so he looked back at Lee.

"I don't understand," he said. "What the hell really happened here?"

"I'm not sure I know," Lee said.

The ambulance attendant lifted a blanket of plain white canvas out of his equipment bag and ripped away the clear plastic wrapping. He spread the blanket over Kang, then stood up and began packing his equipment away.

Tay and Lee sat without moving, their backs still against the wall. They kept their eyes fixed on Kang's canvas-covered body. They didn't want to, but neither one of them could take their eyes off it.

"I let him go in alone," Lee said. "I should never have done that."

Tay continued staring at Kang's body. He didn't reply.

Lee put her hand on his arm. "Are you okay?"

Tay just tilted his head back. He looked at the ceiling and said nothing at all.

23

TAY CLOSED HIS front door and stood wrapped in the comforting darkness of his living room. He tried to remember the last time he had been there. Was it really only this morning? Surely not.

He had been a policeman for nearly twenty-five years and for fifteen years he had been the senior investigator in the Criminal Investigation Department of the Singapore Police Force. He had seen almost a thousand homicides in his career and every single one of them had one thing in common: they had all made him sick to his stomach. In his darkest moments, Tay saw the onset of dementia as something almost inevitable when he grew old, but he also looked at that in one way as a blessing. At least then he would forget what he had seen.

He had seen people shot, people stabbed, people slashed, people beaten, people mangled, people bludgeoned, and people broken. He had even once seen a corpse that had been torn apart by a pack of Dobermans.

But there was one thing he had never seen.

He had never seen the body of a friend lying dead on the dirty carpet of a cheap hotel.

Now he had.

Robbie Kang dead in the second-floor corridor of the Fortuna Hotel.

Robbie Kang shot by…well, by whom?

Tay shook his head and flipped on the light. He walked into the kitchen and filled a glass with water from the tap. After he drained the glass, he put it in the sink, kicked off his loafers, and walked barefooted across the living room, through the French doors, and out into his little garden.

The air was hot and heavy, but the brick pavers felt chilly against his feet and the living room lights cast a pale and calming glow out through the panes of the French doors. He walked to the teak table where he drank his coffee in the mornings, pulled out one of the chairs, and sat down. Then he pulled another chair over and swung his feet up into it. He fished a pack of Marlboros and a box of matches out of the front pocket of his shirt and put them on the table next to the big glass ashtray.

Smoking wasn't much more than a habit for most people, but for Tay it was an undertaking filled with ritualistic meaning. Each cigarette he smoked offered a few moments of escape from the indifference of a pitiless world.

Or maybe it wasn't anything nearly that metaphysical. Maybe he just enjoyed smoking.

He did like unwrapping the pack, feeling the cellophane between his fingers, and listening to the crinkle as he rolled it between his thumb and forefinger. He loved the sudden whiff of tobacco he got when he slit the package with his thumbnail and tore back the top. It pained him that the busybodies who gloried in telling everyone how to live and what to do had stripped the simple act of smoking of all dignity. The more difficult the smug, self-righteous nannies made it for Tay to smoke, the more determined he was to continue doing it.

He would quit smoking soon. Of course he would. Everybody who smoked was going to quit smoking soon. But with all the crap he already sucked into his lungs every day just from breathing the air in Singapore, he couldn't see any advantage to doing it right away. He sure as hell wasn't going to do it tonight.

Tay struck a match, touched it to the cigarette, and felt the first rush of nicotine do its usual fine job of constricting his vascular system and filling body and soul with a sensation of wellbeing. He exhaled and watched as the smoke spiraled away in the darkness until it became part of the darkness, too.

What the hell had really happened at the Fortuna Hotel?

It wasn't the first time Tay had asked himself that question, of course. He had thought of little else while the ambulance crew was taking Kang's body away, while he gave his initial statement to the responding officers, and while he sat in the fast response car as they drove him home. He had thought of little else, but he still didn't know how to answer that question. He knew he would be expected to answer it as well as other questions people would ask tomorrow and the day after and for many days to come, but he had no idea what he was going to say to any of them.

Did Suparman kill Robbie Kang? Somebody had. And as much as Tay wanted to blame ISD, that didn't make sense to him.

Robbie must have come out of the stairwell into the hotel corridor, reacted to the crowd of men there, maybe even recognized Suparman, then turned to retreat and wait for Lee to catch up. And that was when he was shot. Tay couldn't accept the ISD men he saw there in that second floor hallway at the Fortuna Hotel had coolly shot a CID sergeant in the back of the head when he was turning away.

God help him, but he believed Bruce Willis when he said Suparman killed Robbie. He believed him because of the process of elimination if nothing else. There was no one in that corridor but ISD people and Suparman. If ISD hadn't shot Robbie, who else could it have been *but* Suparman?

Then who shot Suparman? Bruce Willis claimed it was Suparman's sister. That was also hard to believe, but again that was where the process of elimination took Tay. No one else was present but ISD men and Suparman's sister. Either ISD shot him, which made no sense at all, or his sister had. Unless, of course, the woman wasn't really Suparman's sister at all.

There was another thing about the whole scene that bewildered Tay. He had gotten a sense during those few minutes in the upstairs corridor at the Fortuna Hotel that Suparman wasn't in the custody of ISD at all, but rather that he was somehow under the protection of ISD, which is also what Bruce Willis had told him, more or less.

But how could that be? ISD set an elaborate trap at the Temple Street Inn to lure Suparman out of hiding. If ISD already had Suparman, what was the point of that? And if ISD did have him, why would they be treating him like an important figure for whom they were providing security rather than one of the world's most hunted terrorists?

Tay got up and went in to the kitchen. He poured two fingers of Powers Irish whiskey into a heavy cut-glass tumbler, hesitated for a moment and added a bit more. Then he took his drink back out into the garden and lit another cigarette.

Robbie Kang had been his friend, and he didn't have many friends. As much as it unsettled him when Kang had asked out of nowhere for him to become the godfather to his unborn child, he had also been profoundly touched. But he hadn't told Robbie that. He hadn't even really admitted that to himself. Thinking back on the conversation now, his failure to do either almost made him weep.

Why hadn't he said something? All he had to do was thank Robbie for asking him and tell him he was honored by the invitation. He supposed he had been unnerved by the subject of the relationship between parents and children coming up and he simply didn't know what to say. He had never married and had no children, so parents and children was something he knew very little about. He had parents, of course, but he hadn't learned very much about the subject from them either.

Tay was the only child of an American-born Chinese man and

a Singaporean-born Chinese woman. His father was an accountant, a careful man who insisted his family live modestly and who died of a heart attack on a business trip to Saigon in 1975. Tay's mother had been shocked to discover she and her son had inherited a small fortune in real estate. She hadn't even known her husband had for decades been buying properties, let alone that his investments would leave her and her son quite comfortably off for the rest of their lives.

Within a year, however, she appeared to adjust to the concept very nicely. She moved to New York and acquired what she described to Tay as a Park Avenue duplex although Tay noticed the address was on East 93rd Street. When his mother married a widowed American investment banker who was a senior partner at some investment firm, Tay was at university. He hadn't gone to New York for the wedding. He couldn't really recall being invited, but he supposed that was beside the point. He wouldn't have gone, he told himself, even if he had been invited.

By the time Tay graduated from university, he had chosen to his mother's horror to make his career in police work. Looking back on his decision now, Tay couldn't for the life of him remember why he had made it. Still, he was a brighter-than-average recruit and suitably conscientious so he rose in the department until he reached the Criminal Investigation Department. It was there that he found his calling. Many times over the years he had been offered further promotions, but he had turned them all down and that puzzled most people who knew him. Why wouldn't someone want to advance in his chosen profession, reaching higher and higher ranks and attaining greater and greater levels of power and prestige? Wasn't that everyone's aspiration, no matter what his profession?

Perhaps it was for some, even most, but it was not for Tay. His refusal to accept promotion had marked him as an oddball to most of his colleagues, but he simply didn't care. He had a reason to stay right where he was. Whether or not it made sense to other people, it made sense to him, and that was all that really mattered.

It was Tay's great good fortune to have stumbled relatively early in his life into a profession for which he perfectly suited. Tay was in his soul an investigator, someone who solved human puzzles. He was not a leader of men and he did not wish to be. He did what he did and he did it best on his own. He was a craftsman whose greatest pride was his individual craft. At first an investigator had been his profession. Now it was who he was.

Tay felt now as if his whole life had been leading him to this particular moment. His friend, perhaps his only real friend, had been murdered. And now it was up to him to use his craft to bring his friend redress.

Was that seeking justice, or was it merely looking for revenge? The more Tay thought about, the less it seemed to him to matter. Call it what you wanted, whoever had taken Robbie Kang from his wife and unborn child—and, yes, from Tay—was going to pay for it. And Sam Tay was going to be the man who made him pay for it.

Tay finished his cigarette and stubbed it out in the ashtray. He stood up and stretched, picked up his glass, and took it back into the kitchen. He had drunk only about half the whiskey, but he didn't want any more. He dumped the rest into the sink and rinsed out the glass.

He felt so tired. He could never remember ever feeling so tired before. All he wanted to do was sleep and crash into the depths of a blackness where no one could find him. He went upstairs, brushed his teeth, and got into to bed, and almost at once he fell into exactly the kind of sleep he wanted.

But someone found him anyway.

24

WHEN TAY OPENED his eyes, his first thought was to wonder what had disturbed his sleep. Everyone has similar thoughts when they are roused in the night, and in the blank space of the empty hours the explanations that crawl from our imaginations are seldom explanations that soothe us.

Had there been a sudden noise or an unusual burst of light? Tay sat up in bed and looked around. The watery glow behind his bedroom drapes looked exactly as it always did. He held his breath and strained his ears, but he heard no unexpected bump or creak. He glanced at his telephone lying on the nightstand next to him. It was not lit up with an incoming call.

Once he had eliminated the usual list of temporal events as possible causes for waking, that left only one explanation, and it was one he did not like.

For nearly a year his mother had been offering all sorts of unsolicited advice. Sometimes it concerned his personal life and sometimes it concerned the cases on which he was working. He would not have considered that remarkable since mothers had been giving their sons unsolicited advice more or less since the beginning of time, but the circumstances here were a little unusual. More than unusual, actually. They were downright creepy.

Tay's mother had died a little over year ago.

"Please leave me alone tonight, Mother," Tay called into the darkness. "I'm depressed and tired and I'm certainly in no mood for a conversation with you."

When his mother was alive, they hardly ever talked. In fact, after she moved to New York and remarried following his father's death, years had gone by without any contact at all between them. Since his mother had passed away, however, she simply couldn't shut up. She appeared quite regularly to him now, always at some God-awful hour in the middle of the night, and gave him all sorts of advice about whatever he might have on his mind at the time. It was driving him mad.

On the first few occasions his mother appeared, he was convinced he was simply being victimized by a particularly acute case of indigestion, but eventually he began wondering if there were not more to it than that. Perhaps in the silence of the night his subconscious was making itself heard. And if that were true, he probably ought to be listening more carefully. As a detective, he had always counted on his intuition to show him the way through the forest, and his subconscious coming to him in his dreams was nothing more than a tangible expression of intuition.

At other times, however, he viewed the whole phenomenon less happily. Those were the times when he wondered if he wasn't simply lonely. He had always been a solitary man and he was generally happy to be one, but he had to admit honestly it was also true that he was sometimes lonely. He thought of his loneliness as a faint and distant ache, like a bruise on the back of his hand. It was not a thing he noticed until he banged it into something, but when he did it hurt like hell.

What else could these imagined manifestations be but his subconscious or his loneliness? After all, he certainly was not a man who normally fraternized with ghosts. He did not see spirits in the street or anywhere else. In the whole of his life, he had only encountered one ghost: that of his mother.

What bothered him a bit, however, was that his mother's occasional appearances did seem...well, terribly real. Tay was not a spiritual man, but sometimes her presence felt so authentic that he wondered in spite of himself if her presence might not actually *be* real.

Still, he could say with absolute certainty that he did not believe in ghosts. When he sat in the garden on a sunny morning with a cup of coffee in his hand and thought about his mother, the idea that she was manifesting herself from beyond the grave to give him advice seemed laughable. In the darkness and the loneliness of his bedroom, however, the idea was far less amusing. Of course, that changed nothing. Daylight was reality. Darkness was not.

When it seemed as if he were speaking to the ghost of his mother, Tay understood perfectly well he was not. No matter how real the conversation might feel, he knew he was simply looking in a mirror and speaking to himself. There was no other rational explanation.

Except, of course, the possibility he wasn't looking into a mirror at all, but through an opening of some sort into a spiritual dimension so profoundly unfathomable that it called into question everything he understood, or thought he understood, about the whole phenomenon of human existence. But Tay was not a spiritual man, so he knew that could not be.

To be entirely fair, he did have to admit his mother's advice sometimes proved quite useful. Tay had once read a magazine story about the American actor, Jack Nicholson, in which Nicholson said something that summed up Tay's feelings on the whole matter quite nicely.

I know the voices in my head aren't real, but they have such damn good ideas I listen to them anyway.

Tay fell back against his pillow and closed his eyes. He knew it wouldn't do him any good, but he did it anyway. He had tried more times than he cared to remember simply to ignore his mother's appearances, but it never worked. She wasn't the kind of woman who tolerated being ignored.

"Go away, Mother. *Please* go away."

"I don't know why I even bother sometimes, Samuel."

Tay knew that if he opened his eyes he would see a light glowing somewhere in his bedroom. His mother's voice generally emerged from a light. At least it did most of the time. Occasionally his mother appeared to him in human form sitting at the end of his bed and she would chat to him in the way he vaguely remembered she had back when he was a small child. But that didn't happen very often. Generally it was just a light, or perhaps several lights.

Tay had never been able to work out the connection between his mother's messages and the manner of her appearance. He thought it stood to reason the way in which she manifested herself had something to do with the message she delivered, but he had never been able to nail down the correlation.

Who was he kidding? Why would he assume a ghost would behave like a rational human being when it was neither rational nor a human being?

"Open your eyes, Samuel. You're being childish."

Tay said nothing and he clenched his eyelids even more tightly together.

"You know you're going to open your eyes eventually, Samuel. You always do. Just do it now and save us both a lot of wasted time and effort."

"Why can't you ever show up at a civilized hour, Mother? Why must it always be at some God-awful hour when I'm exhausted?"

"I come when you need me most, Samuel. That is my job as a mother, to be here when you need me."

"I don't need you tonight, Mother. I really don't."

"Oh yes you do, son. Now open your eyes and sit up."

Tay cracked one eye open in the direction from which his mother's voice was coming and saw her sitting on the end of his bed. She was wearing a black dress of no style to which he could put a name and a round hat he thought was called a pillbox, also black. Her legs were crossed at the knee and her hands were linked around her knee with her fingers interlocked.

So instead of the conventional light show, this was a night for full body manifestation. That couldn't be good.

"Do you have any idea how much effort is required for me to make these little appearances, Samuel?"

"No, Mother, but I get the feeling you're about to tell me."

"It's not as if I can casually drop in on you anytime I feel like it. Arrangements are required."

Tay was intrigued by that in spite of himself. He sat up, both eyes now open, and jammed his pillow behind him to support his back against the headboard.

Was his mother telling him there was some sort of spiritual travel agency through which she had to book passage when she came over to the other side? So what was travel like for a ghost? Did they need to deal with passports and visas and other kinds of paperwork like the sort that was required for temporal travel? Did they have to take off their shoes and put them through an X-ray machine along with their carry-on luggage?

"And yet every time I go through it all so I can come here and tell you something you need to know," his mother continued, preventing Tay's increasingly deranged meditations from getting entirely out of hand, "you act as if I'm imposing on you."

"You *are* imposing on me, Mother. This has been a very difficult day. I can't remember a worse one. And I need to sleep. That was why I asked you very politely not to bother me tonight."

"Yes, I heard you, but I already had everything organized and it seemed such a shame to waste all that effort."

"Yes, well, thank you anyway, but—"

"I'm sorry about Robbie Kang. He was a nice man."

"You didn't know Robbie Kang, Mother."

"Of course I did. I never met him, but I knew him."

Tay's mother uncrossed her legs and crossed them back in the opposite direction. When she did, the bed rocked slightly and Tay wondered about that, too.

His mother was not a large person, and of course she was dead as well, there was that to consider, but she still weighed enough to move his mattress slightly when she shifted her weight. He had always assumed ghosts were spectral, or he would have assumed that if he believed in ghosts, which he didn't, but when his mother sat on the end of his bed it made him think ghosts had weight just like living human beings. How could that be?

"And I do want to tell you, Samuel, that girl seems very nice."

"What girl, Mother?"

"The one you're working with."

"Sergeant Lee?"

"Yes. She's very attractive. Does she cook?"

"I have no idea."

"You should find out. You're not getting any younger, Samuel. You should be married. You may not have many more chances."

"Yes, Mother. Is there anything else? As much as I'm enjoying this conversation, I really do need to get back to sleep."

His mother's figure seemed enveloped in light for an instant, then the light dimmed and she leaned toward him.

"Listen to me, Samuel, I have something to tell you that is very important."

"What is it?"

"Ah-ha! Got your attention now, don't I?"

Tay looked away and sighed. What good would it do him to get mad at his mother? She wasn't there in the first place so getting angry wasn't likely to make her go away.

"Just tell me what you need to tell me, Mother."

"You are in great danger, Samuel."

"What kind of danger, Mother? Do you have another girl to introduce me to?"

"Please stop making jokes and pay attention. Are you paying attention?"

"Yes, Mother, I am paying attention."

"I know what you are going to do."

"How do you know?"

"Oh for Pete's sake, Samuel, I've told you over and over. I know everything. I have universal knowledge. It's one of the few advantages of being dead."

"Do you know I'd rather sleep than have another one of these stupid conversations with you?"

"Always with the jokes, huh? Always the jokes."

"That was not a joke, Mother."

"You know, Samuel, sometimes I think I'm just going to give up trying to help you and leave you to whatever happens."

"That's what I wish you would do, Mother. At least that way I would get a hell of a lot more sleep."

All at once his mother began pacing up and down at the end of his bed with her arms folded tightly across her body.

"I know you are going to try to find the man who killed Robbie Kang," she said, "but everything is much more complicated than you think."

"Complicated in what way?"

"There are things at stake you know nothing about, things so big that people will stop at nothing to prevent you from exposing them. Think about that poor man they pulled out of the Singapore River."

"What are you talking about, Mother? What does that have to do with Robbie's murder?"

Tay's mother ignored his question. "And what about the other body?"

"What other body?"

"You know, the man who...oh wait, never mind. You haven't found that one yet."

"You're scaring me, Mother."

"Don't get involved. Did you hear me? Don't get involved. It will only put you in danger."

"I am involved, Mother. I wish I weren't, but I am."

"If you pursue this, your own life will be at risk."

"And why is that, Mother?"

"That is not completely clear."

"I thought you knew everything."

"I know everything that can be known, but there are things which cannot yet be known."

"Oh, for God's sake, Mother. You sound like a fucking fortune cookie."

"What language, Samuel. I didn't raise you to use language like that."

Tay sighed again and rubbed his eyes. "You didn't raise me at all."

"Such bitterness. It really doesn't become you."

"Are we done here, Mother? Can you go back now to wherever it is you come from and let me go to sleep?"

"Just heed my warning, Samuel. Promise me you won't pursue Robbie Kang's death. Will you do that?"

"It wasn't a death, Mother, it was a murder. And I investigate murders. It's what I do. I find redress for the dead."

"Oh, that's a fine phrase. Very high-sounding. Maybe a little pretentious, but quite grand really. I just hope you don't start thinking you're going to find redress for me."

"I wasn't talking about you, Mother. You're just a figment of my imagination anyway. I was talking about Robbie Kang. You cannot expect me to forget about a friend who was murdered and died right in front of me."

"Of course I can. Let someone else deal with him. You don't have to solve every crime in Singapore, do you? You are not the only policeman in the country."

"May I go back to sleep now?"

"You will thank me for my guidance someday, Samuel."

"Does that come from your universal knowledge, or are you just feeling optimistic?"

"Now you are being tedious. And boring."

"I'm sorry you feel that way, Mother.

"I do feel that way, Samuel. And I think I've had enough of you for tonight."

Then just like that she disappeared. Tay was left sitting in his bed in the dark with his arms folded staring at…well, at nothing at all.

"Mother?" he called out. He felt stupid doing it, but he did it anyway. "Are you still there somewhere?"

There was no reply, so Tay waited for what he thought was a sufficiently polite interval and then stretched out again. He closed his eyes and very quickly drifted off into a deep and blessedly dreamless sleep.

25

TAY WOKE EARLY the next morning with a keen sense of unease about the dream he had in the night. If it had been a dream. Which, of course, he had no doubt that it was.

The glowing red numerals of the clock on his bedside table told him it was not yet even seven. That was a ridiculous hour for him, but sleep always obstinately refused to take him back once he had looked at the clock and knew the time so he put on a robe and went downstairs.

While the coffee maker ran, he stood and watched it and kept his mind as empty as possible. Eventually the coffee maker shut itself off and he took a heavy white ceramic mug out of the cabinet and filled it, then he went out into his garden and sat at the table and sipped his coffee.

Mornings were usually the best part of the day in Singapore and this was a particularly fine morning, cloudless and sunny with low humidity and a sky as blue as a robin's egg. There was a slight breeze from the south and he thought he could smell on it the salt of the ocean and a whiff of exotic lands, but he knew it was probably just his imagination.

Tay finished his coffee. He placed the empty mug on the table and then he leaned back and knitted his fingers together behind his head. Very deliberately he began in his mind to step back through his dream from the night before. He circled and probed at it with all the caution of the airport bomb squad scrutinizing an abandoned suitcase.

What was his mother trying to tell him?

Robbie Kang had been murdered. He died lying on the ground ten feet from Tay, and Tay could do nothing but watch him die. And his mother tells him not to get involved?

What was all that other stuff she had said? A link between Robbie's murder and the body pulled out of the Singapore River? A link between both of those killings and a body he hadn't even discovered yet? Perhaps she was just trying to frighten him by spinning Robbie's murder as part of some vast conspiracy he didn't see or understand.

For God's sake, why was he sitting here trying to interpret what his mother meant? She hadn't meant *anything*. She was a figment of his imagination.

Besides, there clearly *was* no vast conspiracy. He knew who killed Robbie, didn't he? Abu Suparman killed Robbie. That was what the ISD man who looked like Bruce Willis told him, and he had no reason to think otherwise. Either Suparman had killed Robbie or one of the ISD men had killed him, and he simply didn't believe that was possible.

But why were the ISD people at the Fortuna Hotel with Suparman in the first place? If they really were there to protect him as they appeared to be, they had certainly done a crap job of it seeing that his sister managed to shoot him right under their noses.

Tay didn't know for sure Suparman's sister really had shot him, of course. He didn't even know for sure that the woman had been Suparman's sister. He thought back to the man he had seen talking to her outside the Temple Street Inn. The man had given her something. At least Tay was pretty certain he had. Could it have been a gun? Of course it could have. But it could also have been a

148

slip of paper with the address of the hotel or a piece of hard candy or…well, maybe it was nothing at all.

And who *was* that man, anyway? Tay had followed him straight from the alleyway behind the Temple Street Inn to the Australian High Commission and he watched as he breezed inside through their security post. That still made no sense to Tay. Unless, of course, there actually *was* a vast conspiracy.

Tay picked up his mug and took it back into the kitchen to get himself more coffee. He obviously needed it. After he filled his mug he stood leaning against the sink and tried to clear his increasingly muddled mind.

Among all the things Samuel Tay didn't know, there was one thing he knew very well. The universe operated in a kind of balance. It was a fundamental principle of science that for every action there was an equal and opposite reaction and all that. Long ago he had learned that a similar principle applied to his own profession: for every bad act there was an eventual reckoning. Sometimes the reckoning was immediate, and sometimes it did not come until much later, but it always came. He had also learned that it was his calling in life to be the agent of that reckoning.

It felt now to Tay like it was now his sole responsibility to restore balance to the universe, to bring a reckoning for Robbie Kang. And he wasn't going to let an imaginary conversation with his dead mother about an imaginary conspiracy stop him from doing it.

Still, he had to concede the conversation, imaginary or otherwise, had raised a couple of points he needed to keep in mind. A lot of what he knew didn't make much sense. ISD was right in the middle of everything, and everything he knew about who had been responsible for shooting had come from ISD. That made him hugely uncomfortable.

Maybe Bruce Willis had been bullshitting him. Maybe ISD shot Suparman and then shot Robbie to cover it up. But what sense did that make? If ISD wanted to kill Suparman, they wouldn't have grabbed him somewhere and taken him to a hotel in the middle of Singapore to do it. Bruce Willis claimed they took Suparman to that hotel to meet his sister, and that made more sense than any other explanation.

But it also raised a baffling question: why was ISD protecting Suparman and organizing meetings for him with his sister? Wasn't the point of this whole operation to grab Suparman using his sister as bait? If ISD already had Suparman, what in the world had all *that* been about?

Perhaps that was the wrong question to ask, Tay told himself. At least, it was the wrong question to ask right now. He had some huge blank spaces in his understanding he needed to fill in before he even tried to work out what it all meant.

The desk clerk at the hotel had seen everyone's comings and goings. Maybe he ought to have another talk with him. Put together a better time line of who came and went and when they did. That would be a decent place to start.

Then, too, there was something else that bothered him. Another person had been watching the Fortuna Hotel: the girl he saw in the window. Who was she? What was she watching, and who was she watching it *for*? Tay needed to find her. It meant something that she was there, he was sure of it, but he had no idea what it was.

Yeah, he knew the voices in his head weren't real, but sometimes they really did have good ideas.

There was a lot to do. Perhaps Sergeant Lee would be willing to give him a hand. Perhaps he would even ask her if she could cook, just so he would have an answer for his mother the next time she came calling.

Tay finished his coffee. He rinsed out his mug and put it in the sink. Then he climbed the stairs, got dressed, and went to work.

26

TAY WAS IN his office at the Cantonment Complex by a little after eight. He hardly recognized the place at that hour.

After he found the coffeepot and poured himself a cup, he went into his office, closed the door, and sat drumming his fingers on the desk while he sipped the coffee. Did a lot of people go to work at this ungodly hour? Yes, he concluded sadly, a great many probably did. Singaporeans were dutiful people. They obeyed their superiors and showed up when they were told. Most of the poor devils probably went to work at this hour every day, God help them all.

Whatever the time was, he was here. So where to start?

He supposed the first thing he ought to do was go upstairs to see the SAC. He would want to hear about what happened directly from Tay, and he would want to tell Tay he could have no part in the investigation of Kang's death because of his personal connection to it. Tay would nod dutifully and say nothing, and the SAC would understand perfectly well Tay had no intention at all of following his instructions. After that, he would be asked to give a statement to the detectives assigned to the investigation and those detectives would warn him again about avoiding any direct involvement. He would nod a little more and ignore them, too.

Yes, that was what he should do, go upstairs and see the SAC, but he couldn't yet face the expressions of sympathy and concern he would have to wade through to get to the substance of the conversation. Better to stall. But what could he do to look busy enough to keep him from going upstairs for a while? He had no answer to that, but just then his telephone rang, which relieved him for the moment from the necessity of deciding.

"God, Sam, what are you doing in the office?" Susan Hoi asked when Tay answered. "I thought I'd just leave you a message. I heard what happened. I'm so very sorry. I just don't know what else to say. Are you okay?"

Tay wondered briefly if some place in all those words was an actual question to which he was expected to provide an actual answer, but he decided there probably wasn't. Asking if someone was all right was only a pleasantry like saying *Please* or *Thank you*. When people asked how you were, they didn't really want you to tell them. They just wanted you to say you were fine.

"I'm fine, Dr. Hoi," Tay responded dutifully. Hoping that would end the sympathy portion of the conversation, he said nothing else.

Susan Hoi hesitated, but it was clear to her Tay didn't want to talk about Kang's death and she didn't want to press him. So she changed the subject.

"I'm calling about the ID on your floater," she said.

"You found something?"

"Well…"

Tay waited. He wondering if this was going where he thought it might be going. Sure enough, after a moment Susan Hoi said exactly what Tay was afraid she would say.

"Why don't you come over to my office, Sam? It's better if I show you."

"I'm awfully busy, Dr. Hoi. Couldn't you just—"

"My office in ten minutes, Sam. Bye-bye."

152

Then she hung up.

Tay sat looking at the receiver for a long moment before he replaced it in the cradle. He rubbed his eyes and slapped his forehead with his palm a few times. He knew he was trapped.

He had intended to call Dr. Hoi later because of his dream. Just to rule out any possible connection between the floater and Robbie's murder, of course. Not because he was taking anything his mother had said seriously. But that would have only been a phone call. He would rather have a root canal than actually walk over to that place and meet that woman.

On the other hand, it occurred to him there was at least one advantage to going. He could kill an hour or so doing it, and surely spending an hour in a morgue would make the whole idea of sitting down and talking to the SAC afterwards very much more appealing.

The Centre for Forensic Medicine is in a building called Block Nine on the grounds of the Singapore General Hospital. The building itself is a nondescript, modern two-story structure that looks as if it might shelter almost any kind of activity. But of course Tay knew it didn't shelter just any activity, and he understood all too well what took place in Block Nine. Equipped as he was with that knowledge, the otherwise unremarkable structure with the aluminum chimney pipes poking out of it took on a genuinely creepy appearance.

Normally it would take Tay no more than ten minutes to walk from his office in the Cantonment Complex across to Block Nine on the other side of New Bridge Road. In spite of his best efforts to stretch that out considerably, even taking a break for a cigarette when he was halfway there, Tay arrived at Dr. Hoi's office less than twenty minutes later.

Susan Hoi wore a blue, three-button blazer with a pink shirt that was open at the neck. Doctors simply dressed better than cops, Tay decided.

"What took you so long?" she asked after Tay took a seat in one of the straight chairs facing her desk.

"Phone calls," Tay mumbled.

Dr. Hoi looked skeptical. He didn't blame her. It was a lame excuse, but it was the best he could do at the moment.

"You don't much like coming to my office, do you, Sam?"

"Not very much, no."

"I hope it's not because of me."

"It's not. It's because…" Tay trailed off and settled for waving one hand vaguely indicating the area outside of Dr. Hoi's office.

"I see," she said. "I think."

Tay wanted to get away from the whole subject of his squeamishness around dead bodies as quickly as he could. He cleared his throat.

"What was it you wanted to show me?" he asked.

Dr. Hoi plucked a small plastic box off her desk with one hand and pushed a stainless steel tray toward Tay with the other. She dumped the contents of the box onto the tray and what looked like a dozen or so tiny yellow and white pebbles bounced across it making little clicking sounds against the metal. Tay bent toward the tray and peered at the pebbles. When he suddenly realized they weren't pebbles, he recoiled.

"Are those teeth?" he asked.

"From our corpse," Dr. Hoi nodded.

"I assumed they weren't yours," Tay muttered.

"What?"

"Never mind."

Dr. Hoi looked at Tay for a moment, but he didn't say anything else so she went on.

"The upper jaw was substantially destroyed by the gunshot. I found these teeth in his throat when I probed it."

Tay looked away and nodded, concentrating on controlling the bile rising into his throat.

Dr. Hoi reached out and stirred the teeth around with her

forefinger until she found the one she wanted. She scooped it up and thrust it toward Tay.

"What do you see?" she demanded.

"A reminder of the reason I'm not the tooth fairy."

"What?"

"Never mind again."

This time Dr. Hoi smiled and shook her head.

"Look at the dental work, Sam."

Tay saw a spot on the bottom surface of the tooth Dr. Hoi was holding out. It was dark gray and irregularly shaped. Was that what she was talking about?

"Is that a filling?" Tay asked.

Dr. Hoi nodded.

"I don't know anything about dental work," Tay said.

"I don't know much either, but I can tell you one thing. This work certainly wasn't done here."

"So you're saying our corpse was a visitor to Singapore?"

"Or an immigrant."

"Or a local who gets his dental work done in Malaysia because it's cheaper," Tay added.

"I doubt it. From the alloy used for the filling and the way it's applied, my guess is this work was done in Indonesia."

Indonesia?

Tay felt his stomach clench.

An Indonesian shot in the head in Singapore a couple of days before Suparman, another Indonesian, was shot by his sister who was also Indonesian? He didn't think he had ever dealt with the death of an Indonesian in Singapore before, and now suddenly he was up to his ass in violent and deceased Indonesians. Was that just a coincidence? Or had his mother been on to something?

"It's pretty thin, I know," Dr. Hoi said.

Tay nodded, but he didn't say anything.

"That's it," Dr. Hoi shrugged. "You asked me if I had anything that might point to an ID. This is what I've got. It's more than you had before, isn't it?"

"Yes, it is," Tay nodded. "By the way, have you done the autopsy on Robbie Kang yet?"

"I've had a quick look, but the full work-up won't be done for another day or two."

"Any preliminary thoughts?"

"What are you asking me, Sam?"

"What was Robbie shot with?"

"A handgun. Almost certainly a nine millimeter."

"Exactly like the floater."

Dr. Hoi cocked her head and peered at Tay. "What are you saying, Sam? That you think there's a connection between the floater and Robbie?"

Tay said nothing, and Dr. Hoi eventually produced a half smile.

"Maybe we can talk about it some other time," she said.

"Maybe we can," Tay replied as he stood up to leave.

27

WHEN TAY LEFT Block Nine, he lit a cigarette as soon as he could. From the moment he entered the building the unmistakable odor of death had tormented him. He could taste it in his throat and feel the burn in his nostrils. How could Dr. Hoi breathe air all day that was infused with death and putrefaction? All he wanted now was to clean out his mouth and nose. A cigarette would accomplish that quite nicely.

As he walked back to the Cantonment Complex smoking his cigarette, he thought about what Dr. Hoi had told him. What if the floater was an Indonesian? That didn't necessarily mean a connection existed between the floater and Suparman. There were a few hundred million Indonesians. Just because two of them got shot in Singapore within a few days of each other he wasn't going to jump to the conclusion the shootings were related. And certainly not because his mother claimed they were.

Who was he kidding? He knew in his gut they *were* connected someway, even if he couldn't see exactly how. At least not yet.

When Tay got back to the Cantonment Complex, he dumped his cigarette butt into one of the big ashtrays outside the glass doors and took the elevator upstairs to his office.

From the fifteenth floor of the Cantonment Complex, Tay had a glorious view of Singapore. Straight ahead across the Singapore River was the green patch of Fort Canning Park and off to the right were the glass and steel towers of the financial district. If he stood up and walked to the window, he could see all the way north to the long ranks of luxury hotels and shopping malls that walled both sides of Orchard Road. But he wasn't going to stand up and walk to the window. He didn't much like looking at Orchard Road these days.

The ruined façades of the Hyatt, the Marriott, and the Hilton were still under repair from the bombings that had nearly destroyed them. His memories of the chaos and destruction were both raw and personal. Above everything else, he remembered the smell of the dead and dying all around him. He would never forget that smell.

Until the bombings, Singapore had seemed charmed. Life was comparatively placid here in his little corner of Southeast Asia. There was some crime, of course, but Singapore was largely untroubled by the upheavals which regularly swept the rest of the world. Perhaps Singapore was simply too boring for upheavals, but whatever the reason the suffering endured by the rest of the world was only something Singaporeans watched on television.

Then the three American big hotels in the heart of the city were reduced to smoking ruins, and the thousands of dead and dying had not been on television. In that one instant of thunder and blood, Singapore had been transformed. Perhaps, Tay thought, he had been transformed, too.

The question of exactly what Singapore had become, however, was hard to answer. And Tay was even less sure of what he himself might have become.

When Sergeant Lee knocked, Tay was still staring out the window. He said nothing, but she opened the door anyway.

"Can I get you some coffee, sir?"

Tay shook his head. He didn't invite her in.

"Are you okay?" she asked.

"Why does everyone keep asking me that?"

"Because you might not be."

"I've been a homicide investigator almost as long as you've been walking. I've seen a lot of dead bodies."

"But I'll bet none of them were friends of yours."

Tay went back to his desk and sat down. Without being invited, Sergeant Lee closed the door and took one of the chairs across from him.

"I want to help, sir."

"In a moment I'm going to go up and see the SAC. He's going to tell me I can't have any part in investigating Sergeant Kang's murder."

"And you're going to nod and say you understand, and then you're going to go out and do it anyway. That's what the SAC will expect, and he won't do anything to stop you. Tell me I'm wrong about that."

Tay said nothing.

"I want to help, sir," Lee repeated. "Please let me help you."

"Why do you want to do that?"

"I feel responsible."

"You're not."

Lee looked away. "I know how I feel. I don't want to argue with you, sir."

"Did you know Robbie's wife is pregnant?" Tay asked.

Lee shook her head, but she didn't say anything.

"Robbie asked me to be the godfather just yesterday morning."

Lee closed her eyes and looked down. "That's awful, sir. I don't know what to say."

Tay nodded and fell silent.

"Do you believe what that ISD guy said, sir? That the sister shot Suparman and then Suparman shot Sergeant Kang?"

"Somebody shot Suparman and I don't think it was ISD. I guess that doesn't leave anybody else other than the woman they say was his sister."

"But why would she shoot her own brother?"

Tay thought back to the man who met Suparman's sister in the alley behind the Temple Street Inn and decided not to tell Sergeant Lee about following him to the Australian High Commission. He couldn't make any sense out of that and didn't want to talk about it until he could.

"And what about that guy claiming Suparman shot Robbie?" she went on when Tay didn't respond. "That seems a little too neat for me. Maybe Robbie didn't identify himself and came out of the staircase with his gun out. Maybe ISD fired on him by reflex."

"They didn't fire on us when we came out of the same staircase, and you had your gun out."

Lee nodded, but she didn't say anything else.

"Remember, Sergeant, Robbie was shot in the back of the head. My guess is he came out of the door from the stairs, saw Suparman and those five ISD guys, and turned to jump back into the stairwell."

"And that's when somebody shot him."

Tay nodded.

"But not ISD."

"Whatever else I think of ISD," Tay said, "that's not how they would react. They wouldn't have shot him in the back of the head."

"So that leaves Suparman."

"Yes," Tay said, "it appears it does."

Lee took a deep breath and let it out again. "I don't really understand what's going on here, sir."

"Neither do I, Sergeant, but I'm damn well going to find out. And I'd be happy to have your help. Give me a little time. Then we'll sit down and talk."

"Right, sir," Lee said, standing up to leave.

"One other thing, Sergeant."

Lee stopped. "Yes, sir?"

"Can you cook?"

The next few days passed in a blur for Tay. He went to see the SAC, who told him exactly what Tay knew he would. He gave a statement to the detectives assigned to the case, who repeated the same admonitions. He even went to Kang's funeral and he never went to funerals, but he sat in the back and left just as it ended so he wouldn't have to speak to anyone.

Tay didn't like funerals. Funerals were for the living, not for the dead. And mostly they had the purpose of reminding the living they would soon be dead, too. Tay didn't need reminding. Hardly a day passed without the thought occurring to him.

Other than that, Tay mostly stayed in his office. He drank a lot of coffee, made regular trips down the elevator to step outside and smoke a cigarette, and shuffled papers. Among the papers Tay shuffled was Dr. Hoi's preliminary autopsy report on the floater. He hoped the report might contain something pointing to the identity of the corpse other than her speculation about its dental work, but it didn't. The cause of death, Dr. Hoi concluded, was a single shot to the head with a nine millimeter handgun. Tay already knew that.

He also read Dr. Hoi's preliminary autopsy report on Robbie Kang. He didn't want to, but he did. The cause of death, she concluded, was a single gunshot wound. The entrance was seven inches below the top of the head. It penetrated the skull in the left occipital lobe of the brain and was recovered in the left cerebral hemisphere. The track of the wound was back to front, slightly left to right, and at a twenty-three degree upward angle. As if a seated man had fired at one who was standing. And the shooter had used a nine.

Not only didn't that help, it pulled Tay straight down a rabbit hole that felt bottomless.

The floater Dr. Hoi thought might be Indonesian was killed by a shot to the back of the head with a nine. Robbie Kang was killed, presumably by Abu Suparman, with a shot to the back of the head with a nine. On top of that, Suparman, a notorious Indonesian terrorist, had been shot by his sister, another Indonesian, although Tay had no idea what kind of weapon she had used.

Nine millimeter handguns were common enough almost everywhere in the world, that was true, but no handguns were common in Singapore. Gunshot deaths in Singapore were extremely rare. Could these two killings in the same time period using the same caliber of weapon and both involving Indonesians be a coincidence? And if they *weren't* a coincidence, exactly how were they connected?

Tay knew who shot Suparman. At least he knew if he believed Bruce Willis and he supposed he did. But Tay wasn't prepared to believe Suparman's sister also shot the floater and dumped his body in the Singapore River, and he knew she hadn't shot Robbie Kang because by then she was lying dead in Serangoon Road.

So that meant it *was* all a coincidence, didn't it? It meant the shootings *weren't* all connected.

Who was he kidding? He didn't buy that either.

He just wasn't at all sure where that left him.

28

TAY WAS OUT of cigarettes. He had just made up his mind that running out of cigarettes more than justified going home early when there was a perfunctory knock on his office door and the SAC let himself in.

"We need to talk, Sam," the SAC said as he sat down in front of Tay's desk.

Tay was fairly certain no one had ever said anything he wanted to hear after beginning a conversation with the phrase, *we need to talk*. He folded his arms and waited.

"Have you ever considered retirement, Sam?"

Whatever he might have been expecting the SAC to say, it certainly hadn't been that.

"This is a young man's game," the SAC went on without meeting Tay's stare. "I know you're well-off. You don't need the job. You could just toss it in. Particularly after losing Sergeant Kang the way you did, I think you ought to consider doing that."

Tay cleared his throat, but he didn't quite trust himself to speak.

"Or if that doesn't appeal to you, Sam, there's a Deputy Superintendent position opening up in a couple of months. It's an administrative position, of course, but I believe you would be well suited for it. It's a double promotion, but I can swing it for you."

Tay didn't have a lot of friends in the Singapore Police Department. He never had. He understood he could be immensely annoying, but he did his job well and in spite of a few bumps here and there over the years he had mostly been left alone to do it. Some senior officers who didn't like him had made a run at him once. They tried to use a shooting incident in which he had been involved to get rid of him, but it hadn't worked. In the end, CID needed him enough that officers even more senior had overruled his enemies and brought him back.

But now this.

"Why are you asking me this today, sir?"

The SAC shifted in his chair. He looked away and rubbed at his face with one hand. His discomfort was obvious.

"I have a problem with the story you told me about Suparman."

"What kind of problem, sir?"

"We can't find any evidence things happened the way you say they did."

"Has anyone spoken to ISD?"

The SAC nodded. "I did. They deny it."

"They're claiming the sister didn't shoot Suparman, or claiming Suparman didn't shoot Sergeant Kang?"

"They're saying they don't know anything about any of that because no one from ISD was at the Fortuna Hotel when Sergeant Kang was killed."

"They're saying they didn't bring Suparman to the Fortuna Hotel to meet his sister?"

"No."

"Then how did he get there? How did she get there?"

"ISD is saying they have no idea. They had the sister staked out at the Temple Street Inn, but she apparently slipped away and they lost her."

"And Suparman?"

"They say they don't have any idea where he is. Either he never came to Singapore after all, or they missed him."

"They didn't miss him. They had him surrounded by five armed men. I saw it. I was there."

"That's what you say, Sam, but you seem to be forgetting something. You weren't *supposed* to be there. You were assigned to the Santa Grande Hotel in Chinatown to await instructions from ISD."

"That's true, sir, but—"

"And entirely on your own, without informing anyone, you went somewhere else, and you took two sergeants with you. Now one of them is dead."

It was Tay's turn to shift uncomfortably in his chair.

"What's that supposed to mean, sir?"

"I'm just stating facts, Sam. It's going to be up to someone well above me to decide what they mean."

"It sounds like you're blaming me for Robbie's murder."

"If you had been where you were supposed to be, he would probably still be alive. Does that mean you're to blame?"

The SAC's shoulders rose and fell in a very small shrug.

Tay looked away and studied a spot on the wall. For a long time, no one said anything, but then Tay did.

"That's not fair, sir."

The SAC took a deep breath and blew it out. "Yeah, I know it isn't fair, but you ought to get used to hearing it. I'm not going to be the last person to say it to you."

Tay continued to stare at the wall, but he nodded slowly.

"Let's set that aside for the moment, Sam. The immediate problem is the investigation of Robbie's death since we can't find anybody who remembers the men you described being at the Fortuna Hotel."

"The desk clerk says he doesn't remember them?"

"He doesn't say anything. He had some kind of family issue and isn't in Singapore."

"Where did he go?"

"The man we talked to at the hotel doesn't know."

"And you believe that?"

"We have no reason not to."

Tay stood up and walked to the window. He folded his arms and looked at the city.

"ISD was there, sir. ISD has Suparman."

"We can't find anybody who has seen Suparman or has any idea where he is."

"God dammit, yes, you can. You know two people. Sergeant Lee and I both told you we saw him there and that ISD took him away."

The SAC pursed his lips. "This is difficult for me, Sam. It isn't a question of whether I believe you—"

"That's exactly how it sounds to me."

"It isn't a question of whether I believe you," the SAC repeated with exaggerated patience," but you can't ask me to accuse ISD of something like this without corroborating evidence. You've made your views about them well known. If we accused them of protecting Suparman on nothing more than your word, it would look like a personal vendetta and nothing more."

"You have Sergeant Lee's word as well."

"I don't think anyone would see that as genuine corroboration."

"If ISD wasn't there, and Suparman wasn't there, then who the hell shot Robbie Kang?"

"I said we had a problem with the investigation of Kang's death and, in your usual way, Sam, you have put your finger right on it."

"Either Suparman shot Robbie, or ISD shot him. Or hell, sir, maybe you think *I* shot him."

"Don't even joke about that, Sam."

Tay shook his head and looked away.

"To have any chance to put Suparman in the frame," the SAC said, "you need at least one credible witness. Somebody not connected with you who saw pretty much the same thing you did."

"Nobody else saw what happened in the hotel but the desk clerk and the five ISD guys."

"ISD says none of their people were there, and the desk clerk is on leave."

"Don't you think that's awfully convenient?"

"People do take vacation time when they have family issues, Sam. That's not evidence of some vast conspiracy."

The SAC rose to his feet. He stood there awkwardly for a moment waiting for Tay to say something, but Tay remained silent. Finally he sighed and walked to the door. Putting his hand on the knob, he looked back over his shoulder.

"Will you think about it, Sam?"

"Think about what?"

"Retirement. Or at the very least, taking that promotion I suggested."

"You want me out of CID, don't you, sir?"

"I want to avoid any embarrassment to this department, Sam. I don't know how we're going to conclude this investigation. If you're going to continue to insist one of the world's most wanted terrorists killed Robbie Kang, and say without a shred of evidence to support you that ISD is protecting him and knows where he is, it *is* going to embarrass this department."

"That's what's happened, chief."

"Then find yourself a witness. Or take one of my suggestions."

"And what are you going to do if I don't do either of those things?"

The SAC stood quietly for a moment looking at Tay. Eventually his eyes drifted to the window and he appeared to contemplate the city beyond it.

"Please don't make me decide, Sam."

The SAC turned and left Tay's office without another word.

When Sergeant Lee came into Tay's office, Tay was sitting at his desk with a pensive expression on his face. He was leaning forward, his elbow resting on the desktop, and his chin propped on his fist. He made Lee think of a slightly overweight version of Rodin's *The Thinker.*

Lee sat in one of the chairs in front of Tay's desk and waited. After a moment, Tay leaned back in his chair and gave Lee the condensed book version of what the SAC had told him.

"I don't understand, sir." Lee shifted her weight in the chair. "The SAC is saying he doesn't believe that Suparman was at that hotel?"

"He's saying he's not going to say Suparman was there and accuse ISD of protecting him without having something other than our word for it."

"Then who shot Robbie Kang?"

Tay shrugged.

"But we saw what happened, sir."

"Not really. We saw a man we think was Suparman who appeared to be wounded, and we saw Sergeant Kang's body. We didn't see the shots fired. All we really know is what that ISD guy who seemed to be in charge told us."

"Oh, come on, sir. There's no other reasonable explanation."

"The SAC says there's no evidence that ISD has Suparman. They say they don't."

"My God!" Lee snapped. "We've told him they have Suparman and that ought to be good enough for him."

"Maybe it ought to be, but it isn't." Tay folded his arms. "What we need is a witness."

"You think somebody saw the shooting, sir?"

Tay had been thinking off and on about the girl in the window for days. He still didn't have any idea what she had been doing there, but he was convinced it hadn't been a coincidence she was watching the Fortuna Hotel that day. He knew she hadn't seen the shooting, but she had seen everything else. After they ran down the hotel clerk, they would look for her as well, but he thought it might be too soon to go into that with Lee.

"Other than the ISD guys and us," Tay said instead, "there were only three people in that hotel who saw anything: Suparman, his sister, and the hotel clerk. Suparman is in the wind, his sister was run over by a truck in the middle of Serangoon Road, and the hotel clerk is supposedly on leave."

"So what? We just get the hotel clerk back. When he tells the SAC those guys brought Suparman into the hotel and claimed to be cops, everybody will know ISD is lying."

Tay leaned forward and rested his forearms on his desk.

"The hotel doesn't know where the desk clerk is."

Lee looked confused. Tay knew exactly how she felt.

"The desk clerk told the hotel he had some kind of family issue. He might not even be in Singapore now."

"*What?* Bullshit." Lee shook her head. "Just ask Immigration to check their exit records. That will tell us where he went."

"And then what? Say, he flew to Los Angeles. What do we do then?"

Sergeant Lee shook her head and looked away. "This stinks, sir."

"Can you bring your car in tomorrow?"

"My car? Yes, sir. But why do you want me to?"

"We've got things to do and I don't want to use a pool car. Some of them have GPS trackers, and right now I don't trust anybody."

"Where are we going, sir?"

"We're going to find ourselves a witness, Sergeant. Or we're going to die trying."

"I wish you wouldn't put it that way, sir."

Tay nodded. He could see why Lee thought it had been a poor choice of words on his part, but he couldn't think of a better description of exactly where they stood.

29

WHEN TAY AND Lee walked into the lobby of the Fortuna Hotel the next morning, they didn't recognize the man behind the registration desk. The clerk on the day Robbie Kang had been killed had been an elderly Chinese-looking man who was almost bald and wore rimless glasses with thick lenses. This man appeared to be in his thirties and looked vaguely Indian. He was very thin and had long, greasy-looking hair down to his shoulders.

The man turned his head back and forth from Tay to Lee and his lower lip curled into a slight but unmistakable leer. "You want a room?"

Tay took out his warrant card and held it a few inches in front of the man's face. The leer vanished and was quickly replaced by a look of apprehension.

Singaporeans didn't like talking to the police. Growing up in Singapore, no one told you the policeman was your friend. Mostly you were told to obey the police without question and to avoid them whenever possible. When two cops, one of whom was holding his warrant card right in front of your face, confronted you, nothing good could possibly come of it.

"I am so sorry," the man stammered. "I saw you come into the lobby together and I thought...well, I suppose I shouldn't have, but—"

170

"Shut up," Tay said in a quiet voice.

The man shut up.

"Who are you?"

"Rajeev, sir. Rajeev Chandran."

"Are you the manager?"

"No, sir. I am just the desk clerk."

"How long have you worked here, Mr. Chandran?"

"Oh please, sir. Please call me Rajeev."

"How long have you worked here, Mr. Chandran?"

The desk clerk swallowed and looked down. "Almost a year, sir."

"Were you on duty three days ago?"

"No, sir. I had a week off. Yesterday was my first day back."

"Did you hear about what happened here three days ago?"

The clerk hesitated. His eyes flicked back and forth between Tay and Lee as if it would somehow help him to divine the meaning behind Tay's question.

"Three days ago?" the clerk stammered. "I wasn't here three days ago and I don't—"

"Two men were shot here three days ago," Tay snapped. "Are you telling me you know nothing about it?"

"Men shot? Here?" The clerk drew back and his eyes widened. "Oh no, you must be mistaken, sir."

The clerk's surprise appeared genuine to Tay, but how could that be? Surely that had to be the most exciting thing that ever happened at the Fortuna Hotel, and the desk clerk, even if he hadn't been on duty then, hadn't heard anything about it?

"Is the manager here?" Tay asked.

"No, sir."

"When will he be back?"

"I do not know, sir."

"When is he usually here?"

"He only comes in now and then, sir. Mostly when one of us is not here. Like last week. Mr. Wang worked for me when I was away."

"Mr. Wang?" Tay asked.

"Yes, sir. Mr. Robert Wang. He is the manager."

"You're saying Mr. Wang was here three days ago working in your place?"

The desk clerk nodded eagerly, happy to have at last provided Tay with an answer he seemed to like.

"Does Mr. Wang wear glasses?" Tay asked the clerk.

"Why, yes, he does. With very thick lenses."

The clerk made circles with the thumbs and forefingers of both hands and held them in front of his eyes as if Tay might not be familiar with the concept of glasses.

"And he's a rather elderly Chinese man?"

"Oh yes, sir. That is him. You have met Mr. Wang?"

"I think we have."

"How can we contact Mr. Wang?" Lee asked the clerk.

The man slowly shook his head. "I do not know, ma'am."

"Oh come on. Are you telling us you have no way to reach the manager of this hotel? What would you do in an emergency?"

"I would telephone Mr. Wang."

"So telephone him."

The clerk went back to slowly shaking his head. "I fear I cannot. When I came back to work, Mr. Wang told me he was going away. He said he could not be reached for at least two weeks." The clerk seemed to stand a little straighter. "He told me I was in charge until he got back."

"Where did he go?"

"I do not know, ma'am. He said there had been a death in his family. I thought his family was here in Singapore, but perhaps not."

"Give me the telephone number you have for him," Lee said.

The clerk pulled out a drawer and hunted through it. He found a white card and read a telephone number from it. Lee punched the number into her mobile phone, and Tay and the clerk watched Lee in silence until she took the phone away from her ear and pushed the disconnect button.

"No answer, sir."

"Do you have a home address for Mr. Wang?" Tay asked the clerk.

"Uh...perhaps I can find one somewhere."

The clerk bent down, and Tay and Lee listened as he opened and closed drawers underneath the reception desk and poked through their contents. Finally he straightened up, waving a sheet of paper. Lee reached out, plucked it from his fingers, and scanned the contents.

"It's a letter about vacation pay," she said. "It's addressed to an apartment in the Woodlands HDB estate."

Tay looked back at the clerk. "Is this Mr. Wang's home address?"

The clerk nodded.

Tay took a business card from his shirt pocket and found a pen on the check-in desk. He wrote on the back of the card and then pushed it across the desk to the clerk.

"That's the number for my mobile phone. If you hear from Mr. Wang, I expect you to call me at once."

The clerk picked up the card and began nodding so vigorously he made Tay think of a bobblehead doll.

"Yes, sir, I will call if I hear from Mr. Wang. You can count on me, sir."

"If you do not call, I will come back here and arrest you and you will go to prison for the rest of your life. Do you understand?"

The clerk increased the velocity of his nodding to the point that Lee thought his head might pop off his neck. She turned around and pushed out through the lobby doors before she laughed out loud. Tay pointed his index finger at the clerk and followed. As the door swung closed, they could hear the clerk frantically promising them undying cooperation.

"Oh yes, sir, I will call. You can be certain of that, sir. I will not let you down. I am a most reliable man who is loyal to our country and I know that—"

When the closing door finally cut the clerk off, Tay allowed himself a small smile. Sometimes it was good to be a policeman in Singapore.

The Woodlands HDB estate is almost all the way out to the narrow Straits of Johor that separates Singapore from Malaysia. Lee drove and Tay sat looking out the window. It took less than an hour to drive to the Woodlands from the part of Singapore in which he lived, but as far as he was concerned they might as well have been traveling to another planet.

Singaporeans had a particular expression for those parts of their tiny island state that, like the Woodlands, were far removed from the tourist and financial districts most of the world thought of when they thought of Singapore. It was called the heartland, and that was an expression Tay loathed. He thought it was sad to have to come up with a meaningless platitude to make people feel better about places that were cheerless and sometimes even downright creepy.

A government agency called the Housing Development Board had been relentlessly throwing up pre-packaged villages all over Singapore for as long as Tay could remember. Now something like eighty percent of the country's population lived in government-built housing. Every one of the HDB estates looked more or less the same. They were immaculate, of course. Since this was Singapore, the buildings were all in good repair, the walls were all freshly painted, and the landscaping was in perfect order thanks to an army of Indian and Bangladeshi workers permitted into the country on short-term work visas to do the manual labor Singaporeans wouldn't do.

No matter how hard the bureaucrats worked to dress up the HDB estates, however, they still amounted to nothing more than clumps of nearly identical apartment towers pushed together around some community facilities. Every estate had a mosque, a Chinese temple, a Christian church, a community club, a coffee shop, a mini-mart, and a school. What the estates did not have was the feeling that any real, actual life was lived in them. They were not places where the daily stuff of bona fide human existence thrived. The make-believe villages of the heartland had nearly everything, Tay thought, except a heart. He hated them.

The dreary monotony of the Woodlands HDB estate even extended to its street names. Sergeant Lee turned off Woodlands Avenue at a Shell Station and followed Woodlands Street to Woodlands Drive.

They passed building after building, each about a dozen stories tall and all absolutely identical in color and design. In what Tay assumed was a desperate effort to introduce some degree of novelty, the balconies of the buildings had been painted in varying shades of gray, yellow, and green, but if the idea behind either the colors or the apparent randomness of their distribution was to make the buildings appear more cheerful, the effort had been an abysmal failure. There was nothing cheerful about the relentless ranks of buildings that lined both sides of the road.

When they passed Woodlands Circle, Tay pointed into the cul-de-sac. "Robbie and I had a case down there once."

Lee didn't know what Tay was talking about, but she nodded politely.

Once he had brought up the subject, Tay wished he hadn't.

"It wasn't important, Sergeant," Tay muttered. "Never mind."

Even now it was difficult for him to think about that case. When he and Kang had entered the apartment and found the body of a man stretched out on the floor, almost immediately Tay had been seized by a conviction he was somehow connected to the man. He had never met him, he was certain of that, but the sense of some link was overwhelming.

Finding that man's body eventually spun Tay off on a journey of memory that had led him all the way back to a father who had died almost forty years before, a father Tay hardly remembered. It was not a trip he wanted to make again. Ever.

30

LEE PULLED UP to the curb in front of a building exactly like all the other buildings in the Woodlands HDB estate. Ten stories tall, it had about a dozen apartments on each floor, every single one with the same number of windows and an identical narrow balcony. The only visual distinction Tay detected was the variety of junk each resident had piled on his balcony.

The whole area was as deserted as if it had been abandoned. A few cars and motorcycles were parked on the street, but there was no sign of human activity anywhere. No music on the breeze, no conversation in the distance, no flashes of movement. The place was as barren and sterile as anywhere Tay ever remembered being. If it hadn't been for the laundry drying on some of the metal poles that extended out from each balcony, Tay would have wondered if anyone lived here at all.

"Mr. Wang is in 504, sir."

Tay's eyes flicked up five stories. He scanned the apartments on that level and saw absolutely nothing interesting, so he just nodded and got out of the car.

When the elevator opened on the fifth floor, they stepped out into a corridor with a white tiled floor, freshly painted off-white walls, and six black metal doors on each side. There was a faint smell of accumulated cooking odors and something else Tay thought might be urine. He hoped it was from dogs and cats.

They walked down the corridor checking the numbers painted on the doors until they found 504. Lee looked at Tay and raised her eyebrows in the obvious question. Tay nodded.

"Police!" Lee called out. She knocked on the door with her knuckles and the metallic rapping sound echoed in the quiet hallway. "Police!"

No response. After a polite interval, Lee knocked again. Still no response and no sign of life from any of the other apartments on the corridor. Tay reached out and jiggled the doorknob, but it didn't turn.

"I could probably open it, sir. It looks like a simple pin tumbler."

"You know how to pick locks, Sergeant?"

"I have no idea how to pick locks, sir." Lee took out her police warrant card, a laminated card about twice the size of a credit card and a little thinner. "But this works more often than you might think."

Bending over until her eyes were level with the doorknob, Lee slid her warrant card between the door and the jamb and moved it down until she felt the edge of the bolt. She pushed on the door with her left hand, jiggled the card a little further down, and bent it to the left until it almost touched the doorknob. Maintaining her pressure on the door, Lee suddenly bent the card back in the opposite direction and pushed it hard into the jamb. The bolt snapped back and the door swung open.

"It's that easy?" Tay asked.

"Not always, sir, but usually."

Tay just shook his head. He wouldn't have believed that if he hadn't seen it with his own eyes.

The smell came to them the moment they opened the door. Neither Tay nor Lee had any doubt what they would find somewhere inside.

Dead bodies have an unmistakable odor, a sickly sweet stench with stomach-churning undertones that always made Tay think of spoiled cheese. The odor comes from the urine and feces released by the relaxation of muscles at death mixed with the gases from the first stages of organic decomposition. It is a smell anyone who has encountered will remember forever. It is a smell that no homicide investigator can forget no matter how hard he tries.

"He's in here, sir," Lee called from the bedroom.

The body was face down on the carpet just inside the door. The corpse's head was turned to the right and Tay could see the face clearly. He had no doubt, but he stepped to the side so Lee could get a good look as well. Lee just nodded.

It was the elderly Chinese-looking man who had been behind the desk when they rushed into the Fortuna Hotel at the sound of gunshots. Lee squatted down beside the corpse and studied the wound.

"One shot to the back of the head, sir. Looks to me like a nine."

Three men dead from a single shot in the back of the head with a nine millimeter handgun in less than a week. Was there any chance at all that was a coincidence?

Tay didn't want to think about his dream and the conversation he imagined having with his mother, he really didn't, but of course it all came back to him clearly now...

"And what about the other body?"

"What other body?"

"You know, that man who...oh wait, never mind. You haven't found that one yet."

When Sergeant Lee got to her feet, Tay was standing and staring off into space.

"Are you okay, sir?" she asked.

Tay shook off the memory and nodded. He got down on his knees and lifted the corpse's right arm an inch or two. The body was cold and he felt very little rigor in the elbow. The man had been dead for a while, probably two or three days. Tay lowered the arm, put his cheek against the floor, and examined the corpse's face.

"There's no exit wound," he said. "The bullet must still be in him."

"Must have been a low velocity subsonic round," Lee said. "Heavy bullet, slow speed, no penetration. Fired through a suppressor, it wouldn't have made much noise."

A low velocity subsonic round? A heavy bullet fired through a suppressor? That wasn't some robber with a cheap revolver who panicked when he was discovered.

Tay pushed himself up and stood looking down at the man lying on the floor of the dreary little apartment in the Woodlands. He was just an old guy trying to earn a living running a second-rate tourist hotel, and then somebody came into his apartment and shot him in the back of the head. Who would do that? Who would *want* to do that?

Tay could only think of one answer to that question. He tried to put it all together in some other way, but he couldn't.

Somebody was trying to cover up the connection between ISD and Suparman. They were tying up loose ends, getting rid of anyone who knew about it. Tay didn't have a lot of respect for ISD, but couldn't see them as cold-blooded murderers. He simply wasn't prepared to believe the Internal Security Department went around killing people because they knew something they didn't want revealed. But if it wasn't ISD tying up those loose ends, who in the world was it?

There had to be another explanation. He just had no idea what it could be.

"Should I call this in now, sir?"

Tay hesitated. Nothing good could come of their discovery of the hotel manager's body lying on the floor of his apartment. Not for him, and certainly not for them. How would they explain to the SAC what they were doing there, or how they had gotten in?

But what else were they going to do? Just leave the guy's body lying there and walk away?

"Maybe we should call it in anonymously," Tay said after a moment.

"Anonymously, sir? Why?"

"To keep anyone from knowing who made the discovery, Sergeant. That's what anonymously means."

Tay took a couple of steps over to the window, pulled the flimsy curtain aside, and looked out. The glass was grimy and streaked with dirt, but off in the distance he could see the narrow straits that separated Singapore from the southern tip of Malaysia. Just on the other side, indistinct in the afternoon haze, loomed the buildings of Johor Bahru, the slightly shabby Malaysian city at the other end of the causeway.

What if his worst suspicions *were* true? What if ISD had killed the hotel manager and did it because he could connect ISD to Suparman? That meant ISD was willing to go to pretty much any lengths to cover up the fact that they had Suparman and were protecting him for some reason.

Any lengths?

Tay knew of only five people in the world who could link ISD to Suparman. One was the hotel manager, and he was lying dead on the floor right in front of them. The second was Suparman's sister, but she was dead as well, run down by a truck in the middle of Serangoon Road. The third was Robbie Kang, and of course he was dead, too, presumably shot by Suparman.

That left two people, just two people, who could tie ISD directly to Suparman: Tay and Lee.

Tay didn't like looking at it that way. He really didn't. But that was how it was.

31

IT HAD STARTED to rain when they were in Robert Wang's apartment. The rain began with a mist so light it was as if the city were being cooled by a spritz from a gigantic spray bottle, but by the time they got back to the car the rain had turned earnest and fat drops pinged against the windshield with a rhythm that reminded Tay of a song he couldn't quite remember. He watched the raindrops collect at the top of the windshield, join into big rivulets, and streak across it.

Tay walked his memory back through the time they had spent in Wang's apartment. He was pretty certain they left the apartment exactly as they had found it. Neither Tay nor Lee had touched anything but the body and the front doorknob and Tay had used his handkerchief to wipe the doorknob on both sides of the door. It was probably more caution than the circumstances required, but if it was wasted effort it wasn't much effort to waste.

"This isn't right, sir."

"No, it isn't, Sergeant, but we're going to do it anyway."

"We should call it in, sir. We just left that poor man lying there."

"I doubt he cares much one way or the other."

"You know what I mean, sir. For God's sake, we're the police. We can't just ignore a dead body."

"We're not going to ignore it. Tomorrow you will find a pay phone and report it. You're just not going to tell anybody who you are."

Lee looked away and shook her head, but she didn't say anything.

"Look, Linda, don't you see what's going on here?"

"No, sir, I guess I don't."

"ISD is protecting Suparman. You saw them and I saw them."

"Yes, I saw them, sir. But I still don't understand why they would be doing it."

"Neither do I, but the woman they claimed was Suparman's sister saw they were protecting him, and she's dead. Robbie Kang saw they were protecting him, and he's dead. And the hotel manager saw they were protecting him, and now he's dead, too."

"The woman's death was an accident."

"Maybe," Tay shrugged. "Maybe not."

"Are you telling me what I think you're telling me, sir?"

Tay just looked at Lee.

"My God, sir, you can't seriously believe the Internal Security Department is going around murdering people to cover up whatever it is they're doing."

"Somebody is, Linda. You believe all this is just a coincidence?"

"No, sir, but—"

"Think it through. Only five people know ISD was at the Fortuna Hotel with Suparman. And now three of them are dead."

Lee stared at Tay.

"Listen to yourself, sir. You sound crazy."

"It's not crazy at all. We've got four people murdered—"

"Four? You said three: Sergeant Kang, Suparman's sister, and the hotel manager. Who else?"

"A floater that Robbie and I caught just before all this started. Dr. Hoi says he's probably an Indonesian. He was killed with a shot to the back of the head, and the shooter used a nine. Just like Robbie and just like Wang."

Lee just stared.

"It's all tied together somehow. If ISD is protecting Suparman, and if somebody is cutting off the connections between ISD and Suparman, we're the only two connections left."

"You can't really believe ISD would kill two Singapore Police officers, can you, sir?"

"I didn't think so about an hour ago, Linda, but why kill Wang and let us walk away? That's why you're waiting until tomorrow to call this in, and that's why you're going to do it anonymously. Until Wang's body is discovered, they're not going to be in any hurry and we'll still have a chance to get in front of this."

It was the most optimistic thing Tay could say to Lee.

Whether he believed it or not was another story altogether.

They took the Bukit Timah Expressway back to the city. The rain had stopped and they drove in silence. Tay listened to the hissing sound the tires made on the wet pavement and thought about what to do now.

Did he really believe he and Lee were in danger? Did he honestly think ISD would kill two Singapore policemen because they could tie ISD to Suparman? He still couldn't bring himself to believe an agency of the government of Singapore was going around killing people.

On the other hand, if ISD wasn't trying to protect itself from being tied to Suparman, who killed the hotel manager? And who the hell was that Indonesian they pulled out of the Singapore River with a bullet in the back of his head? What did he have to do with Suparman and ISD and all the rest of this?

Tay was just going around in circles and he knew it. It came as a welcome relief when Lee broke the silence.

"How long do you want me to wait, sir, before I make the anonymous call?"

"Not very long, Linda. Right now we know the hotel manager was murdered. Except for whoever killed him, nobody else does."

"I still don't see why that matters, sir."

"Honestly?" Tay shrugged. "Maybe it doesn't matter, but it's the only thing we've got going for us. I don't want to give it up until I know for sure what it tells us about the other killings."

Tay took a packet of Marlboros out of his shirt pocket, shook one out, and lit it. He lowered the passenger window a few inches and the sound of rushing air filled the car. Tay smoked quietly and listened to the rumble of the slipstream.

Several minutes passed like that, then Lee cleared her throat.

"Where are we going, sir?"

"Drop me on Orchard Road and you head on home."

Lee shot Tay a surprised look. "There must be something else we can do, sir."

"There is. We know a lot. We just don't know what any of it means. We need to stop running all over the city and sit down and think."

32

AFTER SERGEANT LEE dropped Tay off on Orchard Road, he walked home and he did what he always did when he needed to think. He sat in his garden with his shoes off and smoked one cigarette after another. He really was going to have to quit. He understood that. He just wasn't going to do it right now.

He and Lee didn't have much time before ISD found out they knew about Robert Wang. The problem was he had absolutely no idea yet what to do with the time they did have.

After a while, the light softened and dusk began to settle over the city, and Tay realized he was hungry since he hadn't eaten any lunch. Before they discovered Wang's body, he didn't wanted to take time to eat. After they discovered Wang's body, he hadn't felt like eating anymore. But now he did. Maybe that was a good sign.

Tay stood up and put on his shoes. Then he went inside, washed his hands, and headed out his front door without any particular destination in mind.

He turned right and walked in the direction of Orchard Road, but as he was passing through Preranakan Place he glanced into the Alley Bar and was surprised to see it wasn't very busy. Tay liked the Alley Bar. It was high-ceilinged and pleasingly dim, and the long bar with the big mirrors behind it stretched for what must have been fifty feet until it almost disappeared into the cool interior shadows. Somehow the scarred wooden bar and hazy mirrors and under-lit interior of the place all combined to make Tay think of what he was sure had been better times, although more and more he wondered if those times had ever really existed.

He took a stool at a section of the bar that was completely deserted and ordered a medium-rare burger and an Irish whiskey. They didn't have any Powers so he settled for Bushmills. It wasn't the same, not nearly, but he could live with it.

While he waited for his order he had the choice of watching himself in the cloudy mirror behind the bar or reading something on his phone. He decided to read the Asian edition of the *Wall Street Journal* on his phone, but he only half registered the words as they scrolled by since his mind was still focused on what he and Sergeant Lee could do to get on top of what he knew would be coming at them all too soon.

Tay was dimly aware of a man wearing a baseball cap walking up to the bar and sitting one stool away. It annoyed him that the guy chose that particular place to sit. There were plenty of empty stools further down the bar. Why did anyone have to pick one so close to him? He didn't want to do anything to suggest he might be open to conversation, so he kept his eyes on his telephone and didn't look up.

At least not until the man spoke to him.

"Just keep your eyes on your phone, Tay. Don't look at me."

So, of course, Tay immediately looked at him. He didn't turn his head, at least he was that subtle, but he did his best to focus on the man's features out of the corner of his eye. He seemed familiar, but the blue baseball cap and sunglasses made it hard to get a fix on his face using only his peripheral vision.

"You looked at me, Tay. I knew you would, you contrary son of a bitch."

The voice was familiar, too, and Tay started clicking through his memory trying to match it to somebody.

"Do you remember," the man went on, "where we met to talk about that kid who was found hanged in his apartment?"

Now Tay *did* turn his head. "Goh? Is that you?"

"My God, Tay, you're the original fucking bull in the fucking china shop. Even the simplest tradecraft is too much for you, isn't it?"

"Tradecraft?" Tay rolled his eyes. "For Christ's sake, Goh, do you have any idea how silly you sound? Grow up, man."

"Do you remember where we met, or don't you, Tay?"

"Of course I remember. We met at—"

"For fuck's sake, don't say it out loud."

Tay just shook his head and looked away.

"Meet me there in half an hour."

Tay sighed and said nothing. He just went back to reading the *Wall Street Journal.*

"Well, are you coming or aren't you?"

"Make it an hour, Goh. I want to finish my burger."

Tay could only think of one good thing about meeting on a bench in Fort Canning Park rather than having a normal conversation back at the Alley Bar like most people would. At least he could smoke there.

Fort Canning Park was one of Singapore's major landmarks. It had seen much of what passed for history there and had been everything from a resort for the Malay kingdoms in the fourteenth century, to the site of the residences of the colonial governors, to the place where the British surrendered to the Japanese in World War II. Now it was a lush, green public garden in the center of the city crisscrossed with meandering walkways shaded by long rows of tall, broad-leafed mahogany trees.

Tay got out of the taxi at the Hill Street entrance to the park and walked west on a winding, brick-paved walk. The glow from the city cast the park in shades of gray, and a warm breeze rattled the trees.

The bench where he and Goh had met before was behind the old Hill Street Police Station. The British built the station back in the thirties and for some reason designed it in the Italianate style. That made it a bit of an oddity in tropical Singapore, but Tay thought its balconies and arcades and courtyards were lovely. Considerably less lovely was the history of the place.

In the thirties, when Singapore was still a British colony, the British fought a nasty little war against the anti-colonialist guerrillas trying to drive them off the Malaysian Peninsula. A good deal of that war had been run out of the Hill Street Station. When the Japanese defeated the British in World War II and took over Singapore, they turned the Hill Street Station into an interrogation center for prisoners. And in the sixties, Singapore's fledgling government dominated by ethnic Chinese made the building the heart of its bloody battle against the Muslim insurgents in Malaysia.

The Hill Street Station was abandoned as a police facility in the eighties and converted into what the government called an arts center. Tay saw that less as a genuine effort to create a public facility of civic worth than it was another fumbling attempt by the faceless men who ran Singapore to sanitize its past. He supposed the truth was it didn't really matter what anyone said the building was now. Singaporeans knew what it had been before.

A lot of Singaporeans even believed the building was haunted. They avoided being anywhere near it, averting their eyes if they were forced to drive past it on Hill Street. Tay knew people who swore that late at night you could hear screams coming from the basement where prisoners had been tortured by first one conqueror and then the next. He had never heard the screams himself, but he had no difficulty imagining them.

Some cities were proud of their past. Others talked mostly about their future. Tay knew Singapore liked to think of itself as being all about the future, but he had always believed Singapore was mostly about the past.

Tay had no difficulty finding the right bench. The first time he and Goh had met there he had wondered whether Goh's choice of a bench right behind the Hill Street Police Station was meant as a subtle touch of irony or if it was only coincidence. He still wasn't certain.

The park was dim and quiet. Off in the distance Tay could hear the traffic on Hill Street. No one else was in sight, not even the occasional dog walker. He was just starting to wonder how wise he was to be meeting an ISD man in a lonely, darkened park when he saw Goh coming up the path from the opposite direction.

Did he really think that Goh might do him harm? No, of course he didn't. At most, Goh would toss out a few threats and that would be that. It might almost be fun. Tay lit a cigarette, shook out the match, and dropped it on the ground.

"You're littering," Goh said after he sat down. "Just like the last time we were here. You're really an anti-social prick, aren't you?"

"I'm not a big fan of yours either, Goh. So can we cut the bullshit? Why am I here?"

"I was sorry to hear about your sergeant."

"I'm sorry to hear about anyone being murdered. I'm even sorrier when he leaves behind a pregnant wife. That he happened to be a friend of mine doesn't really make it any worse."

"I'm not the villain here, Tay."

"You're not?"

"I just want you to know that."

"Then who is?"

Goh chewed at his lip and looked away. "I could guess."

"Guess."

So Goh did.

33

"THE SURVEILLANCE OPERATION at the Temple Street Inn was bullshit," Goh said.

"No kidding."

"They wanted to keep our attention there because something they didn't want us to know about was happening someplace else."

"*Our* attention?"

"Yeah, Tay, *our* attention. They were running me around just as much as they were running you around."

"Who is this *they* you keep talking about?"

Goh bobbed his head and appeared to think about the question, but Tay doubted he really was. He was certain Goh had already decided exactly what he was going to tell him, and what he was not going to tell him.

"My instructions to set up the surveillance operation on the Temple Street Inn came from the top," Goh said after a moment.

"The top of ISD?"

"The *very* top."

Tay thought Goh looked a little uneasy saying that. Goh was not a nervous man, and his uneasiness got Tay's full attention.

"You're saying that—"

"For Christ's sake, Tay, you're going to have to let me tell this my way. I'm not going to sit here and be interrogated by you."

Tay raised both hands, palms out.

"I didn't know what to make of it when I got a call from the Minister's office telling me to include CID in the operation, not at first," Goh went on, "but now I'm guessing they wanted to keep you focused on the Temple Street Inn, too."

Goh looked at Tay and raised one eyebrow. "I should've known you would go off on your own and fuck everything up."

"What did I fuck up?"

"The meeting between Suparman and his sister, if she *was* his sister, and I've got to tell you I'm not absolutely sure about that."

"You don't believe the woman was really his sister?"

"I sure as hell don't think she was sick. That was just a horseshit story somebody dreamed up. And if she wasn't sick, she may not have been his sister either."

"You're losing me, Goh."

"I don't think so. I'd bet both of those things have already occurred to you."

Tay said nothing.

"Here's what I'm trying to tell you. Somebody in Singapore is protecting Suparman. Suparman thought his sister was really sick and he demanded his protectors arrange for him to see her. Some genius decided the best way to hide their meeting was to tell all of us it was going to occur, but point us to the wrong place. Then the sister would slip away and go to a different place to meet Suparman. That way, if you ever need them, you've got a list of witnesses as long as your arm swearing they never met."

"Who's protecting Suparman?"

"There are people in ISD who know it's happening, but not many. Most of us don't have a clue. It goes higher than that."

"Higher than ISD?"

Goh said nothing.

"Higher than the Minister of Home Affairs?"

"You're not going to get me to say any more than I have, Tay. Use your imagination."

Although the Minister of Home Affairs presumably supervised ISD, it was widely assumed in many quarters that the director of ISD actually answered only to the Prime Minister. If that were the case, no wonder Goh didn't want to say any more.

"I still don't understand what you're telling me here, Goh. Why in God's name would anybody here in Singapore be protecting Suparman?"

Goh tilted his head back and took a couple of deep breaths.

"Let's say that somewhere in ISD somebody started running Suparman as an asset—"

"Can we drop the spy movie bullshit, Goh? What does that actually *mean*?"

"It means Suparman was feeding information to ISD on Muslim radicals in Malaysia and Indonesia, giving them warnings of impending attacks. At least they thought he was. Can I go on now?"

Tay nodded.

"And let's also say they started doing it well back before the Bali bombings, and finally let's say what they were doing was cleared at the high level of government. So all those folks are sitting behind their big desks in their big offices and Bali gets hit and other places get hit and they slowly start to realize that their prize asset may be shoving one up their ass. So somebody goes out and has a heart to heart with Suparman and he tells them, *not me, brother, you've got this all wrong.* And they decide to believe him."

"And the somebody who believed him was high up in ISD."

"Very high up."

"And he cleared his decision to believe Suparman all the way to the top."

"I have no doubt a decision like that would have been discussed at the highest levels of government."

Tay nodded. "Go on."

"So they keep running Suparman and, because he's been linked to all of these big events and because he feeds them just enough about each one to make them believe him, ISD keeps telling these high levels of government they've got a prize asset on the inside and he's giving them the good stuff. No matter what happens, they keep saying that. If they ever admit they've been burned, half the people at the top of ISD will go down and take some of the people above them down, too."

"So they protect Suparman no matter what he does, and they keep hoping the intelligence they get will be worth more in the end than the damage he does."

"See, Tay, you've figured it out already. I knew you were a smart guy."

Tay thought back to the ISD men he had seen at the Fortuna hotel. Even then, they looked to him like close protection, which would make sense if what Goh was telling him now was true. But then who was the woman who had apparently shot Suparman? And how was the guy from the Australian High Commission involved?

Tay felt like he had been asked to assemble a giant jigsaw puzzle with a thousand little pieces, but someone had thrown the box away and he had no idea what it was supposed to look like. He could have been trying to put together a picture of the Eiffel Tower or one of a pot of petunias.

"Why are you telling me all this, Goh?"

"Because this is fucked up and it's got to be stopped. I hate to admit it, Tay, but you have a better chance to stop it now than I do."

"How am I supposed to do that?"

"I have a lot of confidence in you, Tay. Now that you know your sergeant died because a bunch of bureaucrats are trying to cover their ass, you'll figure it out. There's just one other thing."

Tay looked at Goh and waited.

"Be careful, man. They're in so deep now they won't hesitate if they think you're getting too close. They will drop you without a second thought. You have to find a way to get to Suparman before they see you coming."

"And what am I supposed to do if I do get to him?"

"You'll have to decide that for yourself, Tay. I don't have any doubt what I would do, but then you're not me." Goh scratched at his neck and looked away. "You see what I'm getting at here?"

Tay saw what Goh was getting at all right, but he didn't see what use there was in acknowledging it. So he didn't.

"I've got something else to ask you," Tay said instead. "Is it possible ISD had the Fortuna Hotel under surveillance?"

Goh looked exasperated. "Haven't you been paying attention to anything I said, Tay? I'm telling you the people there with Suparman were protecting him, and they were ISD."

"I don't mean them. I mean somebody else. Somebody watching the hotel from another building."

"What the hell are you talking about?"

"There was a woman in a building across the street. She was watching the Fortuna Hotel when all this happened."

"Across the street?"

Tay nodded.

"Did she make contact with the ISD team covering Suparman?"

"Not that I saw."

"Or the so-called sister?"

Tay shook his head.

"Fucking hell," Goh laughed, shaking his head. "You mean somebody *else* is involved in this thing, too?"

"Then you're saying she wasn't yours?"

"She sure as hell wasn't mine, and it doesn't sound to me like she was anybody else's at ISD either. I don't see why anybody at ISD would want a witness when they had just gone to such elaborate lengths to get rid of all the witnesses."

"Then who was she? Who else could have possibly known

something was going down at that hotel?"

Goh chuckled. "It sounds to me, Tay, like you've got yourself another player somewhere out there."

"Any ideas?"

"Nope. This just gets better and better, doesn't it?"

Tay shook out a cigarette and lit it. Goh didn't seem to be in any hurry to leave, but he didn't say anything else either.

Tay smoked quietly for a while, then asked, "Is that it, Goh?"

"That's it."

"You're not going to give me anything else to go on?"

"I *got* nothing else for you to go on."

Tay thought about that briefly, and then he stood up and nodded at Goh. He turned and strolled away up the bricked pathway. He didn't say anything, and he didn't look back.

When he got out to Hill Street, he flicked away his cigarette butt and started looking for a taxi.

34

THE NEXT MORNING Tay drank far too much coffee and ate a couple of pieces of toast while standing over the sink to keep the crumbs from falling on the floor. After that, he walked through Preranakan Place to Orchard Road and got in the first taxi he saw.

"The Fortuna Hotel," he said to the driver.

"On Serangoon Road?"

Tay nodded and the driver started the meter.

He was missing something. He was sure of that now. And whatever he was missing was important. He was sure of that as well.

He needed to go back over everything and think it all through from the beginning. That was why he was doing this alone. Thinking, he had learned long ago, was always best done alone.

Tay got out of the taxi across the street from the Fortuna Hotel and stood there looking around. The vegetarian restaurant from which he and Kang and Lee had watched the hotel was closed. A steel shutter had been pulled across the front and secured on both sides by heavy padlocks attached to U-bolts sunk into the concrete walls of the building. He went into a few of the neighboring businesses, but his inquiries as to why the vegetarian restaurant was closed were answered with shrugs that varied only in their intensity. After ten minutes, he was back on the sidewalk and no wiser than he had been before.

Was it just a coincidence that the restaurant was closed, or was that too somehow connected with the events of the week before at the Fortuna Hotel? He couldn't see the connection, but that didn't mean there wasn't one.

Tay leaned back against the metal shutter, folded his arms, and contemplated the Fortuna Hotel on the other side of Serangoon Road.

The traffic was heavy. Serangoon Road was a major traffic artery and now that artery was in full thrombosis, clogged with so many trucks, buses, and passenger cars Tay could barely see across it. It was well after rush hour, but these days the city seemed to be jammed with traffic regardless of the hour. He wondered if he drove around at three o'clock in the morning whether the traffic might be lighter. It probably would be, but he wasn't going to drive around at three o'clock in the morning just to find out.

The older Tay got, the less pleasant he found many things. He knew most people would dismiss such thoughts as nothing but evidence of a man growing crotchety in his old age, but that was unfair. It wasn't him. The world really *was* less pleasant than it used it be.

Tay's eyes roamed over the scene. He tried to see it as it was the evening they had watched the hotel from the vegetarian restaurant. He picked out the spot near the intersection with Owen Road where Kang first noticed the two men sitting in the dirty white Toyota. He pictured the silver blue Hi-Lux van, unmarked and without windows, pulling up behind the Toyota and the three men getting out. He pictured the two men from the Toyota going into the hotel, then the other men getting back in the van and rolling up to the entry before getting out again with the fourth man and going into the hotel, too. But none of that told him anything he didn't already know.

So Tay started over at the beginning and worked his way methodically through each of the events again, trying to recall exactly what each of them had said at the time. And this time he added in the piece of the puzzle about which he had the least understanding.

"Now who the hell is that?"

Tay glanced at Kang to see what he was talking about. Kang pointed at the apartment building across Owen Road from the hotel.

"Third floor, sir. The corner window."

Tay counted up to the third floor and his eyes found the corner of the building where Owen Road and Serangoon Road met.

"Do you see her, sir? The girl in the window?"

Tay did see her. She was standing close to the glass and appeared to be watching the same men he and Kang were watching.

"If those men are ISD," Kang said, "who is the girl watching them? She's not one of ours, is she?"

Tay shook his head.

"Okay, so we're CID and she's not ours, and they're ISD and she not theirs since she's watching them. So who is she?"

It was a good question. A very good question. Tay had no answer for it so he said nothing.

The entrance to the building was unlocked. The double glass doors were scratched and pitted and they opened into a small and dreary lobby with a black-and-white tiled linoleum floor and several dozen black metal mailboxes on the wall opposite a staircase.

There was no elevator so Tay trudged up the stairs to the third floor. By the time he passed the second floor, he was already short of breath. He kept telling himself he had to get some exercise, maybe lose a little weight, but it was only at times like this he really thought about it seriously. Was fifty too old to start exercising? It probably was. Diet and exercise programs were meant mostly for young people, weren't they? Maybe he ought to just stop walking up staircases instead.

The third floor hallway was floored in the same black-and-white linoleum as the lobby. The walls had once been white, but the paint had yellowed into a sickly looking color that caused Tay to think of things he would rather not have thought about. The lights along the middle of the ceiling were surprisingly bright and they showed every crack and chip in the walls.

Tay stood still for a moment orienting himself. The third-floor corner window in which they saw the girl had to be at the end of the hall to the left, he finally decided. The apartment door all the way at that end was whiter and cleaner than the hallway walls, but not by much. The two brass numerals screwed into it at eye level said 62. How could apartment number 62 be on the third floor? Tay had no idea. He knocked on the door and it opened almost at once.

"What you want?"

The man was short and heavy and wore baggy brown pants and an undershirt that barely stretched over his belly. He had a Chinese face framed by a few wisps of white hair and a pair of gold-rimmed glasses low on his nose. His feet were bare.

Tay held out his warrant card, but the man didn't even glance at it.

"What you want?" he asked again.

"I'm Inspector Tay from Singapore CID."

The man closed the door.

Tay stood there a moment feeling like an idiot. The old man had just closed the door in his face, but what could he do about it? Arrest him? Not bloody likely. He would have considered shooting him, but he had left his gun at home. He settled for pounding hard on the door with his open hand.

Once again the door opened almost immediately.

"You come to wrong place. I no call police."

"I know you didn't call the police. I want to ask you a few questions."

Tay thought the old man was going to close the door for the second time so he pointed at him with his index finger.

"If you do that again," he said. "I'll kick it down and shoot you."

The man looked unimpressed by Tay's threat, but the door stayed open.

"Who lives here with you?" Tay asked.

"Nobody. Just me here."

"I'm looking for a young woman. Perhaps thirty, European looking?"

The old man snorted, but he didn't say anything else.

"We saw her." Tay gestured into the apartment. "Through the window."

"No woman here. Only me. You not hear me say first time?"

"Perhaps she was here when you were out."

"You think this woman break in when I gone and stand in front of window?" The man snorted again. "You stupid."

"Listen to me, sir. We saw this woman in your apartment. We need to understand what she was doing here. It is necessary for you to tell me the truth."

"Fuck off!" the old man shouted. "No woman here! No woman break in when I gone!"

Tay put his hand on the old man's shoulder, gently moved him aside, and walked into the apartment. He went directly to the window on the opposite wall, raised the shade, and looked out.

He was at the end of the building furthest away from Serangoon Road, not the end closest to it. He had turned the wrong direction in the hallway.

He was in the wrong apartment.

35

TAY WAS MORTIFIED and mumbled an apology as quickly as he could. The old man just stared at him and said nothing.

Tay walked to the other end of the hall and found the correct door. It was indistinguishable from the first door he knocked on other than for the brass numbers reading 13 instead of 62. He was still baffled at the numbering system in the building, but he had more important things to think about.

He knocked and no one answered. He put his ear to the door and heard nothing. He knocked again. Still no answer. He tried the knob, but of course the door was locked.

What should he do now? He certainly wasn't going to kick the door down. He wished for a moment he had brought Lee with him. Maybe she could do that trick with her warrant card that had opened the hotel manager's apartment.

Tay still had his own warrant card in his hand from having shown it to the old man in the other apartment. He tentatively pushed it into the crack between the door and the jamb right next to the lock, but of course nothing happened. He thought back to what he had seen Lee do and tried to imitate it. Leaning against the door, he applied as much pressure as he dared and bent the warrant card to the left up against the lock. He thought he could feel the card slide past something, but he wasn't sure. Perhaps that was just wishful thinking. He jiggled the card up and down a few times and then snapped it back in the opposite direction just as he had seen Lee do, all the while keeping pressure on the door with his shoulder.

There was a click, and the door swung open so abruptly Tay almost fell into the apartment.

"Hello?" he called out. "Anyone here?"

He got no response and knew he wouldn't. He could feel the emptiness. He stepped quickly inside and closed the door behind him.

Tay crossed the room to the window, raised the shade, and looked out. He had the right apartment this time. He was looking across Serangoon Road directly at the metal shutter on the front of the vegetarian restaurant from which he and Kang had seen the girl in the window.

This window.

It took Tay only a few minutes to search through the apartment. He was pretty sure he would find nothing, but he did it anyway. The apartment consisted of a living room a bit longer than it was wide, a Pullman kitchen, a dingy bedroom, and a tiny bathroom. The bedroom had only a stained and lumpy looking mattress sitting on a frame. No sheets, no pillows, no blanket. The bedroom closet was empty, as were the drawers of the chest. There was nothing at all in the bathroom.

Except for a smell.

It took Tay a moment to put a name to it, but then he did. It was disinfectant. Probably bleach.

He stepped back out into the bedroom and sniffed the air. The smell was fainter there, but now that he knew what he was looking for it was unmistakable. Could the landlord have just given the place a thorough cleaning, preparing the apartment for the next tenant? In a building like this? Not likely.

The floors, the furniture, everything had been scrubbed with disinfectant. This apartment hadn't simply been cleaned; it had been sanitized. Somebody had intentionally obliterated all traces of whoever had been in it.

Tay went back to the window. Down and to the left he had a perfect view of the entrance to the Fortuna Hotel. The emergency exit from which Suparman's sister had fled into Serangoon Road was also clearly visible. It was the ideal surveillance location. There was no better place than this window to monitor everyone who came and went at the Fortuna Hotel.

But who had the Fortuna Hotel under surveillance? And why?

Tay glanced around the apartment again. He saw nothing he had not already seen and let himself out.

He knocked again on the first door he had gone to and the same elderly Chinese-looking man again jerked it open almost instantly. Tay wondered if the old man spent his entire day just standing behind the door waiting for someone to knock on it.

The man looked at Tay without saying anything. Tay had always thought the description of Chinese faces as inscrutable was an awful cliché, but he was beginning to reconsider his opinion.

"Who do I contact about the apartments in this building?" he asked.

At that, the man unaccountably perked up and his face took on a glimmer of life.

"You want apartment?" he asked Tay.

"I want to know who I talk to about renting an apartment here, yes."

The old man was almost smiling now. He stepped aside, gestured Tay into the apartment with little pulling motions of both hands, and pointed to a chair. Tay sat down and glanced around. The apartment was nearly identical to the empty one at the other end of the hall. Same layout, same shades on the windows, even the same furniture.

The old man sat down opposite him. "When you want move in?" he asked.

"I don't want to move in. I only want some information about who rented the apartment at the other end of this floor."

The old man stopped smiling.

"You no rent apartment?"

Tay shook his head.

The man shot to his feet, took three surprisingly nimble steps across the room, and jerked open the door to the hallway. Tay smiled politely, but he didn't move.

"Who owns this building?" he asked in what he thought, under the circumstances, was an exceedingly restrained and civil voice.

The man said nothing.

"I am prepared to sit here all day," Tay said. "I want to know who the owner of this building is and how to contact him and then I will leave. But I am not leaving until you tell me."

Tay could see the old man thinking about that. He leaned back and crossed his legs in a gesture he hoped would underline his willingness to remain sitting exactly where he was until he got answers to his question.

The man said nothing for a long while. Finally he closed the door, turned toward Tay, and folded his arms across his chest.

"Me," he said.

It took Tay a moment to realize what the man was telling him, and even then he didn't quite believe it.

"*You* own this building?"

The man replied with a single jerk of his head.

"The *entire* building?"

Another jerk.

"And you manage it, too? You rent out the apartments?"

A third jerk of the head.

"In that case," Tay said, "please sit down. We are going to have a conversation whether you want to or not."

The old man looked sullen, but he walked back to the chair he had previously occupied and sat down.

"I need to see everything you have about whoever has been renting the apartment at the other end of this hall, number 13."

The old man's eyes flicked from side to side, and Tay had no doubt he was thinking about how he could lie and get away it.

"Have nothing."

Tay sighed. "Okay, let's take this one step at a time. Who rents apartment number 13?"

"Nobody rent. Empty."

"But it has been rented to somebody, hasn't it?"

The old man shrugged.

"Who was it last rented to?"

"Man."

"When did he leave?"

The old man shrugged again. "Went to collect rent today. Apartment empty. Very clean. He gone."

"You don't know when he left?"

The man shook his head.

"When did he rent the apartment?"

"Two month ago. Pay two month in advance and deposit."

"How did he pay you?"

"How you think?" the old man snorted. "I take cash. No check, no credit card. Only cash."

"Did he fill out a rental application?"

The old man snorted again.

"So you don't have a name or an address for him?"

A shake of the head.

"You can at least describe him, can't you?"

"All foreigners look same."

"He was a foreigner?"

"What I just say? Foreigner, yes."

"What kind of foreigner?"

"How I know? Maybe English. Maybe American. Maybe anything. White people. All look same."

205

Tay continued pushing the old man for another ten minutes, but he learned nothing else of any use. A white man, neither young nor old, had paid the old man cash to rent the apartment two months ago. The old man had no idea who he was, and he hadn't seen him again. When we went to the apartment to collect another month's rent, he found it empty and clean.

It was obvious someone had rented the apartment to use as an observation post for watching the Fortuna Hotel, but who would have known two months ago that the Fortuna Hotel was worth watching? And why had they cleared out so fast? Were they spooked by the ISD dustup that left Suparman wounded and both the woman and Robbie Kang dead? That must have been why they had not only cleared out, Tay concluded, but also gone to great pains to erase any trace of whoever had been in the apartment.

Okay, so who had rented the apartment to watch the hotel? Not ISD. If ISD had a surveillance post in the apartment, he and Kang would almost certainly have seen some interaction between it and the men who took Suparman into the hotel. The ISD men hadn't even known the surveillance post was there. He was sure of that.

Did the surveillance post belong to some branch of the Singapore Police? That didn't make any sense either. If the Singapore Police had set it up, they wouldn't have sent a white man out to rent the apartment. Besides, he would have heard something by now if the police had a surveillance post anywhere near the Fortuna Hotel.

So who did that leave? He had no idea.

All he knew for sure was that the people who used the apartment were professionals who didn't want to be identified, not even by accident. But professionals at what? And professionals working for whom?

Tay took the stairs down to the lobby. He hadn't found out enough to be ready to leave, but he didn't know what else to do. There was nothing left to look at and nobody left to talk to.

At the bottom of the stairs, Tay reached to open one of the glass doors. He was halfway out when he stopped, turned around, and came back. He stood in front of the wall filled with mailboxes and looked at them. It took him a moment, but eventually he located box number 13 in the center of the bottom row.

When he pulled it open, all he saw was the usual litter of supermarket circulars and food delivery menus. He scooped it all out and shuffled through it hoping to find something which pointed to whoever had rented the apartment. He didn't have the slightest idea what he was looking for, but he looked anyway and hoped a flash of genius would strike him.

But a flash of genius didn't strike him, and neither did anything else.

Tay finished going through the junk in the mail box and was just about to cram it all back in when the sharp corner of what looked like a postcard slid out from between the folds of one of the food delivery menus and poked him in the hand. He clamped the postcard between his thumb and forefinger and held it up to take a look at it.

It wasn't a postcard at all, but an advertising flyer printed on a heavy piece of glossy cardboard touting a girly bar. On one side there was a garish photograph of about a dozen attractive young girls wearing red bikinis and high heels and swinging from polished chrome poles on some sort of elevated platform. On the other side was the name and location of the bar. It was called Baby Dolls, but it wasn't in Singapore. It was located in a shabby beach resort in Thailand called Pattaya.

Tay almost laughed out loud.

He shoved the rest of the mail back into the box and slammed the cover closed. He jammed the card in his pocket and pushed out through the lobby doors to Serangoon Road in search of a taxi.

36

THE TAXI DRIVER was a middle-aged man who looked Indian or perhaps Pakistani. Tay slid into the back and pointed to the radio which was emitting sounds he gathered were considered music by some, but not by him.

"Would you cut that off, please?"

The driver rotated his head just far enough to see Tay out of the corner of one eye. He looked as if he were about to say something, but apparently thought better of it and reached out and pushed a button that blessedly enveloped the interior of the taxi in silence.

Tay gave the man his home address and automatically recited the short explanation he gave all taxi drivers of the best way to get there. Emerald Hill Road was in central Singapore and within shouting distance of several prominent landmarks, but the street itself was short and one-way and surrounded by so many other one-way streets that getting to it baffled most taxi drivers. This driver said nothing at all when Tay finished his explanation. He just pulled away from the curb into traffic and Tay assumed he had been understood.

Leaning against the lumpy backrest, Tay pulled the card for Baby Dolls out of his pocket and examined it again. It wasn't really an advertising card for a girly bar. Tay had known that from the first moment he saw it. It was a message to him from John August. August wanted him to know the observation post Tay had discovered had been his, and the woman watching from it worked for him.

But how had August known Tay even realized the observation post was there, let alone that he would come around trying to find out who was watching from it? Tay had learned not to ask questions like that. There were a great many things John August simply knew.

John August was...well, the truth was Tay didn't really know *who* John August was, at least not for sure. August was a ghost.

He had been introduced to August a couple of years back by a member of the American Diplomatic Security Service, a woman who was then the Regional Security Officer at the American Embassy in Singapore. August was retired, she told Tay then, and he had a retirement gig running a go-go bar called Baby Dolls that was located in Pattaya, a cheerfully seedy Thai beach resort a couple of hours drive south of Bangkok. She was professionally imprecise about exactly what August was retired *from*, but she left Tay with the impression that August had worked for the United States State Department in some capacity. Tay didn't think August was really retired at all, and he was even more certain he had never had any connection with the State Department.

Naturally, Tay had jumped to the conclusion that August was CIA. When he encountered Americas wandering around Asia who were vague about their affiliations, he *always* jumped to the conclusion they were CIA.

After a while, however, Tay realized it was more complicated than that. August wasn't just another freebooting intelligence operative bouncing around Asia on contract to the CIA. He wasn't a spy.

John August solved problems the old fashioned way. He killed them.

August had ties to the American security establishment all right, Tay had no doubt of that, but Tay understood now that August was connected with something far scarier than the CIA. And he wasn't sure he even *wanted* to know what that was.

Whoever August really was, Tay genuinely liked the man, but in spite of that he had kept his relationship with August to himself. For a CID detective in Singapore to have connections with American intelligence, whatever brand of American intelligence August might be, raised all sorts of questions he didn't want anyone to ask. He hadn't found it particularly difficult to keep his relationship with August quiet since the truth was they didn't really have all that much of a relationship. They certainly weren't pals, and they didn't hit the bars together. Which was just fine with Tay.

Tay had asked August for a couple of favors, and August had never appeared to mind. Violence wasn't Tay's first choice for solving problems, but it beat the hell out of doing nothing. Justice might be blind, but it didn't have to be stupid.

August hadn't asked Tay for any favors in return, at least not yet, but Tay figured if his bill ever came due the payment was likely to be a doozy.

Okay, so the girl in the window was someone connected with John August. He got that, but it still didn't tell him anything about what she was doing there.

Tay could always try to call August, of course, but that wasn't easy. He had a telephone number with a Los Angeles city code, but neither August nor anyone else ever answered the telephone. Tay just called the number and hung up. Then an hour or a day or a week later August either called back or he didn't. Tay assumed the number functioned as a caller ID system that couldn't be blocked, but that was only a guess on his part. He considered a couple of times borrowing someone else's telephone and calling the number to see what would happen, but he never did it. John August wasn't a guy you played games with.

So what was going on here? Putting a flyer for Baby Dolls in the mailbox of an abandoned apartment just so Tay would know August had been there was pretty exotic, even by John August's standards. And it offered him no hint at all as to why August had someone sitting on a hotel where ISD had brought one of the world's most wanted terrorists, presumably for a meeting with his sister. Regardless, at least now Tay knew something he hadn't known before. He just couldn't figure out exactly what it was he knew.

American intelligence, at least whatever part of it John August was connected with, had been using that apartment to watch the Fortuna Hotel. But why? Did they know in advance that Suparman was going to be there? They must have or they wouldn't have been there either. Unless the surveillance was for somebody else altogether, and that was way too big a coincidence to swallow. So what did that tell him? Were the Americans trying to grab Suparman, too?

The more Tay thought about it, the less sense that made. The old man told him somebody rented the apartment two months back. To do that, somebody in American intelligence would have to know Suparman was going to be at the Fortuna Hotel more than two months before he turned up there. How could that possibly be?

Tay also thought back to the man who spoke to Suparman's sister in the alleyway behind the Inn at Temple Street before she went to the Fortuna Hotel. Tay had followed the man from Temple Street to the Australian High Commission and watched him pass through security like someone who worked there. That hadn't made any sense at the time, actually it still didn't, but did the Australians have something to do with John August and his people watching the Fortuna Hotel from a rundown apartment across the street?

Both things pointed to involvement in all this by western intelligence agencies, that was clear enough, but Tay still couldn't see exactly what that involvement was or what it meant.

While he pondered the mysterious layers of the hidden world of national security operations, Tay watched the city sliding by outside the cab's windows. All at once it occurred to him he didn't recognize where they were and he leaned forward and tapped the driver on the shoulder.

"Where are you going?"

The driver shot a glance over his shoulder. "You say Gilstead Road."

"*What?* I did not. I said Emerald Hill Road."

The driver shook his head. "No, you say Gilstead Road."

He sounded so certain that for a second Tay wondered if he really *had* said Gilstead Road, but since he didn't think he had ever heard of Gilstead Road, he thought that was unlikely.

Tay turned his head from side to side trying to figure out where they were, but nothing looked familiar. Then he peered through the windshield over the driver's shoulder and finally saw something he thought he recognized.

"Is that Newton Circus in front of us?"

The driver grunted, which Tay took as a yes.

"Then go around it past the hawker center and take Clemenceau Avenue. I'll show you where to stop."

Emerald Hill Road dead-ended just south of Clemenceau Avenue, and a short pathway with a flight of stairs allowed pedestrians to walk down to it from Clemenceau. If Tay got out of the taxi on Clemenceau and walked to his house, he would spare himself having to guide this nitwit through the maze of one-way streets they had to navigate to drive into Emerald Hill Road. It was only a few hundred meters. The walk would do him good anyway. He wondered for a moment how much weight he would lose by walking three or four hundred meters, but he knew it probably wasn't very much.

A few minutes later Tay leaned forward behind the driver and pointed to the curb.

"Stop right here," he said.

The driver grunted. "Double yellow line," he said. "Cannot stop."

Tay pulled out his warrant card and held it in front of the man's face.

"Police," he snapped. "Stop the goddamned taxi right here."

The driver stopped.

Tay looked at the meter and counted out the exact fare. He usually tipped cab drivers at least a little although most people in Singapore didn't bother. He didn't want to be petty, but he had no intention of tipping this driver because he had been such a surly jerk. The man accepted the money Tay handed him without comment and Tay got out and walked away.

A short flight of concrete stairs with a green metal railing led from the sidewalk on Clemenceau Road down to the end of Emerald Hill Road. Because of all the one-way streets there was very little automobile traffic there. People owned the streets in Tay's neighborhood, not vehicles. Actual human beings walked along them and talked to the neighbors they saw as they passed. Even if you didn't know your neighbors personally, and almost no one did, you recognized their faces when you saw them and that was part of what made the area feel like a real neighborhood.

Tay took the stairs two at a time and walked briskly toward home. He had always liked the upper end of Emerald Hill Road. It was lined on both sides by brightly painted row houses with wooden shutters and iron balconies. Clumps of banana trees peeped over garden walls, their big flat leaves draped on whitewashed concrete like drying laundry, and lush vegetation sprouted from every patch of earth. The area was almost a museum of colonial Singapore. All over the city, government bureaucrats had ruthlessly bulldozed neighborhoods like Emerald Hill and replaced human-scale structures with nondescript high-rise apartments and ugly office buildings. Somehow this tiny pocket of old Singapore still survived, but Tay knew it would not survive forever. Nothing in Singapore did.

There was a smell of ozone on the breeze. It would rain soon. Tay quickened his pace toward home.

37

TAY SPOTTED THE van as soon as he crossed Saunders Road. It was parked at the curb on the left side of Emerald Hill facing toward his house. He stopped behind a beige Mercedes parked on the opposite side of the street and took a long look.

It was a silver blue Hi-Lux, unmarked and without windows. It looked exactly like the van ISD had at the Fortuna Hotel.

That might just be a coincidence, of course. The Toyota Hi-Lux was a common commercial vehicle in Singapore, and Tay imagined a fair number of them were silver blue, but he didn't remember ever seeing a commercial vehicle that didn't display the name and the telephone number of whatever business operated the vehicle. Nobody wanted to waste a perfectly good billboard like the side of a van that plied the city's streets all day.

Poised halfway between caution and paranoia, Tay stood behind the Mercedes and contemplated the van. Something about it sitting there didn't feel at all right.

Was ISD waiting to snatch him when he came home? Even if they were, surely they wouldn't do it on a public street in broad daylight. Maybe that meant they were already in his house and that they would grab him the moment he set foot inside. Or maybe they had something in mind more permanent than grabbing him.

Tay and Lee were the only people left alive who could connect ISD with Suparman and the Fortuna Hotel. If ISD wanted to hide that connection badly enough to have been involved already in the deaths of at least three people, wouldn't they be willing to kill Tay, too? ISD was in pretty deep already if that's what they had been doing. Was getting in a little deeper really much of an additional risk for them?

His best protection, Tay knew, was to nail ISD in public for protecting Suparman. Once that was all out there, ISD would no longer have any reason to move against either him or Lee. Once that was all out there, there would be nothing to protect any longer.

Could John August be the key to doing that? Maybe that was why he left the Baby Dolls card. To tell Tay he could help him out.

ISD didn't know about the girl in the window, at least he didn't think they did, and now that Tay knew the observation post across from the Fortuna Hotel had something to do with John August and that John August *wanted* him to know that it had something to do with him, Tay was willing to bet that August had something good to tell him. Maybe it was something he could even use to nail ISD on all this.

Tay took a deep breath and thought about it. Was he getting carried away here? It was probably just a neighbor's silver blue Toyota Hi-Lux van parked there on Emerald Hill Road. If not, it was probably one belonging to somebody who was visiting one of his neighbors.

Looking at everything that way made him feel better.

But not for long.

The sliding door in the side of the van started to move and Tay reacted quickly. Two large trees were right next to the Mercedes and he stepped behind them to block the line of sight from the van. He duck-walked forward until he was next to the front right tire of the Mercedes and, keeping his head well below the hood, he very slowly pressed himself up enough to see the van again.

A man was standing next to the open door smoking a cigarette. As Tay watched, the man turned and spoke to someone inside the van. Tay was too far away to hear what he said, but he was plenty close enough to recognize the man. He had been at the Fortuna Hotel. Tay didn't have the slightest doubt.

Tay eased his head down until he was concealed behind the Mercedes again. Then he dropped to his hands and knees and scuttled back behind the trees. Sitting down, he leaned against the trunk of one of the trees and thought about what to do.

Okay, he wasn't being paranoid. It was the same van and it was the same ISD guys, and they were parked on Emerald Hill Road just down from his house.

What were they doing there? That much, at least, was easy enough to guess. They were waiting for him to come home. Were they going to kill him? Were they going to kidnap him? Were they going to kick the unholy shit out of him? Tay had no idea, but he was pretty sure they weren't there to present him with a public service award.

So what the hell did he do now?

It was easier to decide what he didn't do.

He didn't go home. He had no idea what ISD's plan was, but he was absolutely certain he didn't want to walk right into it, whatever it was.

He could always phone for a couple of fast response cars, say there were suspicious people outside his house and bang these guys up, but that would end up accomplishing nothing. The ISD men would just tell the cops they had no interest in Tay and were there on some other surveillance mission, the details of which they were not allowed to talk about. Who was going to challenge that? The men would go away, of course, but that would be a temporary fix because they would be back. It would be some other time or perhaps even some other place, but they would be back.

No, he had it right the first time. The fix here was to get

everything out in the open. He and Lee were a threat to ISD because they knew ISD was protecting Suparman, even if they had no idea why. Once it was public knowledge ISD was protecting Suparman, he and Lee would no longer be a threat. But to make it public knowledge Tay knew he needed some kind of evidence, something to corroborate his claim. Without that, no one would believe him.

He needed to talk to August. He had to find out whether August had something that might help him. He could call him, of course, but the only way he had to reach August by telephone was so awkward it wasn't particularly useful when you were in a hurry.

His passport was in a desk drawer at his office, so maybe he should get it, go straight out to the airport, and grab the next flight to Thailand. He could be in Pattaya in four or five hours, and he didn't remember August ever returning a call in less time than that.

The problem there was Tay had never been a keen traveler. He thought all that business about how you broaden your mind when you visited other countries was nonsense. When you went to other countries mostly what you discovered was how good you had it at home. He would just telephone August and hope for the best. At least that way he didn't have to leave Singapore and go blundering around some third world shithole.

A few moments later Tay heard the sound of the van's sliding door again and he peeked cautiously out from behind the tree. The smoker must have gone inside and shut the door because now the van once again sat closed up and silent. If he was going to make a move, this was the time to do it.

So he did.

Tay retraced his steps back to the end of Emerald Hill Road and climbed the concrete stairs up to Clemenceau. Traffic was still running heavy and it took only a moment to find a cab driver hungry enough for a fare to be willing to stop on a double-yellow line.

He told the driver to take him to the Cantonment Complex and pulled out his telephone. His first call was to the switchboard at New Phoenix Park where he identified himself with his warrant card number and got Sergeant Lee's number. Then he dialed Sergeant Lee.

"Where are you, Linda?"

"At the Cantonment Complex, sir." Lee hesitated. "Is everything okay?"

"Listen to me very carefully. Do not leave the building for any reason until I get there. Is that understood?"

"Yes, sir. But why—"

Tay broke the connection without another word and scrolled through his contacts list until he found the number he had for August. When he called it, of course nothing happened. The number just rang until Tay hung up. Maybe John August would call him back, maybe he wouldn't, but Tay wasn't sure what to do if August didn't call. The advertising card for Baby Dolls sure hadn't gotten into that apartment's mailbox by accident. August was trying to tell him something. Tay didn't have any idea what it was, but he knew it was important. August didn't do anything that wasn't important.

The rain Tay smelled coming a while ago began falling and he sat watching the big drops roll down the taxi's windows. There was something comforting about rain. It dampened the noise of the world and hid the misery of it.

Maybe it would rain forever.

38

TAY PAID OFF the cab driver and was showing his warrant card at the security post in the lobby of the Cantonment Complex when his telephone buzzed.

He stopped in front of the elevators and looked at the screen. He saw an unfamiliar number and a text message.

Where are you?

Almost no one ever sent him a text message. He couldn't even remember the last one he had gotten so he figured it had to be from John August. Who else? All this cloak and dagger crap really drove him mad.

Fortunately, the phone's software displayed a box right below the message and invited him to type a reply into it. Otherwise he wouldn't have had any idea how to do it.

Tay laborious picked out his response on the keyboard using one finger.

My office. The Cantonment Complex.

An elevator opened and the passengers flooded out. Tay stepped to the side, stared at the screen of his telephone, and waited for another message. None came.

Tay had never really understood the whole concept of text messages. If you had something to say to someone, why didn't you simply telephone and say what you had to say and then hang up? What was the point of sending words and phrases back and forth in staccato bursts until everyone figured out what the hell the conversation was really about? More and more things about modern life utterly eluded him.

When he got tired of waiting for what would probably be another cryptic question from August to appear on his screen, Tay jammed the telephone in his pocket and got on the next elevator that opened. Unfortunately, he discovered it was going down, not up. All the way to the garage and back up to the lobby, Tay berated himself for not noticing before he got on. That was one more thing for which he could blame the whole ridiculous concept of text messages.

Tay was at his desk contemplating the piles of paper that had accumulated since the last time he had been in the office when Sergeant Lee's head appeared around his door.

"Good day, sir. Am I interrupting anything?"

Tay waved her in and was pleased to see her carrying two mugs of coffee. She placed one in front of him and settled into a chair facing his desk. While Lee drank her coffee, Tay told her about going home, walking up his street from a different direction than usual, and discovering the men waiting for him in the van.

"Are you sure they were ISD, sir?"

"It was the same van we saw outside the Fortuna Hotel, and the man who got out to smoke was one of the men we saw there. If those guys were ISD, so were these."

"So that's why you were so weird on the telephone. You think they're watching me, too?"

Tay said nothing, but saying nothing answered Lee's question.

"That really does sound a little crazy, sir."

"We're the only two people left who can tie ISD to Suparman. And there are people who don't want us to be able to do that. It's just that simple, Linda."

"So you're saying ISD might kill two cops in the Criminal Investigation Department to keep us quiet? You can't be serious."

Tay didn't say anything. He just looked at Lee.

"Oh shit," Lee said. "You *are* serious."

"Somebody is killing the people who can expose all this. If it's not ISD, it's Suparman. I suppose he wouldn't want his cozy arrangement with ISD to be public information either."

"But you think it could be ISD?"

"We're targets either way," Tay shrugged. "Is there someplace you can lie low for a few days?"

"You mean, not go home? Not go to work?"

"That's exactly what I mean."

Lee took a deep breath and looked away.

"I'm working on something, Linda. I need to know you're safe for the next couple of days. I can't be worrying about you along with everything else."

"Are you going to tell me what you're doing, sir?"

Tay hesitated. He didn't want to tell Lee about the girl in the window, partly because he wasn't sure why that mattered yet and partly because he had absolutely no intention of telling her anything about John August. So Tay just shook his head.

Lee looked a little annoyed, but she didn't say anything.

"Is there some place, Linda?" Tay pressed. "Some place you can go?"

"I have a friend I can stay with. She and her husband recently moved to JB, and she's always after me to come out and visit them."

JB was Johor Bahru, the Malaysian city right across the Straits of Johor. Getting Lee completely out of the country was even better than Tay had hoped for.

"When do you want me to go, sir?"

"Right now. This afternoon. Turn your phone off and keep it off. Do not turn it on under any circumstances. Is it one of those you can take the battery out of?"

"Yes, sir."

"Do that, too."

"But shouldn't you be able to reach me?"

"When you get to JB buy yourself a prepaid cell phone. Text the number to me. Just the number and nothing else, but type it backwards. Last number first and so on."

"You're scaring me, sir."

"Good. Stay scared. You'll be safer that way."

"Where are you going to be, sir?"

Tay said nothing.

Lee held up both hands, palms out. "Okay, never mind. Forget I asked. How about that call? Are you ready for me to make it yet?"

For a moment Tay had no idea what Lee was talking about, but then he remembered he told her he wanted her to make an anonymous call about the body of the hotel manager. So much had happened since they found it that he had completely forgotten.

"Make it this afternoon on your way home to pack." Then all at once something occurred to Tay. "Do pay telephones still exist? They do, don't they?"

"I was thinking of going to the airport, sir. They have them there and the location won't help to identify who made the call."

Tay nodded. It was a good idea. He should have thought of it himself.

"Fine," he said. "Go home, get your passport and pack a bag. Take a cab to the airport and kill about an hour. Then make your telephone call and right away take another cab from there straight to JB. If anybody's watching, they'll assume you're on an airplane. By the time they figure out you aren't, you'll be in Malaysia."

"I really don't understand any of this, sir. What's really going on here?"

"I don't know, Linda. Not yet. But when I do, I'll tell you. Besides, it's probably better that you don't know too much right now anyway."

"Then everything must be peachy keen, sir, because right now what I know is fuck all."

A minute or two after Lee left Tay's office his telephone buzzed. He took it out of his pocket and looked at the screen.

Sure enough, there was another stranger number and another message.

Walk south on Cantonment Road, west on Neil Road, south on Everton.

Why the hell couldn't August say left and right like everybody else? Tay was still sitting there picturing a city map in his mind and trying to turn August's text into directions he could follow when his phone buzzed again.

Stop overthinking this. Just do it. Right now.

Tay had to admit August knew him pretty well.

39

TAY LIKED WALKING in Singapore, although most people avoided it unless it was absolutely necessary. The city was generally so hot and muggy that any exposure to air that hadn't been comprehensively cooled and thoroughly dehydrated by industrial strength machinery was pure misery.

If Singaporeans were absolutely forced into the streets for some reason, they ducked and dodged from one tiny patch of shade to the next like soldiers picking their way through a minefield. When there was no shade, he had even seen women holding their purses in front of their faces to keep the sun off. Did that do any good? It seemed a bit silly to Tay, but what did he know about such things?

For Tay, one of the things he liked most about walking in Singapore was that it usually constituted an almost solitary pursuit. He frequently had the sidewalks more or less to himself and he could soak in the unique feel of every neighborhood and tune in to its sounds and smells without battling other people. Even so, Tay very much preferred walking when he had at least a rough idea where he was going and why he was going there. And right then he had no fucking clue about either of those things.

Tay turned right outside the Cantonment Complex and walked along Cantonment Road. The blue and silver glass of the high-rise towers shimmered in the bright sun and Tay felt like most of the heat was being focused directly onto him. By the time he got to Neil Road, he was already sweating. He turned right and walked along in front of one of those massive, soulless apartment complexes that had taken over most of Singapore.

It wasn't an especially interesting neighborhood for walking. If Tay had chosen his own route, he would have gone north up New Bridge Road toward Chinatown where the streets were still lined with the little shophouses of another era. But he had not chosen his route, of course. John August had. Tay assumed August had some specific reason for sending him this way, and he hoped to hell August would reveal it before he died from either heatstroke or boredom.

When Tay got to Everton Road, he turned left, exactly as he had been instructed. He still didn't see why he was there. On one side of the road more bland and nondescript apartment buildings were grouped behind an arched gateway that said *Everton Park* at the top, and on the other side a line of two-story shophouses had been converted into modest private residences. Tay warily examined the shophouses as he passed. He peered into the shadows cast by the overhangs of the upper levels and looked for anything that seemed off. He saw nothing.

All at once in his peripheral vision he caught sight of a silver-blue van. It came out of a side street, turned into Everton Road about a hundred yards in front of him, and drove straight toward him. ISD had found him and here he was stranded out in the open.

Crap.

Tay glanced around, but he couldn't see any obvious refuge. Unless he forced his way into one of the shophouses there was no safety on this side of the street. But even if he could, what would he do after he got inside? He was pretty sure there were no back entrances to any of the little houses so he would be trapped.

More by default than because of any clear idea why he was doing it, Tay jogged across the road toward the entrance arch to Everton Park. Maybe he could somehow lose himself among the apartment buildings inside. It felt like a forlorn hope, but he had no other ideas.

The silver-blue van suddenly accelerated. It bounced over the sidewalk, roared up a driveway, and slammed to a stop right in front of him. The sliding door on the side flew open.

"What the *fuck* are you doing, Sam?"

John August was comfortably slumped in a black leather captain's chair in the back of the van. His legs were stretched out and crossed at the ankle, and his arms were folded. He was swiveling the chair briskly left and right and looked downright annoyed.

"We're as conspicuous in this concrete wasteland as tits on a bull," he snapped. "Now would you please get the fuck in here before somebody calls the cops?"

When Tay had climbed into the van and settled into a similar chair, August reached into an ice chest and handed him a bottle of water. Tay cracked the cap and took a long pull. The bottle was wet and cold and crystals of ice clung to the plastic. Tay leaned back and rolled the bottle against his forehead.

"I don't know how you people live in this place," August said as the van accelerated away. "It's so goddamned hot here a scorpion would go shopping for an air conditioner."

Tay drank some more water and looked around the van. He was sitting in another captain's chair facing August across a small table. They were alone in the back, but he could see a driver in the front and a woman in the passenger seat. Both of them were facing forward and he could make out nothing about either.

"Nice van, John. It looks exactly like the ones ISD uses."

"Yeah, sorry about that," August grinned. "I guess we spooked you, and when you started running away—"

"I wasn't exactly running."

"No, you weren't, but I suppose you were moving as fast as you could. I was trying to be kind."

"That's not what I meant."

August grinned again. Tay just drank some more water.

"What are you doing here, John?"

"I know why you called me, of course. We need to talk."

Tay drank some more water and waited.

"I'm sorry about your sergeant, Sam. I really am. That was rotten luck. He never should have been there in the first place. *You* never should have been there."

"Robbie was there because that's where I told him to be."

"Don't be so tough on yourself, Sam. Shit happens to good people. That's not our fault. We're both in hard businesses."

Tay looked over August's shoulder and out through the windshield of the van. They were on New Bridge Road heading north toward the Singapore River.

"Where are we going, John?"

"We have a safe house off Nassim Road. I thought we could talk there."

"That must be handy for you. You can just about walk to the American Embassy from there."

"I wouldn't know," August said. "I don't hang around embassies."

Tay took out his Marlboros and a pack of matches. He shook a cigarette from the package and automatically offered it to August, but August shook his head as Tay knew he would. Tay lit it for himself and returned the pack and the matches to his pocket.

"This is a United States government vehicle," August said. "Absolutely no smoking is permitted."

"What an enlightened and forward-looking policy that is, John. I'm sure all Americans are better human beings simply for knowing such a policy exists and that it is rigorously and impartially enforced at all times by the government of the United States."

Tay took a long pull on his cigarette, exhaled slowly, and stared at August expressionlessly.

When the van stopped and the door was opened from the outside, Tay climbed out and looked around.

"Nice digs."

"Come on, Sam. You didn't expect me to hang around in some shithole, did you?"

Back in the late 1800s and early 1900s, Singapore's British rulers built lavish villas all over the island to house high-ranking officials and civil servants. Called black and white bungalows because of their dark timber beams and whitewashed walls, the structures were stately two- and three-story houses of vaguely Tudor design, but with tropical touches such as wide, shady verandas. Only a few hundred were left now. Tucked away in genteel enclaves, they were throwbacks to the country's colonial past.

"It's owned by a shell company in the British Virgin Islands," August offered. "The company even leased it out for a while to the Iranian ambassador. We had a lot of fun with that."

August's safe house was one of the most lavish black and whites Tay had ever seen. Surround by a rolling, emerald-green lawn mowed to the smoothness of a golf green, the two-story structure was capped with a sloped roof of red tile that overhung the house and cast it into deep, cooling shadows. A wide veranda on the ground floor had groupings of thick-cushioned rattan furniture scattered here and there, and the louvered windows around the upper floor rattled and clicked in the light breeze.

"Some people say these old houses are haunted, John."

"Yeah, I've heard that, too. The Japanese used this one as a prison camp during World War II."

August pointed down to where the rolling lawn ended at a thick stand of long-leafed gum trees.

"One day the Japs are supposed to have dragged something like a hundred sick and wounded prisoners down there, lined them up, and shot them in retaliation for an attack on a Japanese officer. To this day, people claim to hear gunshots and screams coming from down there late at night. Never heard them myself. You don't believe in ghosts, do you, Sam?"

Tay wondered if he had ever in a moment of weakness told August about his occasional visits with his mother. Surely he hadn't, but he wasn't absolutely certain.

To his relief, August dropped the subject without saying anything else and started walking across the lawn to the veranda. Tay followed.

They sat on two facing rattan couches that had big, fluffy cushions covered with white sailcloth. An elderly woman who looked to Tay to be a Filipina sat a tray on the coffee table between them and immediately disappeared. The tray held a large pitcher of water with chunks of ice floating in it, three tall glasses, and three bottles of Tiger beer.

"Help yourself," August said.

"I gather someone is joining us."

"She'll be along in a minute."

"She?"

August half shrugged, but he didn't say anything else.

Tay wasn't a beer drinker, but the sweating bottles on the tray looked refreshing so he took one, tilted it back, and took a long drink. All at once it came back to him why he wasn't a beer drinker. Was it just Tiger beer that tasted this bad, or did all beer taste terrible?

He set the beer down on the table and took his cigarettes out of his shirt pocket.

Tay looked at August. "Another United States government facility that is absolutely non-smoking?"

August nodded slowly and reached for a beer.

Tay shook out a cigarette, lit it, and sat smoking quietly. It certainly tasted a lot better than the beer.

"When are you going to tell me what's going on here, John?"

August seem to consider the question for a moment, and then he grinned. "How about now?"

"Now would be good," Tay said.

So August told him.

40

"YOUR INTERNAL SECURITY Department—"

"It's not my Internal Security Department," Tay said.

August even didn't bother to smile.

"Regardless of whose responsibility ISD is," he said, "they started running Suparman years ago. They believed he gave them access to the inner circles of—"

"Running?" Tay interrupted again. "You guys just love the spy movie bullshit, don't you?"

"Would you feel less annoyed if I said Suparman was an informant for ISD?"

"How could Suparman be an informant for anyone? He's one of the most hunted terrorists in Asia. He's been responsible for bombings all over Indonesia, Malaysia, Thailand, and Singapore."

"Opinions on that vary. Some say he's mostly a creation of the press, a bogeyman to frighten children, and he wasn't really involved in most of the things people say he was."

"He wasn't involved in the hotel bombings here?"

"Some people think not."

"What do *you* think?"

"I think the people who say he wasn't are full of shit."

Tay considered that for a moment. He took a final puff and

flipped the butt of his cigarette into the grass.

"I don't see the connection between ISD thinking Suparman was their informant and John August watching the Fortuna Hotel."

"It started when we heard that ridiculous story from the Indonesians about his sister supposedly having cancer."

"So it's not true?"

"Of course it's not true. The woman at the hotel wasn't even Suparman's sister. The real sister was grabbed a couple months ago trying to sneak into Australia. That's when ASIO dreamed up this stunt. The idea was—"

"Wait…what? ASIO? The Australian Security Intelligence Organization?"

"Sure. Counterterrorism in Australia is their patch."

"What's Australia got to do with all this?"

"They think Suparman is as much a threat to them as he is to you. When they grabbed his sister, they saw an opportunity to lure him out into the open and take him. But that was when they discovered there are people here in Singapore heavily invested in the belief Suparman is really *your* guy. ISD didn't want ASIO or anybody else to take him down."

"So ASIO abandoned the whole idea?"

"Don't be ridiculous, Sam. That was when they decided to kill him instead."

Tay thought back to the man in the alleyway behind the Temple Street Inn who appeared to slip something to the woman they thought was Suparman's sister.

"The woman worked for the Australians?"

August nodded.

"And the Australians provided the weapon?"

August nodded again.

"But this woman screwed it up and didn't kill Suparman," Tay finished.

"It was a stupid fucking idea from the beginning," August

shrugged. "Australian Intelligence dreamed it up. That's an oxymoron if I ever hear one. What else do you need to know?"

"I still don't understand what you were doing at the Fortuna Hotel."

"The Australians convinced ISD the sister was for real, but ISD wanted to use a little misdirection in setting up the meet to give them an extra layer of deniability. ASIO was happy enough with the plan when they heard it. It gave them a nice quiet location to stage their stunt."

"You haven't answered my question yet."

"We wanted Suparman taken down," August said. "We've been trying to get ISD on board to do that for nearly a year and we had come to the conclusion it wasn't going to happen. When we found out about this Aussie shit show, it was too good an opportunity to pass up. We decided we'd solve the problem ourselves if they didn't."

"You mean you were going to try to take Suparman away from ISD?"

"Don't be silly, Sam. We wanted to kill him, too. ISD thinks he's their bitch, that he'll tip them off to all kinds of nefarious shit. Personally, I'm convinced they know they've been had, but you've got people at high levels here who don't want to admit they made a mistake."

"How high?"

August wiggled his hand in a gesture that could have meant almost anything.

"So you were…what, John? Planning to sit in that apartment until you saw Suparman and then run down and shoot him?"

"I don't do manual labor anymore myself, Sam. Haven't you heard? I'm an executive now. Besides, we decided on a sniper shot and there are better people for that than me."

"So why didn't whoever you had up there take the shot?"

"Why, funny you should ask, Sam. At the last minute these three Singapore cops showed up. We were already coping with

Suparman being surrounded by his ISD security detail and the crazy female assassin the Aussies had running around. The cops made it all just a little too complicated for us so we decided to fold our tent and wait for a better day."

"But you haven't given up?"

"Not a chance, my friend. Especially not now that it's gotten personal."

"Personal?"

"That body you pulled out of the Singapore River was our man in Indonesian intelligence. Suparman found out and killed him. You lost one of yours, and we've lost one of ours. That makes it personal in my book."

"Do you know about the hotel manager?"

"Of course I know about him. Suparman did him, too. The bastard's got a good gig here. He's willing to do whatever he needs to protect it."

"Then Suparman was responsible for all the murders? It wasn't ISD cleaning up, eliminating anybody who knew they were protecting Suparman?"

"ISD might be a bunch of clowns, Sam, but they don't murder their own. At least not as far as I know."

"So why was ISD waiting for me when I went home, John? They were in a van parked up the street. I would never have seen them if I hadn't walked home from an unusual direction. Otherwise, I would have walked straight into their trap."

"It wasn't a trap, Sam. They were just keeping an eye on you. They were afraid Suparman might come after you, and two CID detectives going down in the same day would have been downright embarrassing."

Tay reached for the beer he had abandoned. He didn't want it, but he needed a second to let what August had just told him sink in. He sipped at it absentmindedly, but it was warm and he almost spit it out.

"You haven't told me yet why I'm here, John. You didn't go to all this trouble just to explain everything to me."

"You're right, Sam. You're here because I need your help."

"With what?"

"I don't see how we can get this bastard without you."

"I'm flattered, John, but what do you need me for? I'm sure you have all sorts of capabilities I can't even imagine. I'm just a local cop."

"There's somebody I want you to meet and then we'll talk about that." August stood up. "I'll be right back."

Tay was halfway through another Marlboro when August returned with the woman who had been in the front passenger seat of the van when they picked him up.

She was relatively tall and her long blonde hair was pulled back in a ponytail. She was lean and fit looking with a tanned face, and the khaki shirt, jeans, and aviator sunglasses she wore gave her a slightly masculine look. Tay assumed she was an American, but nothing about her appearance confirmed it. That was only one of many things that disconcerted Tay about Americans. There was no template for an American. They could look like anything.

"This is Claire," August said. "She's my best sniper."

"Inspector," Claire nodded and sat down on the couch opposite him.

Tay wasn't sure whether he should stand up and offer his hand or not. What was the etiquette on shaking hands with a sniper? Then he noticed that August was sitting down so he decided that was the end of the greeting portion of the program and let it go.

"Is Claire your real name?" Tay asked

"Don't be fucking stupid, Sam," August chimed in. "Of course it isn't."

Claire said nothing. She just smiled. A little.

"Okay, here's the deal," August said. "Suparman could be anywhere. We're not going to find him by blundering around the city. We need to make him come to us, and I have a way to do that."

"Don't you think ISD will throw a blanket over him after all this?"

"They'll try, but they aren't going to want to piss him off. Remember, they're treating him like a valued informant, not a prisoner. And he's had enough freedom of movement to kill at least two people and not get caught at it. He knows how to get around the city, he knows how to avoid his handlers, and he's willing to do whatever he thinks needs to be done."

"So what you need is a motivation powerful enough to convince him to surface and go after somebody else."

August nodded.

Tay took a long drag on his cigarette, flipped away the butt, and thought about what August had just told him. He shifted his eyes back to August.

August nodded again.

"Oh shit," Tay said.

"Yeah, that's pretty much the deal, Sam. He knows you're coming after him, but he also knows either you or that woman sergeant who was with you can blow him up even if you don't find him just by going public with what you know. He has to stop you before you do that or his cushy gig is over. Where's your sergeant now?"

"She's…" Tay hesitated. "Out of the country. I told her to lie low for a while."

"So that leaves you," August said.

"That leaves me. I gather you want me to be the bait."

"Doesn't matter what I want, Sam. You *are* the bait. Suparman is coming after you anyway. I'm just proposing we use that to set a little trap for him."

Tay looked out across the lawn, thought about it, and then he looked back at August. "You better explain that to me."

"We just want you to go about your life as you always do. Don't do anything that might scare him off."

"You're going to have a group of armed guards following me

everywhere just in case Suparman shows up?"

"He's not going to come after you on the street, Sam, and he's sure as hell not going to come to the Cantonment Complex and take an elevator up to your office. He wants to walk away after he gets rid of you."

"Then what do you think he has in mind?"

"Suparman will come for you when you're at home. He'll have you alone then. There's really no other way he can do it."

"So you think—"

"Your house will be completely covered. And Claire will be there to take him when he shows up. She's the best. She's not going to waste another chance."

Tay shifted his glance to the woman. She had said nothing at all. He couldn't see her eyes behind the sunglasses, but he thought there was a hint of a smile at the corners of her mouth.

"You were the girl in the window," Tay said to her.

"I would have waved, but I never wave at strange men."

"I'm not strange."

"That's not what John says."

Tay looked at August.

August shrugged.

August's van carried Tay up to Orchard Road and he found a taxi to take him home. The taxi dropped Tay in front of Preranakan Place where he usually asked taxis to drop him, and he walked up Emerald Hill toward his house exactly the way he always did. As he walked, he examined the vehicles parked further up Emerald Hill Road with as much subtlety as he could muster. The ISD van that had been there before was gone, but did any of the other vehicles contain a new set of watchers? Tay had no idea.

He assumed August would have his people in place soon. For all he knew, they were already there. If they weren't and Suparman made an early appearance, Tay figured he was pretty much screwed. He doubted he would be any match for Suparman one on one, so he was largely in August's hands. He trusted August, that wasn't the problem, but he also recognized that people made mistakes. He only hoped he wouldn't be one of August's.

Tay went straight to the kitchen, poured himself a couple of inches of Irish whiskey, and took it and his cigarettes out into the garden. August had told him to behave normally, hadn't he? And this was as normal as life got for him.

As he smoked and sipped his whiskey, he thought about how it felt to be the cheese in John August's mousetrap.

He couldn't blame August, no matter how much he wished he could. He alone was responsible for the position he was in now. It was his decision to freelance and not tell anyone else what he was doing that had started all this. It was his decision that left Robbie Kang dead and him hoping very much now not to become dead.

On the other hand, it was also true that his decision to freelance had accomplished something of real value, too. That was how he found Suparman, and how he found out ISD was protecting Suparman to save face for the men who ran ISD and the politicians to whom they reported.

The idea of face was very much an Asian concept. When Westerners heard people talk about saving face, they generally thought it meant avoiding embarrassment, but losing face was far more serious to an Asian than suffering an embarrassment. Lost face was something never regained. When you lost face you were permanently diminished. You mattered less than you did before. You *were* less than you were before. To most Asians, their face was their very existence, and protecting it was everything.

Had Robbie Kang and other people died because some bureaucrats feared losing face? Was it possible that people above them, politicians at the top levels of government, knew and approved the plan because they would lose face too if it became known how badly they had screwed up?

If that was what had happened here, Tay thought, maybe

August was killing the wrong man. If bureaucrats or government ministers had known who Suparman really was and what he had done and they had said nothing to save face, they deserved shooting as much as Suparman did. Maybe more. Perhaps he ought to see what he could do about that.

Tay stubbed out his cigarette, finished his whiskey, and went upstairs to bed.

41

TAY WAS FULLY awake in an instant. He had felt the foot of his bed move slightly, but he didn't open his eyes. If he did open his eyes, he was certain he would see one of two things. Either a murderous terrorist waiting to kill him, or the ghost of his mother preparing to give him advice. On the whole, he thought he might prefer the murderous terrorist.

"Samuel, I can see you're awake. Don't try to pretend you're sleeping. That's childish."

Tay sighed and buried his face in the pillow.

"Oh, for God's sake, Samuel, cut it out," his mother snapped. "You're a grown man. Act like it!"

Tay yawned. He realized there was no point in trying to ignore her. She had always been able to wait him out. Better to let her have her say and get it over, then he could go back to sleep.

He pushed himself up on his elbows, jammed a pillow behind him, and leaned back against the headboard. A very realistic manifestation of his mother was sitting at the foot of his bed. Usually his mother's little visits didn't amount to much more than a few swirling lights, but this was the second full-body materialization within a few days. This was getting serious.

"Good evening, Mother. To what do I owe the pleasure tonight?"

"You owe the pleasure, as you put it in that snarky tone of yours, to the same thing you always do. I'm your mother. It is my responsibility to try to help you in any way I can no matter what obstacles I must overcome to do it."

"And is one of those obstacles the fact that you're dead?"

His mother unfolded her arms and gave an airy little wave with one hand. "That's the least of my problems. It's your obstinacy and pigheadedness that make helping you so difficult."

"Can we skip the part where you criticize my character just this once, Mother? I'm really very tired. It's been a hell of a few days and I'd like to go back to sleep. Please tell me what you've come to say and then bugger off."

"Such language, Samuel, such language. I swear I don't know why I go to all this trouble for you. It's not as if doing these materializations is a day at the beach, you know. Do you have any idea how much energy I have to put into this?"

"Perhaps next time, you could just send me an email."

"You don't read emails."

"Yes, exactly."

Tay's mother shook her head, and then she stood up and walked across the room to the low dresser between two windows that overlooked his garden.

"Every single time I'm here I hope to see a framed picture of a woman on your dresser, Samuel, but I never do."

"You'd only start asking me a lot of questions about her."

"Of course I would. Shouldn't a mother be interested in the woman with whom her unmarried and I should also say increasingly elderly son is keeping company?"

"I'm hardly elderly."

"Getting close, Samuel. Getting very close."

"And I'm not keeping company, as you put it, with anyone."

"Yes, I can see that," she said, waving vaguely at the top of the dresser. "More's the pity."

Tay's mother strolled around the room casually peering here

and there, and then after a bit she returned to the foot of Tay's bed and resumed her seat.

"Why are you here, Mother?" Tay asked.

"I heard what you and your friend were talking about yesterday. And I wanted to tell you—"

"What friend?"

"That August person."

"I wouldn't really call John August a friend."

"Whatever you call him, when he asked you to—"

"Wait a minute. You're saying you heard what August and I were talking about yesterday?"

"Yes, that's what I just said. Don't you ever listen to me, Samuel?"

"How could you have heard us, Mother? You weren't there."

Tay wasn't certain what to make of the rather humorless smile on his mother's face. He had never seen an expression quite like it before.

"*Were* you there, Mother? Somewhere?"

Tay's mother shook her head and looked away.

"Why must we always have the same tiresome conversation, Samuel?"

"Are you saying you know about my conversation with John August yesterday because of your universal knowledge?"

Tay's mother just looked at him. "I've told you over and over. It's one of the few advantages of being dead."

"You know everything I say? All the time? Regardless of where I am or who I'm talking to?"

"More or less. Sometimes I don't really pay any attention to you, but you haven't paid any attention to me in forty years so I think that's only fair, don't you?"

"You're telling me you hear—"

"For God's sake, Samuel, would you stop talking long enough for me to say what I came here to say?"

"Sorry, Mother. Yes, please, by all means. Say whatever you

would like to say so I can go back to sleep."

"I wanted to tell you I'm proud of you for doing this."

Tay couldn't ever remember his mother telling him she was proud of him about anything before. For a moment, he had no idea what to say.

"Did you hear me, Samuel?" his mother prodded.

"Yes, I heard you. I'm just too surprised to speak."

"You really can be an ass sometimes, Samuel. Can't I even tell you that I'm proud of you without getting a dose of sarcasm?"

"I'm sorry, Mother. You're absolutely right. I am glad you're proud of me, but…well, I'm not exactly sure what it is you're proud of."

"You went after Robbie Kang's killer in spite of my advice, and I realize perhaps I was wrong to tell you not to. Now you've found him—"

"Not exactly, Mother. August thinks he's going to find me."

"Same thing. Anyway, I'm sure you're going to get this man before he hurts anybody else. Superman? Isn't that what they call him?"

"Suparman, Mother. Not Superman."

"Whatever." Tay's mother lifted one hand languidly. "What matters is that you and this August person are going to get him."

"I'm only the cheese in the trap, Mother. The cheese isn't entitled to take much credit for nabbing the rat. It's the trap that does all the work."

"Now you're being modest, Samuel, and modesty bores me. What matters is that soon this Superman—"

"Suparman, Mother. Suparman."

Tay's mother gave him a hard look. "What matters is that soon this man will be dead and you will have had a part in killing him."

"Not if I can help it."

"What? I don't understand."

"I am willing to be the bait, Mother. But if Suparman takes that bait, I'm going to try to arrest him if I can. Not just stand there and let August's people kill him."

Tay's mother cocked her head at him.

"Arrest? Are you out of your mind, Samuel? You arrest the little shit and the people who have been protecting him will put him right back on the street."

"Mother, please. Watch your language."

"Oh, shut up, Samuel. Let August kill the bastard or you do it yourself."

"I will only kill him if I have absolutely no choice."

"I've seen you shoot, Samuel. You probably couldn't kill him even if you had absolutely no choice. If it's you pointing a gun at this man, he's as safe as he'll ever be."

"Thank you, Mother."

Tay's mother looked away and shook her head.

"Please remember, Mother, that I am a policeman. We arrest people and then they are punished according to the law. We don't set them up to be killed, particularly not by some assassin working for the American government."

Tay's mother leaped up and began pacing furiously back and forth at the foot of Tay's bed.

"Samuel, I swear you are the biggest fuddy-duddy I have ever known. This man isn't a purse-snatcher. He's responsible for the murder of hundreds if not thousands of completely innocent people. He killed Robbie Kang. You get him when you have the chance. You do not arrest him and let the politicians set him free. The barbarians no longer live in a land far, far away. They're right next door."

Tay said nothing, hoping his mother would run down of her own accord.

"You have to take a stand, Samuel. Life has always been nasty, brutish, and short, but never—"

"Hobbes. Thomas Hobbes."

"What?"

"That was written by the English philosopher Thomas Hobbes

in the seventeenth century. 'The life of man: solitary, poor, nasty, brutish, and short'. "

"What in the world are you on about, Samuel? Who cares? It's just something I heard somewhere."

"Look, Mother, let's stop arguing about this. I'm going back to sleep."

At that Tay's mother levitated about three feet over the end of his bed and began shaking her finger at him.

"Do not mess this up, Samuel. Do not try to arrest this man. Let August kill him if he gets the chance. And if he doesn't, you kill him."

"I already told you, Mother, I'm not killing anybody unless I have to."

"Don't you want revenge for Robbie's murder?"

"I want justice for his killer, Mother. Justice is civilized. Revenge isn't."

"Oh, that is the way you see it, is it? Are you really that naive?"

"It's not naïve, it's—"

"Justice is nothing but revenge dressed up in a nice suit so we can pretend it's not what it really is."

Tay said nothing. He knew there was a lot of truth to what his mother was saying, but he certainly wasn't going to admit that to her. Not right now, anyway.

"Maybe you should just toddle off and have a cup of tea, Samuel, and leave protecting the world to real men like August."

Tay felt a pulse of anger in spite of himself, but he pushed it away.

"I don't drink tea, Mother."

"No? I would have thought coffee might be too strong for you."

"May I go back to sleep now?"

"Do whatever you want. I'm leaving."

"Thank heaven," Tay muttered.

"What did you say?"

"I thought you heard everything, Mother."

Tay's mother waved one hand at him in a gesture of dismissal.

"Honestly, I don't know why I bother. I came here tonight to tell you I was proud of you for standing up for what is right—"

"I *am* standing up for what is right."

"—and now I am leaving here filled with disappointment. You are a dinosaur, Samuel. You belong in a museum."

"Good night, Mother. Don't be a stranger."

As Tay watched, the image of his mother begin to fade away until all that remained was a single point of light that quivered like a candle flame in the darkness. After a few moments the point of light disappeared, too, and Tay was left sitting in his bed with a pillow behind him wondering if he was asleep or awake.

As usual, he decided he was asleep, and almost at once he was.

42

TAY CLOSED THE door behind him and was halfway down his front walk when an unsettling thought crossed his mind. Shouldn't he be carrying his service weapon?

He almost never carried a gun. In fact, he couldn't remember the last time he even looked at his old Smith & Wesson .38. Was it still in the drawer in his nightstand next to his bed? Unless someone had stolen it, he supposed it had to be.

There wasn't really much point in him carrying it, he supposed. He was such a terrible shot that the gun wouldn't be much use to him even if he had it with him. Did other people know what an awful shot he was? His mother seemed to, which was pretty embarrassing.

Still, if there was ever a sensible time for him to carry a gun, this was probably it. He didn't really want to haul the thing around with him, but he didn't want to be surprised by Suparman somewhere and have no way to defend himself either. Whether he could defend himself successfully even if he did have his gun was another question altogether. He supposed he would find out if the time came when he had to try.

Tay turned around, took out his key, and let himself back into the house.

He sat on the side of his bed and lifted the .38 and its leather holster out of the drawer. Sliding it out, he spun the cylinder and saw it was fully loaded. When had he loaded it? He couldn't remember. He couldn't even remember the last time he had fired it or, worse, the last time he had cleaned it.

It didn't seem very wise to entrust his life to a dirty handgun so Tay fumbled around in the back of the drawer until he found his cleaning kit. It was a black zippered pouch that held several brushes of various sizes, a sack of cotton patches, and plastic squeeze bottles of lubricating oil and gun solvent.

Downstairs at the table in the garden, Tay opened the cylinder and tipped the gun up. The five rounds slid out of the cylinder and he caught them in his palm and stuck them in his pocket. At least he remembered that much about cleaning a weapon: to do it, you had to unload it first.

He unzipped the cleaning kit and took out one of the brushes. He squeezed a little Hoppe's Number 9 solvent on it and pushed it through the bore. After that he wiped the brush through each of the five chambers in the cylinder. When he was done with the Hoppe's, he wrapped one of the cotton patches around the brush and repeated the entire procedure, checking the cotton patch after it passed through the bore to confirm it was reasonably clean.

He fished the five rounds out of his pocket and looked at them. Did ammunition get old? Should he reload with fresh rounds? Did he even have a box of ammunition at home?

Screw it, he thought. *They'll either go bang or they won't.* He pushed a round into each of the chambers, spun the cylinder, and slapped it shut. Then he holstered the gun, stood up, and reached underneath his shirt to slip the paddle holster over his belt at the two o'clock position.

He sat down, testing the holster position for comfort. Somehow the shirt felt a little snug over the holster. He didn't remember it being snug the last time he carried a gun. He would have liked to tell himself that this was a bigger gun than he had carried before, but it wasn't. It was exactly the same gun. What was bigger was the stomach against which it rested.

Tay set that depressing thought aside, shoved all the cleaning gear back into the kit, and zipped it closed. Back inside the house, he dropped the kit on a chair and headed for the front door. Thinking about his stomach had made him hungry. He would stop for breakfast before he went to the office.

Tay stood for a moment outside his front gate and looked around. The sun had disappeared behind a shelf of low-hanging clouds and there was a scent of rain in the air.

Were John August's people out there somewhere watching him right now? He could see no suspicious vehicles parked on Emerald Hill Road nor was anyone loitering on the sidewalks. It was a quiet residential street and August's people could hardly be standing around pretending to read newspapers. If they were there, they had to be behind one of his neighbors' windows. That didn't make a lot of sense to Tay either, but he couldn't think of anywhere else they might be.

Tay turned right and walked toward Orchard Road. There was a Coffee Bean and Tea Leaf where he sometimes went for breakfast when he was in a hurry. Coffee and a roll was all he needed this morning. The Coffee Bean would do just fine.

He ordered a drip coffee and examined the breakfast offerings in the glass case next to the cash register. The muffins looked awful and the cinnamon roll looked worse, so he settled for a toasted cinnamon bagel with cream cheese. When it was ready, he took it and the coffee to an empty table in the corner and sat down. His holster dug uncomfortably into his belly and he shot a look around the room. It was almost empty and no one was paying any attention to him so he half rose from his chair, pushed the holster a little further around to the front of his belt, and sat down again. Better.

As Tay sipped his coffee and chewed at his bagel his thoughts drifted back to the dream he had the night before and the conversation he had, or imagined he had, with his mother. Dream or not, his mother probably had the right idea. He ought to let John August's people shoot Suparman and be done with it.

He understood that really did make sense, but there was still a problem: he simply couldn't bring himself to do it. He arrested the people who ought to be arrested and let the justice system sort them out. That was what he had done for twenty-five years or more. He didn't set people up to be killed just because they were poor excuses for human beings, even if sometimes he arrested people he thought deserved killing.

A chair scraped the floor table right behind him and reflexively Tay scooted his own chair a bit closer to his table to make room for whoever just sat down. But he didn't look at them. People in Singapore seldom acknowledged strangers unless they absolutely had to.

"How can you drink hot coffee in weather like this?" the woman behind him said.

Tay glanced over his shoulder and his surprise must have shown on his face because Claire giggled slightly.

"Look straight ahead and drink your coffee," Claire said. "We can hear each other fine. Don't make it too obvious we're having a conversation."

"You don't think our lips moving might give that away?"

"I can talk without moving my lips. Can't you?"

Tay didn't know what to say to that, so he said nothing at all. After a moment Claire went on.

"I'm kidding, Sam. You've got to lighten up a little."

"Everyone tells me that."

"Everyone's right."

Tay cleared his throat. "Could you at least tell me what we're not having this conversation about?"

"I saw you looking for us this morning."

"I didn't see you."

"Well, Sam, you do understand that's really the whole idea, don't you?"

Tay nodded, but immediately realized that was pretty pointless since Claire had her back to him.

"So relax," she added. "We've got you covered. We're there. Don't worry about it."

"Easy for you to say."

"Not really. I'm responsible for you. If anything happens to you, I'm dead."

Claire paused. Tay said nothing.

"Okay," she went on, "maybe that was a bad way to put it, but you know what I mean."

"That's the best you can do? Tell me not to worry?"

"Look, Sam, we've got your house zipped up so tight a roach can't get in there without me knowing it."

"What if Suparman shows up somewhere else?"

"Like where? When you're in the Cantonment Complex surrounded by about five hundred armed cops?"

"I guess that's not likely."

"And where else do you go?"

"Gee, you make me sound so dull."

"Dull is good. Dull makes you easy to cover."

"You know, I'm on the street sometimes. I do have to go back and forth between places. I even eat in cafes and restaurants occasionally. Like now, for instance."

"It wouldn't make any sense for him to try to take you on the street or in a public place like this coffee shop. Why would he take a risk like that in front of a ton of witnesses? No, Sam, that's not the way Suparman works. He wants you static and in a nice quiet place where no one else is around. And that's at your house right here on Emerald Hill Road."

"You're sure of that?"

"You bet your life." Claire giggled slightly in what sounded to Tay like genuine embarrassment. "Another poor choice of words, I guess."

Tay chewed his bagel without tasting it. He took the napkin that came with it and wiped the crumbs off his lips.

"What if something unanticipated happens? I mean, what if I have to go someplace unexpected?"

"Like where?"

"How the hell should I know?" Tay snapped. "I'm a cop. I investigate crimes. I don't just sit around and shuffle papers all day."

"That's not what John says."

Tay had only been talking to this woman for a few minutes and already he wasn't sure he liked her. Fortunately, she started talking again before Tay could say something he would no doubt later regret.

"Look, Sam, have you got your cell phone with you?"

"Yes."

"I'm going to send you a text in a few minutes. If something happens to disrupt your routine, text me at that number and we'll figure it out. Stay cool, Sam. We've got this."

Before Tay had decided what to say, he heard the chair behind him scrape and he felt rather than saw Claire standing up and moving away. He didn't look back at her.

Tay finished his bagel and coffee and had just wiped his mouth and wadded up the napkin when his phone buzzed in his pocket.

He took it out and looked at the screen.

I don't really think you're dull.

Buzz.

Just a little old for me maybe.

Funny. Very goddamned funny.

43

TAY HAD BEEN at his desk for nearly an hour trying to think of something to do other than sit at his desk when there was a knock at the door. A patrolman he didn't know leaned in.

"Inspector Tay?"

Tay acknowledged with a nod that he was.

"You're wanted upstairs, sir. The SAC asked if you would come up right away."

Tay nodded again and the patrolman closed the door.

He sat drumming his fingers and wondering what this could be about. What he and August needed right now were routine days without surprises. A sudden assignment to some case would only screw things up. Maybe he would plead he was suffering from traumatic stress and beg off from any new assignments. The SAC already thought he was a little crazy so he figured he wouldn't have any difficulty selling that.

With a sigh Tay stood up and headed upstairs to the SAC's office. He would take the stairs. He needed the exercise. And it would take longer to get there.

"How are you feeling, Sam?"

"Fine, sir. Just fine."

"Good. Ah, good."

Tay waited with his features arranged in an expression of polite interest, but nothing more was immediately forthcoming. Tay's patience quickly ran out.

"What was it you wanted to see me about, sir?"

The SAC pursed his lips and hesitated, but then he cleared his throat. "Well, Sam...have you thought about that conversation we had?"

Tay was baffled. What in the world was the SAC talking about? What conversation? He tried to keep his face empty, but his puzzlement must have been apparent because the SAC started talking again.

"I meant a few days ago when I asked you to consider the possibility of retirement, Sam. Have you thought about that?"

Tay hadn't. He remembered the conversation now, but so much had happened since then it felt like it must have happened several years back.

"I've been a bit busy, sir."

"Yes, of course, you have. But this is still something I have to ask you to focus on right now."

"I don't want to retire, sir. I still have a lot to contribute to this department."

"If you're not willing to retire, Sam, I'm going to have to insist you accept that promotion to Deputy Superintendent."

"Didn't you say that was an administrative position, sir?"

"Yes. It is. The position supervises public affairs, legal, procurement, and..."

The SAC hesitated, but Tay waited him out.

"And...uh, traffic," he finished quickly.

"I'm a criminal investigator, sir. It's what I do. I don't want to become just another paper-shuffling dolt."

"Careful, Sam."

"I didn't mean you, sir."

"No, of course you didn't." The SAC studied a spot on the wall just above Tay's head. "Then I think perhaps retirement would be the right option for you after all, Sam."

"What's really going on here, sir?"

"What do you mean?"

Tay said nothing. He simply sat and looked at the SAC and kept his face completely blank.

"Okay, Sam. It's like this. They want you out of CID. Completely out."

"They?"

The SAC waved his hand in the general direction of the Ministry of Home Affairs compound at New Phoenix Park.

"The Minister," he said.

The SAC paused. Tay waited.

"And...ah, others."

"You mean the Prime Minister, don't you, sir?"

The SAC looked away and said nothing. That meant yes.

"My hands are tied here, Sam. You know the Minister has wanted you out for a long time, and after this..."

The SAC trailed off, flapping one hand in a way that could have meant almost anything.

"After what, sir?"

"Goddamn it, Sam, don't be naive," the SAC snapped. "You went off on your own. You embarrassed ISD and your sergeant ended up dead."

"I didn't kill him, sir."

"I know you didn't, but if you'd just done what you were told to do he would still be alive."

Tay didn't want to hear that. Particularly because it might be true.

"Here's how I'm reading this, sir," Tay said. "The politicians need a scapegoat for something they knew about and which should never have been allowed to happen. And I've been selected for the role. Isn't that what you really mean?"

The SAC looked out the window for a while without saying

anything, and then he leaned back in his chair and laced his fingers together behind his head. The sweat rings in the armpits of his shirt looked to Tay like the rings of a freshly cut tree.

"What's it going to be, Sam?"

Tay crossed his legs and studied his foot, but his foot appeared to have no useful suggestions to make. It remained studiously silent.

"How long do I have to decide?" Tay asked.

"I was hoping to get an answer right now."

"How long do I have to decide, sir?" he repeated.

The SAC scratched at his ear and looked around the room as if he might find the answer written on one of the walls.

"I suppose I could leave it to the end of today," he finally said, "but no later than that. Do I have your word you'll call me by five o'clock this afternoon and tell me what you're going to do?"

Tay felt boxed in, and he felt that way because he *was* boxed in.

"Yes, sir. I will call you by five o'clock today."

"Okay, Sam, then that's it. I'll be waiting for your call."

The two men stood and shook hands. It was an automatic gesture of civility with no substance to it. Tay walked out of the SAC's office without looking back and closed the door behind him.

Instead of going back to his office, Tay took the elevator to the ground floor and went outside for a cigarette. It was almost midday and the sidewalk was already crowded with groups of people on their way to lunch. Singaporeans went to lunch in groups, and they went early. It was frequently the most exciting part of their day.

Tay walked far enough away from the main entrance to avoid the casual conversations that sometimes sprung up among huddled smokers, shook out a Marlboro, and lit it. He smoked the first cigarette rapidly and efficiently and thought about nothing at all while he did it. When he was done, he almost immediately lit another, but this time he smoked it slowly and ran his conversation with the SAC back and forth through his mind.

They really did seem determined to get him this time, didn't they? Senior officers had tried to get him before, of course, more times than he could remember really, but he had always had a few friends among officers who were even more senior. If the word had come down this time from the Minister of Home Affairs or even the Prime Minister himself, he had clearly been outbid. He had no higher cards to play. Nobody did.

Maybe, he told himself, he even deserved to be put out to pasture this time. Robbie Kang's death was ultimately his responsibility. He didn't want to look at it that way, but he had to look at it that way because it was. Maybe this time things were different.

But a choice of retirement or being shuffled off into an administrative position where he was no longer involved in solving cases? What choice was that? He was an investigator, not an administrator. He didn't even know what administrators did all day, other than shuffle papers and try hard not to offend anybody. He couldn't do that. He simply couldn't.

On the other hand, what would he do if he retired? He had no idea what retirees did either. He could stay home and read books and not have to talk to anybody, he supposed. That part seemed attractive enough right now, but he imagined the attractiveness would fade before long. Retirement was the beginning of a long slide that led nowhere but to total irrelevancy. Nobody took retired people seriously. Retired people were invisible.

Tay walked over to one of the sand-filled pedestals that had been placed here and there to entice smokers out of dropping the cigarette butts on the ground. He stubbed out what was left of his Marlboro, wiped his hands on a handkerchief, and headed back into the Cantonment Complex. He would give himself exactly one hour upstairs in his office to decide what he was going to do, and then he was going home.

Tay was waiting for the elevator when his telephone buzzed in his pocket.

Did he have another text message? He had gone most of life avoiding text messages and suddenly they were coming in almost faster than he could read them. He took out his telephone and looked at the screen.

Maybe you're not really too old for me.

Was Claire trying to apologize for the message she sent him before, the one saying he wasn't dull, just old? Before he could decide, his phone buzzed again.

How old are you anyway?

The elevator arrived and a crowd surged off on their way to lunch. Tay stepped away from the closing door and let it leave without him. He moved to a relatively quiet corner of the lobby and stared at the screen of his telephone.

Was Claire flirting with him? If she was, she had picked the lousiest possible day on which to do it. Bringing up the question of his age, even in a joking way, on the very day the SAC was trying to push him into retirement was like mashing on a bruise. It damn well hurt.

Of course, Claire didn't know anything about that. Should he just tell her and be done with it? No, he couldn't. Then he would have to explain the whole business about the Minister trying to get rid of him, and he didn't want to talk about it. Worse, if Claire wasn't flirting and was simply asking a genuine question, he would look like a complete fool.

Buzz.

Come on, Sam, how old are you really?

Tay stared at the screen of his telephone. Claire *was* flirting. He had no doubt about it now.

Nothing good could come of this. He had to find some way to cut it off right now, but he didn't want to seem rude or make it appear he was casually brushing her off. When your life is resting in somebody's hands, it was always good policy not to piss them off unnecessarily. He had absolutely no idea what to do.

The lunch rush was largely over and a degree of quiet had returned to the lobby. When the next elevator arrived, Tay saw it was empty and jumped in just as the doors closed. He punched the button for his floor, leaned against the back of the elevator, and folded his arms.

When in doubt do nothing at all. It was a policy that had served him well for most of his fifty years. Why look around now for a new approach?

He left the elevator and was no more than a dozen steps down the corridor toward his office when...

Buzz.

I'm sending you a picture I want you to see.

Christ, now what? They were right in the middle of a dangerous operation to trap one of the world's most wanted terrorists and Claire wanted to send him a picture? What kind of picture could she be sending him? One possibility immediately popped into Tay's mind and just as quickly he pushed it out again. Surely *that* wasn't what she meant, was it?

He read back through the message in hopes of divining some further understanding, but he found none. Then he noticed something odd. The message had come from a different number than Claire's other messages had, a number he didn't recognize. Had Claire switched telephones for some reason?

Oh God, had she switched to a personal telephone because she wanted to send him a picture that was...well, personal? He still couldn't believe that, but what else could switching telephones mean? Claire wouldn't do that for no reason and the only reason he could think of was that she wanted to keep this picture just between the two of them. And if she wanted to keep this picture just between the two of them, Tay could think of only one reason *that* might be.

Buzz.

Tay shoved the phone back in his pocket without looking at the screen and walked into his office. He closed the door, sat behind his desk, and placed the phone face down on the blotter in front of him. He stared at the back of the phone for a bit, and then he took a deep breath and turned it over.

He thought he was completely prepared for whatever he might see.

He wasn't.

44

TAY SAT STARING at the screen of his telephone, but what he was looking at made no sense to him.

The photograph that had arrived by text message was one of Sergeant Lee seated in a straight wooden chair in front of a white wall. She was lashed to the chair with bands of silver duct tape around her legs, her arms, and her shoulders. Two more strips of duct tape covered her eyes and mouth. *What the fuck?*

The answer to Tay's unspoken question arrived almost immediately.

Buzz.

> *You have thirty minutes.*

Buzz.

> *If you're not here by then, I'll kill her.*

Buzz.

> *If I see anybody but you, I'll kill her.*

Buzz.

> *Answer me right now or I'll hurt her.*

Tay could hardly bring himself to touch his telephone again. If he just ignored the messages, maybe nothing would happen. But of course he knew that was nonsense. Whoever sent the messages could easily see they had been read, couldn't he?

He thought for a moment, took a deep breath, and picked up the telephone. He pecked out a message with his thumbs and hit *Send*.

Who is this?

Buzz.

You know who this is.

Buzz.

So you also know I will kill her.

Suparman had Linda. Tay didn't know how that could be, but it was obviously true. Linda must have come back from Johor Bahru without telling him, and Suparman had somehow surprised her.

They hadn't prepared for that. What he and August had talked about was Suparman coming after *him*. He thought Linda was safe, so they had given no thought to protecting her.

Now Suparman had Linda, and Tay had no idea what to do. He felt responsible for her, just as he felt responsible for what happened to Robbie Kang. If he had only done what they told him to do and let his suspicions go, none of this would have happened.

Tay pecked out another message and hit *Send*.

Where are you?

Buzz.

Her house.

Tay typed with his thumbs.

I don't know where that is.

Buzz.

You're the detective. Figure it out.

Buzz.

Thirty minutes. Or she's dead.

Tay hesitated, then typed.

It will take me an hour.

He thought for a moment and added one more thing.

If you hurt her, I will kill you.

Buzz.

LOL

It took Tay only a minute to get Linda Lee's home address from the CID operations center: Joo Chiat Avenue. It sounded familiar to him, but he wasn't certain where it was so he pulled up a city map on his telephone.

Joo Chiat Avenue was in a middle-class neighborhood about halfway between the Cantonment Complex and Changi Airport. A pretty nice place to live on a sergeant's pay. Was Linda married? No, he was pretty sure she wasn't. Maybe it was family money. Tay pushed the thought away, annoyed to have had it. How she acquired the house hardly mattered now.

What *did* matter was that he needed to figure out how to keep Suparman from killing both of them and he had less than an hour to do it.

Tay knew Suparman wasn't going to let Linda go just because he followed instructions and showed up at her house. If he went there, Suparman would kill them both. If he didn't go there, Suparman would kill Linda and come after him later.

Should he call Claire? He had no doubt she would produce half a dozen hardened killers within the hour, surround Linda's house, and take Suparman down.

No, that didn't make any sense. If he called out August's troops, they would get Suparman, he had no doubt they would, but Suparman would still kill Linda. Suparman wasn't going to turn her loose just because a bunch of armed men showed up. He must have anticipated already that might happen and he had to be prepared for it.

Tay could only look at this one way: he was responsible for Linda being tied to that chair and he had to get her out of that chair unharmed. Whatever the risk to him. Whatever it might cost him. It was as simple as that. The only choices he could consider were ones that made that possible.

THE GIRL IN THE WINDOW

Which meant he was going. And he was going alone.

Anyway, what did he have to lose? Everybody he had ever been close to was already dead: his father, his mother, Robbie Kang. It was a short list, but they had all left him. He was at the front of the line now. His turn to leave would come soon enough. Why did it matter exactly when it came?

Tay knew he could make it to Joo Chiat Avenue in thirty minutes, a little more if traffic was bad. He ran for the elevator.

He would figure out what to do when he got there while he was driving.

Probably.

Down in the garage where they kept the pool vehicles, Tay found a fast response car that had been left for repairs and not yet returned to New Phoenix Park. It was a white Toyota Altis equipped with lights and siren.

Unlike most cars imported to Singapore, fast response cars had no speed governor, which made the fast response car exactly the right vehicle for the job. Tay was not a particularly good driver, but he had long ago discovered the faster he went the less that seemed to matter.

It took Tay fifteen minutes to get to Joo Chiat Avenue.

When he reached the general area, he cut the siren and lights and pulled to the curb to take a closer look at the map on his telephone. Joo Chiat Avenue and Joo Chiat Place formed a rectangular cul-de-sac in front of Telok Kurau Park. Both of the streets dead-ended into the park, but a narrow alleyway that ran along the front edge of the park connected the two streets and formed the base of the rectangle.

Tay punched in the house number he got from the CID operations center. Linda's house was right at the end of the street. It was just across the alleyway from the Telok Kurau Park.

He switched to Google Street View and took a look around.

Joo Chiat Avenue and Joo Chiat Place were both narrow streets that appeared to carry very little traffic since they didn't go through to anywhere. Linda's house was the last unit on the end of a group of two-story row houses set back about twenty feet off the road. There must have been at least a dozen separate houses, but they were all joined in a straight line by common walls and a common red-tiled roof.

The houses were small and most had whitewashed front walls and narrow casement windows on both floors. Fences separated front parking areas from the houses on both sides and gates separated them from the road. The fences and gates were mostly made of open iron railings in various styles and provided no privacy for the houses. Worse, from Tay's point of view, they exposed anyone on the street to full view from inside the house.

Telok Kurau Park was fairly large, but it didn't amount to much. Some clumps of scrubby trees and a little scruffy grass were about all it offered. On the opposite side of the park from Joo Chiat Avenue was some kind of canal or drainage ditch. Tay didn't recall having seen it before so he wasn't sure what it really was, but it looked fairly wide on the map. Nothing in the area crossed it other than a single pedestrian bridge. Suparman had chosen well. Vehicles could only approach Linda's house from one direction.

Tay was momentarily stumped. He could hardly drive up and park right out front of Linda's house. A fast response car with POLICE painted in blue on both sides would announce his presence long before he wanted it announced. So what to do?

He took a closer look at the park. That was a possibility. He could leave the car somewhere and approach the house on foot across the park. That would make his appearance about as stealthly as he could hope for it to be.

He worked out a route on the map he could drive to get to the other side of the park, one that would keep the fast response car out of sight of Linda's house, and then he pulled away from the curb.

Lor Telok Kurau was a residential roadway that ran along the south side of Telok Kurau Park all the way down to the canal. Tay drove to the end and stopped. The canal turned out to be a twenty-foot wide stream with cemented walls and a chain-link fence on both sides. Other than the water being a surprisingly rich and cooling shade of blue, it looked like a miniature version of the Singapore River.

The park was walled with an ornamental iron fence painted in a shade of green that was apparently meant to blend in with its surroundings, but the park's vegetation wasn't up to the challenge. There were several small groves of twenty or thirty foot gum trees, although most of the park was bare other than for some scruffy looking grass burned brown by the relentless Singapore sun. Here and there small trees and bushes had been planted in what looked like an effort to increase the density of the vegetation, but the effort had clearly been a failure.

Tay turned the car around and drove away from the canal until he came to an entrance to the park. He pulled the wheels of the car up on the sidewalk and got out.

He followed a brick walkway through a break in the iron fence and into a stand of gum trees that sheltered a tiny playground. Two red-painted slides, a yellow swing set, and a green teeter-totter were arranged in the shade of the trees and all of them were empty. When he walked through the trees, he found himself looking straight at the end wall of Linda's house no more than a hundred feet in front of him.

The wall was completely exposed to Singapore's blistering sun so the white paint was washed out and yellowed. It looked more like a bad case of jaundice than a coat of paint. There were only two windows, one on the bottom floor and one on the top, and they were both small and covered with drapes or shades.

There wasn't much open space in Singapore and Tay couldn't imagine why a house right next to a park wouldn't have big windows through which the view could be enjoyed, but he was glad this one didn't. At least now he had found an inconspicuous way to approach the house. He just didn't have a clue what he was going to do when he got there.

Tay stepped back into the trees, went over to the yellow swing set, and sat down in one of the swings. It hung very low and he had to hold his feet straight out in front of him to keep them from dragging on the ground. Without thinking, he began to push with his heels and he drifted back and forth in the swing while he considered what to do.

If he simply knocked on the front door and went inside, Suparman would surely shoot him and then shoot Linda. That made no sense at all. Linda would still be dead and then he would be dead as well. What would that accomplish? On the other hand, staging some kind of an assault on the house made just as little sense as walking up and knocking on the door. Suparman would no doubt shoot Linda then, too.

Tay glanced around him to make certain he was still alone, and then he lifted his shirt and slid his Smith & Wesson .38 into his lap. He opened the cylinder, made sure it was fully loaded, and snapped it shut again. He had five rounds. He wasn't going to do much assaulting with that, was he? As lousy a shot as he was, he wasn't going to do much of anything with five rounds. He pushed his old .38 back into its holster and smoothed his shirt down over it.

Tay sat swinging gently back and forth and turning the problem over in his mind. He was missing something here. He could feel it. He just couldn't figure out what it was.

What was Suparman trying to accomplish?

The answer appeared obvious. Suparman wanted to keep his sweet deal with ISD intact and he wanted to be free to keep operating like he was now. Tay and Linda could blow all that up. As long as either one of them was alive to talk about what happened at the Fortuna Hotel, Suparman had a problem. That was why he wanted them both dead. It was the only outcome that guaranteed the continuation of his collusion with ISD.

And that was when Tay realized what he was missing.

Suparman might want them dead, but he certainly didn't want himself dead. He had a way out of this.

He didn't know Tay and he couldn't be certain what Tay would do when he saw that picture. Maybe Tay would show up just as he asked, but maybe Tay would be willing to sacrifice Linda to take Suparman down. Maybe Tay would have just called in a Special Tactics and Rescue team and let them hit the house.

Suparman had to have a way out if Tay did something like that. Anything else would amount to suicide.

But what was his way out?

Tay was still pondering that when he felt rather than saw someone walk up from behind him and sit in the other swing facing the opposite direction.

When he glanced over, Claire smiled at him.

"What the fuck are you doing here, Sam?"

45

"YOU TOLD ME you weren't watching me when I was at work," Tay said.

Claire gave a little push with her feet and began swinging in a slow counterpoint to Tay.

"I lied. So sue me."

Tay said nothing.

"I figured you might try some kind of crazy shit," Claire went on. "I didn't know what, but I thought keeping an eye on you at the Cantonment Complex would be worth doing."

She spread both her arms to encompass the playground and the rest of the park beyond.

"So here we sit, gliding back and forth together on a children's swing set in one of the dreariest parks I've ever seen, and I've got no idea at all what's going on. Are you going to tell me, Sam, or do I need to torture you a little first?"

"That sounds like it might be fun."

Claire didn't smile. "It wouldn't be. Trust me on that, pal, it wouldn't be."

Tay looked at his watch. He had less than half an hour to meet Suparman's deadline. Not nearly enough time to get rid of Claire and still somehow pull off a miracle. It looked like Claire was part of this now whether he wanted her to be or not.

Tay took out his telephone, opened the message app, and showed Claire the picture of Linda duct-taped to a chair.

"Who's that?"

"It's Sergeant Lee. She was with me at the Fortuna Hotel when Robbie was shot."

Tay beckoned to Claire. He pushed himself out of the swing, walked to the edge of the grove of gum trees, and pointed across the park to the house at the end of Joo Chiat Avenue.

"That's her house. I thought she was in Malaysia, but she must have come home without telling me. Suparman has her. They're in there. Suparman sent me that picture and some text messages. He said if I'm not there a half hour from now, he'll kill her."

Claire looked from Tay to the house and then back to Tay again.

"And if you *are* there a half hour from now, he'll kill both of you. That doesn't do anybody any good, Sam."

Tay nodded, but he didn't say anything.

"John warned me you were a loner, but it doesn't make any sense for you to take *this* on by yourself."

"Sure it does."

"Look, Sam, no matter how much—"

"I'm not going to leave her in there. I'm not going to let Suparman kill her. I'm already responsible for one sergeant being killed and I'm not going to lose another one."

"That's ridiculous, Sam. You're not responsible for—"

"Look, could we debate this some other time? I've got things to do right now."

"Who else knows about this?" Claire asked.

"Nobody."

"You could have called me."

"I could have. But I didn't. Anyway, you're here now. How many of your people are with you?"

"None."

"Seriously? *None?*"

"Yeah, it's just me."

Tay turned around and walked back into the grove of gum trees. He stopped at the swing set, but he didn't sit down. Instead, he folded his arms, leaned back against the frame, and focused his eyes somewhere off in the distance.

Claire stood patiently next to him for a while, but eventually she broke the silence.

"If you'd called me, I could have brought out half a dozen guys and—"

"Do what? Surround the house? Kick in both doors? And what do you think would happen then?"

"I understand. He'd kill her. But, Sam, Suparman is going to kill her anyway. At least then we'd have him, too."

"I don't think so."

Claire cocked her head, looked at Tay, and waited.

"When Suparman set all this up, he had no idea what I would do. He doesn't know anything about me. He would have to believe there was at least a pretty good chance I'd just call out Special Tactics and Rescue. Then he would have looked outside and found fifty heavily armed men surrounding the house."

Claire nodded and waited some more.

"He's not suicidal, Claire. Killing Linda or me or both of us serves no purpose if he gets killed at the same time."

"Unless he wants to go out in a wave of what he considers glory."

"Yes…" Tay thought about that for a moment. "Unless that."

"Even if you're right, Sam, how does that help us?"

"Because now we know he's got a way out. If we attack the house, he kills Linda, and he's got a way out."

Claire looked in the direction of the house, although it wasn't visible from where they were.

"All I saw was a front door and a back door. What did I miss?"

Tay shrugged.

"So what's his way out, Sam?"

"I have no idea. But he has one. We attack the house, he kills Linda, and he's gone. You can make book on it."

Tay fished his cigarettes out of the front pocket of his shirt and automatically held the pack out to Claire. When she shook her head, Tay lit one for himself and pushed the pack back in his pocket. He stood smoking quietly and saying nothing. Claire sat back down in one of the swings.

"Linda only has one chance of walking out of there," Tay said without looking at Claire. "I have to go in and get her."

"That's crazy, Sam. He'll shoot you the second you walk through the door. Then he'll shoot her, too. What does that accomplish?"

"It's the only way, Claire. I'm responsible for Linda being in there, and I'm responsible for getting her out. Besides, we know that woman at the hotel shot Suparman at least once. Maybe it wasn't serious, but he can't be a hundred percent now. That's something."

"No, Sam, it's nothing. Remember who you're up against here."

"You're wasting your breath arguing with me. I'm going in. The only question open for discussion is exactly *how* I'm going in."

Tay finished his cigarette. He dropped the butt on the ground and mashed it out with the toe of his shoe.

"Take a little stroll with me," he said and walked off toward where he had left the fast response car.

Tay went around behind the car and opened the trunk. He leaned in and pulled a black metal chest toward him. It was about the size of a footlocker.

"This is the equipment box," he said with a glance at Claire. "Our cars carry around a lot of good stuff."

Tay unsnapped the catches and opened the lid.

"We switched to concealable vests last year," he said reaching inside the chest and taking one out.

Tay unbuttoned his shirt and took it off. Then he slipped the vest on over his T-shirt and cinched up the straps. He was a little embarrassed in front of Claire to discover how tightly it fit him. He was going to have to lose some weight. He really was.

Tay pulled his shirt back on and buttoned it. Fortunately, the shirt was big for him and it covered the body armor without any telltale bulges.

"You're going to let him shoot you," Claire said. "That's your plan?"

"Well, when you put it like that, you make it sound stupid."

"That's because it *is* stupid."

Tay shrugged, but he didn't say anything.

"Do you know what Suparman is armed with?" Claire asked.

"He shot both Robbie and the hotel clerk with a nine, not to mention that guy we fished out of the Singapore River. Since he used a nine on all three of them, my bet is he's got a nine aimed at Linda, too."

"Is that thing rated for a nine?"

"Yeah, it's a level III vest. It'll stop a nine."

Claire tapped him on the chest with her index finger. "What if he's got something bigger? Say something loaded with .44 Magnum hollow points?"

Tay shrugged. "In that case, I'll lose my bet."

He reached under his shirt and pulled the paddle holster off his belt. He slipped out his old .38 and laid the holster and the gun down separately in the trunk.

"Is that little popgun all you've got?"

Tay reached into the chest with his free hand and lifted up a Mossberg tactical shotgun.

"What do you think? Maybe I could shove it down one pants leg? That might make it a little hard for me to walk, but I'll bet Suparman would never notice it."

Claire didn't bother to answer.

Tay put the shotgun back in the trunk and took a role of duct tape out of the chest. Propping his right foot up on the car's bumper, he used his teeth to tear two strips off the roll. He pulled up his pants leg, held the .38 tightly against his ankle, and secured it with the two strips of duct tape. He stood up and shook down his pants leg. It covered the .38 perfectly.

Tay bent back into the trunk and took an H&K semi-automatic pistol out of the chest. It had a longer barrel than his .38 and was a little thicker, but he was able to get it into his paddle holster by giving it a hard shove. He lifted his shirt and snapped the paddle back over his belt.

"You didn't even check the magazine," Claire said. "How do you know what it's loaded with?"

"I don't. And I don't really care since I'm not going to shoot it. I just need something to give to Suparman when he tells me to take off my gun. Maybe he'll overlook my .38 if I give him this one."

"I don't see much chance of that."

"It's my best idea," Tay shrugged. "If you've got a better one, I'm listening."

"You're damn right I've got a better idea, and my better idea is for you to get out of the way and let me take care of this."

"This is my city—"

"I'm not going to stand around and let you go in there alone, Sam, no matter what you say. I'm just not."

"This is my city, Claire," Tay repeated patiently. "I'm doing this my way."

"Sam, don't be foolish. I kill people for a living and I'm good at it. Certainly better than you are."

"I'm not going in there to kill Suparman. That's not what this is about. I'm going in there to get Linda out."

"But you'll have to kill him to do that."

"No, what I have to do is make him run."

"I don't understand."

"The only way this plays out well is if I get Suparman separated from Linda. Then if I can make him feel threatened enough, maybe he'll throw in the towel without killing her and take whatever exit route he's mapped out."

"That sounds more like a hope than a plan."

"Maybe, but it's all I've got."

"And you think you're going to make Suparman feel threatened enough to run just with that little popgun you've got taped to your ankle?"

"Well, now that you're here and apparently have nothing better to do, I've got an idea. You want to hear it?"

Claire nodded.

"Here's what I'm thinking. You take up a position close to the front door when I go in. As soon as you hear a shot, no matter who fired it, I want you to start shooting and making as much noise as you can. You need to sound like all fifty of those armed men I didn't bring with me are storming the house."

Claire pursed her lips, but she didn't say anything.

"If I've managed to get Suparman far enough away from Linda by then," Tay continued, "maybe he won't take the time to go back and kill her and just follow his escape plan, whatever it is. I guess that depends on how persuasive your noise is."

Claire took a deep breath and let it out again, but she still didn't say anything.

"So what do you think?" Tay asked. "You willing to do that?"

"I still think we've got a good chance to take him right up front if we both go in."

"And I think that would get Linda killed. I've already told you why. Do this the way I've asked you to do it or leave. Your choice."

"I thought you might say something like that."

"So why did you waste time asking? What's it going to be, Claire?"

"You got a box of shells for that shotgun?"

Tay took the Mossberg out of the trunk and handed it to Claire, and then he rummaged around in the chest until he found a box of twelve gauge shells. She checked the shotgun's action and began methodically snapping shells into the magazine. When it was full, she scooped the rest of the shells out of the box and pushed them into her pockets. She jacked a shell into the chamber and propped the shotgun on her shoulder.

"All set," she said.

"You want one of these?" Tay asked her, pulling another ballistic vest out of the chest.

Claire shook her head. "A man's vest doesn't fit me very well."

Tay started to ask what she meant by that, but then the reason suddenly came to him and he swallowed the question just in time to avoid embarrassing himself. He slammed the car trunk and looked at his watch.

"Time to go," he said.

46

THEY REACHED THE edge of trees on the other side of the playground and stood quietly looking at Linda's house. The sky was ice blue and broken only by a few wads of puffy white clouds that appeared to have been swept up into piles by a giant broom.

Tay and Claire could take an angle across the park that would keep them out of sight of both the front and back windows in the house, but there was nothing they could do to avoid the two little windows on the side. Suparman couldn't be watching out of all the windows at once, Tay told himself, and he wouldn't be expecting anyone to approach from across the park. The front and back of the house were the points of entry. That's where Suparman would focus his attention. At least Tay hoped that's where Suparman would focus his attention. To pull this off, they needed a little good luck, and this was where that good luck needed to start.

By the time they had crossed the open ground of the park and taken refuge in a sliver of shade at the end of the house, Tay had sweated through the T-shirt underneath his vest. He felt the rivulets of moisture streaming down his back and accumulating in the waistband of his shorts. If this were the day he died, he would die in sweaty underpants. It felt unseemly, but there it was. There wasn't anything he could do about it.

Claire looked around. The park was empty and the streets were empty. She didn't hear a sound.

"Where is everybody?" she asked.

"Residential neighborhoods in Singapore are pretty quiet during the day. Everyone is at work."

"Quiet I can see. But this is comatose. It's like a bomb went off and wiped out all human life."

"We should count ourselves lucky. The last thing we need is an audience."

The line of houses facing Joo Chiat Avenue backed up to a narrow alleyway not much more than a single car in width. On the other side of the alleyway was the back of another line of similar houses. Tay peered around the corner up the alleyway. The rear of Linda's house had a tiny concrete pad separated from the alleyway by a black metal fence. Other than two green plastic trashcans and a stepladder leaning against the back wall, the area was empty.

"Maybe I should cover the back door," Claire said.

"Remember, we *want* him to run. Boxing him into a corner is going to get people killed. Maybe us."

Claire stood next to Tay and studied the alleyway. "I don't see how he thinks he can run. If people hit the front and the back doors at the same time, there's nowhere for him to go. Not unless he's got a tunnel in there."

Tay and Claire moved around to the front of the house and looked cautiously down Joo Chiat Avenue. The area between the house and the road at the front was bigger than in the back, but it didn't look much more hospitable. It too was entirely concreted and separated from the road by an open metal fence. There was a double drive gate in the fence and one of the gates stood open by about three feet.

Directly in front of the house's front door was a car shelter made from a green plastic roof supported on four aluminum poles. Next to it was a rusty metal table with three chairs that looked even rustier. A single red Chinese lantern dangled from a gold cord right in the center of the car shelter, but otherwise it was empty.

"As soon as I close the door behind me," Tay said, "come in through the gate and stand up against the front wall. Suparman's attention will be on me and he won't see you. Remember, do absolutely nothing no matter what happens unless you hear a shot. If you do, use that shotgun to shoot into the roof of the car shelter. Just keep banging away at it and it will sound like we've got about twenty guys out here all shooting at once. Don't fire into the house and don't come inside. I want him to have plenty of opportunity to get away."

Tay pulled up his pants leg and checked that his .38 hadn't become dislodged during the walk across the park. He bent down and wiggled it, but it appeared secure. When he straightened up, he shook down his pants leg and looked at Claire.

"Are you ready?" he asked.

She clicked off the safety on the Mossberg. "I think the right question is whether *you're* ready."

"I guess I'm about to find out."

Tay took his telephone out of his pants pocket and pushed buttons until he found the thread of text messages he exchanged with Suparman. With one finger, he picked out a new message and hit *Send.*

I'm here.

Tay could feel Claire holding her breath as they both stared at the screen of his telephone waiting for an answer. Tay was holding his, too. Then…

Buzz.

Where?

Tay tapped with one finger again.

In front.

Buzz.

Door is open. Hands out to your sides.

Buzz.

You won't see me. I'll see you.

Tay took a deep breath and stepped out from behind the corner of the house. Staying close to the fence, he walked quickly to the gate, turned sideways, and slipped through without touching it.

He was in the open then. Twenty feet from the front door. If Suparman was going to ambush him, this was when he would do it.

Tay walked slowly toward the front door, his hands just below his waist, palms out. His eyes flicked from the drapery-covered windows to the door and back again.

No sign of movement.

Nothing happened.

When he got to the front door, he stopped. It stood open about two inches. He bent forward and listened, but he heard nothing.

Tay put his fingertips against the door and pushed. It swung back without a sound. Through the open doorway he could see across the room to the back of a couch covered in what looked like imitation black leather and, beyond it, a low table with a television set. He saw no sign of either Linda or Suparman in the narrow section of room visible to him.

Tay took a deep breath, lifted one foot onto the threshold, and stepped inside.

Now he was all the way into the living room of Linda's house, but he still saw no one. Not Linda, not Suparman. Reaching back with his left hand, he closed the door behind him.

The living room was on the small side, but Tay's first thought was that might be an advantage. The less space he had to deal with, the better it ought to be for him. If there was anything at all that could make this lousy idea better. Which he seriously doubted.

Right in front of him was the couch he saw when he first pushed open the door. A love seat upholstered in the same fake leather sat at a ninety-degree angle to create an L-shaped configuration in front of the television set. On the right-hand side of the living room was a door, but Tay could only see a few feet of the hallway behind it and couldn't tell what was back there. A kitchen probably, and maybe a dining room. On the left, a wooden staircase with a white metal railing led to the upper floor where he assumed the bedrooms were located.

Tay still saw no one. He still heard no one. He stood motionless, holding his breath and straining his ears for any clue where Suparman and Linda were. Nothing.

He shuffled a couple of steps to his right. He tried to make as little noise as possible although he supposed he didn't really make any difference. His presence wasn't exactly a surprise to Suparman.

He needed to pin down where Suparman was and where Suparman had Linda. The whole idea of this stupid plan was to get between them. That obviously required him to have at least some idea where they were.

Tay kept his hands at his waist, palms out, and continued to shuffle slowly in the direction of the hallway at the right side of the living room. He didn't want to do anything to spook Suparman and cause him to start shooting, at least not yet. Until he knew where Linda was, that wouldn't do any good.

He reached the end of the couch, took a step past it, and stopped.

47

TAY COULD SEE down the hallway now. He caught sight of the entrance to a kitchen area just past the doorway and he was willing to bet the space beyond the kitchen was a dining room. Was it possible Suparman had Linda in the dining room? Tay thought back to the picture of Linda taped to a straight wooden chair. A chair from a dining table? Maybe.

Tay took another step and felt rather than saw someone watching him from the stairs. He shifted his eyes slowly in that direction, but he saw no one. He took another step toward the hallway.

"Stop!"

The voice came from the top of staircase.

Tay stopped.

White sneakers and jeans-clad legs appeared on the highest stair. The legs began to descend slowly and Tay watched transfixed as Suparman showed himself.

Suparman was tall and very thin, but nothing else about him came anywhere close to matching the sketch ISD had passed out at their briefing. His hair was jet-black and shiny and it was brushed back in a kind of modified pompadour. He had a long, patrician nose, high cheekbones, and a small white scar above his right eyebrow. His eyes were almost black and his mouth was thin-lipped and turned slightly down at the corners.

His languid face and slight build made Suparman appear curiously old fashioned. Tay was suddenly seized by the bizarre idea that he was staring at a 1940's saloon singer, something like Frank Sinatra might look if he were reincarnated as an Indonesian terrorist. He wouldn't even have been surprised to hear Suparman break into song:

"It's a quarter to three,
there's no one in the place
except you and me…"

Tay shook his head to clear it. He was going mad from the stress. He had to hang in there.

When Suparman reached the bottom of the stairs, he stood looking at Tay for a long while. His face was empty and he held a large, black semi-automatic pistol with what looked like a five-inch barrel.

Oh shit, Tay thought. *Maybe that's not a nine. If it's a .45, I'm screwed.*

"You by yourself?" Suparman finally asked.

"Do you see somebody else with me?"

Suparman didn't say anything. He just looked at Tay some more.

"Yes," Tay said. "I'm by myself."

"That is either very brave or very foolish."

"I'm still trying to make up my mind about that myself."

"Take your gun out and place it on the floor," Suparman instructed Tay.

Tay raised his shirt and lifted the H&K he took from the fast response car out of his holster. He bent down and placed the gun on the floor at his feet.

"Push it away. Toward the front door."

With his left foot Tay pushed the pistol past the end of the couch. It skidded about ten feet across the wooden floor and bumped to a stop against the wall.

Tay kept his hands open at waist level. He didn't move a muscle, but his eyes gave Suparman a thorough going over.

"You look pretty good for a guy who got shot a few days ago," Tay said.

"I do, don't I?"

"Where is Linda?"

"Here."

"I want to see her. I want to know she is all right."

Something that looked almost like a smile creased Suparman's face.

"You do understand that I am going to kill you, don't you?"

"I understand you are going to try."

Suparman looked at Tay for a long time. The smile, if that's what it was, disappeared.

"You are very strange man," he said.

"A lot of people say that," Tay nodded.

"I want to see Linda," Tay told Suparman again after a moment, mostly just to keep him talking.

"She's all right. I had to keep her alive until I could be sure you would come."

"Where is she?"

Suparman gestured with the muzzle of his gun toward the hallway that led back to the kitchen. "She is there."

So Linda was in the rear of the house and Suparman was at the bottom of the stairs in the front of the house. Tay was standing exactly between those two points. So far, so good.

"I want to see her."

"No."

Tay began moving, but very slowly. He shuffled a few half steps toward Suparman, acting more like a man who was confused and frightened than one who was any threat. He found that a remarkably easy impression to create.

"Stop!" Suparman snapped. "Get down on your knees."

"If you're going to shoot me, you can shoot me standing right here. I'm not getting on my knees."

Tay shuffled another step toward Suparman and looked around the room as if he didn't quite know where he was.

Suparman raised his pistol. Tay's watched Suparman's trigger finger out of the corner of his eye. It didn't whiten like a finger squeezing against a trigger so he risked sliding his feet a little closer. And he kept talking.

"Why not let me see her? If you're going to kill me anyway, what difference does it make?"

Another small slide forward. Now Tay was about three feet behind the love seat. It was the only thing between him and Suparman.

All at once, just outside the front door, there was the sound of a sneeze. Immediately after that, two things happened almost simultaneously.

In an instinctive reaction to the sound, Suparman turned slightly toward the front door, which also pulled the muzzle of his pistol in that direction. Tay saw his opening and dived for the floor behind the love seat.

Suparman brought the pistol quickly back to Tay and fired, but Tay was already on the floor behind the couch and he missed. Tay began ripping desperately at the tape holding the .38 to his ankle.

When she heard the gunshot, Claire did just what she was supposed to. The noise of the shotgun firing into the plastic roof of the car shelter was deafening. Maybe it didn't sound exactly like fifty guys were attacking the house, but it couldn't have sounded to Suparman like anything good was about to happen to him.

From where Tay was huddled on the floor, he couldn't see how Suparman was reacting, but he figured he had to be at least a little unnerved. The *boom-boom-boom* of the Mossberg sure unnerved the hell out of him.

Tay finally got his gun free from his ankle and he ripped away the strips of tape that had come off with it. Staying prone, he pushed himself along the floor with his free hand and peeked around the end of the couch. He wasn't concerned about noise. The blasts from the Mossberg were so loud they would have drowned out a motorcycle starting up.

When Tay's eyes cleared the end of the couch, he saw Suparman in a crouch with his handgun pushed out in front of him in a two-handed grip, and he was concentrating on the front door. Tay extended his gun hand around the couch and braced his elbow on the floor. A sense of calm settled over him and all his training seemed to come back at once. He brought the front sight of his .38 up until it rested on what he could see of Suparman's chest, took a breath, and let half of it out. Then he slowly squeezed the trigger.

Right at that moment, Claire unleashed a furious series of blasts and Suparman jerked his body a little further toward the front door. The movement reduced the size of Tay's target, but it was too late for Tay to hold back the shot.

He missed.

At the sound of Tay's revolver, Suparman wrenched his head back in Tay's direction and loosed off a wild shot. He hit nothing but the back of the couch. He hesitated briefly, and then he abruptly turned and ran up the steps.

Tay came to his knees, led the running man up the stairs with his front sight, and fired a second time, then a third. Both shots missed. Just as Suparman got to the top of the stairs, he reached back with his pistol and fired in Tay's direction once more.

This time Suparman was lucky and Tay was not.

The shot caught Tay high on the left side of his vest about halfway between his heart and the center of his chest. The impact drove Tay backwards onto the floor.

His head slammed into the wood.

He didn't move.

48

WHEN THE MOSSBERG was empty, Claire pulled shells from her pocket and slammed them into the magazine until it was full again. She racked the pump to push one into the chamber and then she stepped up and kicked the front door of Linda's house.

She was willing to follow Tay's instructions, but only to a point. And wherever that point was, she figured they were now well past it.

Leading with the Mossberg, she leaped through the door, dived, and rolled behind the couch. When nothing happened, she raised her head cautiously and glanced around. Tay was off to her left toward the staircase. He was down, but he was moving slightly, so she looked away and scanned the rest of the room for threats.

The open doorway to her right worried her. It wouldn't do Tay any good if she went to him only to have Suparman come out of there behind them and start shooting. She didn't hesitate. She rose out of her crouch, took half a dozen quick steps to the doorway, and plunged through it.

The small kitchen area to her left was clear, but she could hear a grunting sound coming from the room beyond it. With the Mossberg straight out in front of her, she followed the sound. Against the far wall of the next room a woman was duct-taped to a straight wooden chair.

Claire went to her and ripped the tape off Linda's mouth and eyes.

"Are you okay?"

"Yes, but who—"

"Tay is down in the front room. I've got to check on him. Then I'll come back and cut you loose."

"What do you mean down? Is he—"

But before Linda could finish her sentence, Claire was gone.

"Are you hit?" she asked Tay.

"He got me in the vest," Tay mumbled. "It knocked me backwards and I hit my head."

Tay was prone, but he was rolling his head tentatively with very small movements. He looked like he was checking to see if it was still attached.

Claire was down on one knee next to him, but her head was up and she was scanning the room.

"Relax," Tay said. "He's gone."

"Where did he go?"

"He went upstairs, but he's not there now."

"What are you talking about?" Claire asked, giving Tay a look. "How hard did you hit your head?"

Tay ignored the question.

"Where's Linda?" he asked instead.

"She's in the back room. She says she's fine, but I haven't cut her loose yet. I've been a little busy."

Tay held out a hand. "Help me up."

Claire stood and reached down for Tay's hand. He held it and pulled, but he only made it as far as a sitting position.

"Son of a *bitch*, that hurts!"

Tay's hand automatically went to the spot where Suparman's shot had hit his vest.

"*Shit!*" he shouted again and jerked his hand away.

"Let me take a look at that," Claire said.

Tay shook his head. Carefully, but he shook it.

"It didn't penetrate. Just get me up. Suparman is running."

"I thought you said he was upstairs."

"I said he *went* upstairs, but he's sure as hell not up there now. He has some way of getting out on the roof. Nothing else makes any sense. There's no other way out of here."

"What good would that do him? He'd just be trapped up there."

"All these houses have a common roof. Once he gets out on it he can walk three hundred feet away before he comes down. That gets him all the way to the next street. If he has a vehicle there, he's gone."

"But how can you be certain—"

"Stop talking and *get me the fuck up!*"

When Tay was finally on his feet, he stood perfectly still until he stopped swaying.

"You can let me go now," he said to Claire.

"Are you sure?"

"I'm sure."

Claire dropped his hands, but she stayed close just in case.

"Do you want me to cut Linda loose?" she asked.

"No time. If we don't get Suparman before he comes down the other end of the roof, he'll be gone."

Tay looked around on the floor until he saw his .38. He started to bend down to pick it up, but a wave of nausea washed over him. He stopped moving, stood very still, and pointed at it.

"Would you hand me my gun?" he asked Claire.

She scooped it up and put it in Tay's hand. He shifted it around until the grip felt right.

"Suparman has a head start," he said, "but he has to climb up on the roof and then climb back down again. We might still be able to catch up."

"Are you sure you can do this, Sam? Do you feel up to it?"

"Stop asking me how I feel and get moving! Take the alley in back, but stay close to the houses. You don't want him getting above you."

Claire nodded. She turned and trotted toward the back door.

Tay took a couple of steps in the direction of the front door. He wanted to glide like a tiger, but instead he waddled like a penguin. He stopped, took a deep breath, and tried it again.

Better. A little.

At least he made it to the door without falling over.

Out the front door, past the parking area, through the gate.

Tay stood in Joo Chiat Avenue and craned his neck to look at the roof. He saw no sign of Suparman. Either Suparman was on the back section of the roof or he had already made it all the way to the end. Or perhaps he had never gone out on the roof at all, but was somewhere else altogether. Tay didn't even want to think about that possibility.

Tay began to lumber along Joo Chiat Avenue as fast as he could without falling down. He stayed close to the houses to keep Suparman from surprising him from above exactly as he had told Claire to do, but every twenty feet or so he lurched out into the road to get a better view of the roof.

Nothing.

Tay glanced at the .38 in his hand. Five shots and a two-inch barrel. It would take an expert using a full-sized handgun with fiber optic sights to shoot a running man fifty or a hundred feet in front of him and twenty or thirty feet above him. But to do it with a small, short-barreled revolver that had open iron sights? For almost anyone, that would be like winning the lottery. For him, it would be like winning *all* the lotteries at the same time.

Even if he still had five rounds, he knew he wouldn't have much of a chance, and he didn't have five rounds. How many shots had he already fired? Three? Or four?

He couldn't take the time to stop and open the cylinder and count so he tried his best to remember. He was pretty sure he had fired three shots at Suparman on the staircase, which meant he had two rounds left. But maybe he had fired four times. Then he had only one round left.

Two rounds? One round? What different did it make? He would need a machine gun to have any confidence about his chances of bringing Suparman down.

About halfway along the line of row houses Tay realized he was still alive and he forced himself to move faster. He broke into something that was almost, but not quite, a jog.

After thirty feet or so he dodged into the roadway and looked up at the roof again.

This time he did see something, or at least thought he did. It was motion down near the very end of the line of row houses almost to the next cross street. It could have been a man climbing down from the roof. But it could just have easily have been a flock of birds flying away.

Tay bit back the pain and loped on down the street.

49

CLAIRE TROTTED PAST the kitchen and into the dining room.

"Whoever you are," Linda began, "would you—"

"Sam's okay," Claire said as she headed directly to the back door. "Suparman is running and we're trying to cut him off. I'll be back."

"Oh, for God's sake—"

The slamming of the back door cut Linda off.

"Shit," she muttered.

Claire stepped out into the alleyway and lifted the Mossberg to her shoulder. She moved away from the house and looked down the length of the roof.

She spotted Suparman right away. He was on the roof at the end of the line of row houses almost all the way down to the cross street. Tay had been right. Claire pulled the Mossberg down across her chest and broke into a run.

She tried to keep one eye on Suparman as she ran, but she didn't want to fall over anything so she kept shifting her glance back and forth between the alleyway and the roof. About halfway to the end, she glanced down long enough to sidestep two large black trash barrels and then looked up again.

Suparman was gone.

She slowed to a jog.

There weren't that many possibilities as to where he might have gone. If he had gone over to the front of the roof and doubled back, Sam would have him. If he hadn't, he must have started down somewhere. She couldn't see him coming down her side of the row of houses, and if he went down the other side Tay would be there, so her guess was Suparman had gone over the end of the last house. He was somehow getting down into whatever the street was there.

Tay thought Suparman must have parked a vehicle somewhere. It had to be there.

Claire started to run again.

The last house at the end of the alley had a four-foot wide strip of dirt behind it. The part of the strip closest to her was bare and whoever lived there was using it to park his motorbike, a shiny black Kawasaki.

The part of the strip closest to the end of the alley was covered with a clump of banana trees so thick it looked almost solid. The banana trees rippled in the breeze as she ran toward them and she made a mental note that the trees would make a good place to take cover if they got in a gun fight with Suparman.

She slowed as she approached the corner and slid up close to the banana trees. She ducked her head around the corner quickly and pulled it back.

She didn't see Suparman. She didn't see anything. The street was quiet and empty. No people. No vehicles.

What the hell?

Where did he go?

Claire edged around the corner keeping as close to the building as she could. She crept toward Joo Chiat Avenue where Tay was covering the other side of the roof. Suparman had to be over there somewhere. Where else could he be? He sure as hell hadn't gotten past her.

Everything was so quiet it made her edgy. Half a dozen shotgun blasts and another half dozen shots from handguns and nobody was even a little curious? Even if the neighborhood was mostly deserted during working hours, there had to be somebody around. She gathered Tay was right about Singaporeans. They were good at minding their own business and they really didn't want to get involved in anyone else's.

Where the hell *was* Suparman? He sure wasn't going to walk away through a neighborhood this quiet. But if he had stashed a car somewhere like Tay thought, where was it? There wasn't a single car anywhere in the alley and there were none here on the cross street at the end of the line of row houses. There might be a few in the parking areas along Joo Chiat Avenue, but what good would those do him? Even if he stole one, he would have to break through locked gates to get it out and that wasn't something you wanted to do when you were in a hurry.

When Claire left the alley she had dropped the shotgun down next to her leg to make it as inconspicuous as possible, if a shotgun could ever really be inconspicuous, but now she swung it up across her chest again and got ready to fire.

Suparman was somewhere, and it looked now like he had to be just around the corner. There was nowhere else he could have stashed a vehicle.

Claire suddenly stopped dead. In some corner of her consciousness she suddenly remembered she had seen a vehicle. The black Kawasaki motorcycle behind the house she was creeping along right next to. She had been thinking about a car so she hadn't paid much attention to the bike when she jogged by, but a motorbike would be even better than a car to disappear on. Faster, more maneuverable, and less conspicuous.

The Kawasaki, she thought, *I am so damn stupid!*

Claire was just turning to go back when Tay rounded the corner not twenty feet in front of her. She opened her mouth to tell him about the motorcycle, but the words froze on her lips.

Tay had his .38 thrust out in front of him, and he was pointing it at her. She stopped and stared.

"What are you doing, Sam?"

Tay didn't say anything. He just aimed directly at her and pulled the trigger.

BANG!

The shot passed so close to Claire she could feel it buzz past her cheek.

"What the fuck?" she screamed. "*What the fuck are you doing, Sam?*"

Tay shifted the muzzle of his gun slightly and pulled the trigger again.

Tay kept jumping out into Joo Chiat Avenue, looking up at the roof, and veering back as close to the row of houses as he could, but he didn't see any more signs of motion or catch a glimpse of Suparman.

Where *was* he? He had to be on the back of the roof where Claire would have him in sight. Unless of course he wasn't on the roof at all. But Tay didn't even want to think about that. Had Suparman hidden upstairs until they left and then come downstairs, killed Linda, and run away? No, that didn't make any sense. At least Tay hoped it didn't.

If that had been Suparman he had seen on the roof, Tay thought it was likely he had gone over the end of the row of houses and somehow gotten down into the cross street. That must be where he had left his vehicle. But Tay hadn't heard a car start and he certainly hadn't seen a car pull out up ahead of him, so perhaps Suparman hadn't made it down to the ground yet. Maybe there was still time.

The corner was fifty feet away.

Tay ran as hard as he could.

Thirty feet away.

He raised his .38, brought it around in front of him in a two-handed grip, and held it in front of his chest with the barrel slightly elevated.

Ten feet away.

He took a deep breath and steadied himself.

At the corner.

He thrust his .38 out in front of him and lifted the sights to eye level.

Then he was around the corner...

And he stopped dead.

Twenty feet in front of him Claire stood holding the shotgun across her chest. She started to speak, but stopped and just stared.

Over her shoulder, a rustling in a clump of banana trees that poked out from behind the house caught his eye. He shifted his eyes there just in time to see Suparman step out and point his pistol at Claire's back.

Tay was eighty or a hundred feet away, but what choice did he have?

He focused on his front sight, put it squarely on Suparman's center mass, and lifted his point of aim to compensate for the distance.

"What are you doing, Sam?" Claire asked, but Tay barely heard her.

He didn't say anything. He just squeezed the trigger as smoothly as he could.

BANG!

He missed.

"What the fuck?" Claire screamed. "*What the fuck are you doing, Sam?*"

Although he had missed, the shot wasn't completely wasted. It caused Suparman to hesitate, lower his weapon, and move to one side. It bought Tay some time, just not very much time.

Suparman crouched, rose slightly, and began moving his pistol once again toward Claire's back.

Did he have another round in the cylinder, Tay asked himself, or had he already fired all five?

But even as he formed the question, Tay realized that the answer didn't matter now. He either had another round or he didn't. If he did, that gave him one more chance to take Suparman down. If he didn't, they were both dead.

Tay stopped trying to count the shots he had fired and put his whole being into a single-minded focus on the tiny front sight of his .38. He shifted it to the right until Suparman's shirt slid out of focus behind it, and then he lifted it a little above the neckline of the shirt to somewhere around Suparman's head to compensate for what he thought would be the increased bullet drop over that distance. He breathed out and steadied himself.

With hope in his heart, Tay squeezed the trigger.

50

WHEN CLAIRE LOOKED into Tay's eyes and realized they were focused somewhere over her shoulder, she finally understood what was happening.

She dropped to the ground and rolled, bringing the shotgun across her body and aiming it between her feet. But she held her fire.

Suparman was sprawled in the street, and he wasn't moving.

Claire got up quickly. With the shotgun leveled at Suparman, she edged cautiously toward him. She found his pistol lying near the curb, stepped over it, and pushed it further away with her heel. She inched closer, and then she saw his face.

Tay's last shot had entered Suparman's right eye. She could see blood pulsing from it in little spurts.

There wouldn't be an exit wound. That was the thing about those little popguns like Tay carried. Small bullet, low velocity, not enough power to punch back out of the skull. If you placed a head shot perfectly, that little sucker just ricocheted around inside and mushed up everything like it had been run through a Cuisinart.

No point in calling an ambulance. It wouldn't do Suparman any good now.

Tay walked up beside Claire and they stood there together looking down at Superman's body.

"Goddamn, Sam," Claire said. "You told me you couldn't shoot."

"I can't."

She pointed at the blood still pulsing from Superman's right eye. "You're saying that was just luck?"

"That was just luck."

Claire looked at Tay for a long moment, and then she shook her head. "I don't believe you."

"Sometimes the best plan is to have a little good luck," Tay said. "Exactly the way I did when you sneezed."

Claire looked puzzled.

"You distracted Superman just when I had to take cover," Tay explained. "I'm not sure what would have happened if you hadn't sneezed."

Claire smiled, but she didn't say anything.

Tay lifted his eyes from Superman's body and looked around. He saw no sign of anyone on the streets. Still, a bunch of shotgun blasts and a few more shots from handguns would have attracted a lot of attention. There was no doubt in Tay's mind people had called the police by now. He strained his ears for the sound of sirens, but he didn't hear anything. They had a few minutes yet. Probably no more than five. Ten, if they were fortunate.

Whatever time they had, Tay needed every minute of it to get this organized.

"You can't be here," he said to Claire. "You're *not* here."

Tay took the Mossberg from her, safetied it, and pointed to the alleyway behind the line of row houses.

"Let's get back to Linda's house."

"What about…" Claire pointed down at Superman's body.

"He's not going anywhere," Tay shrugged. "But you are."

They walked down the alleyway as briskly as they could without running. Tay didn't want to draw any unnecessary attention, but then he remembered he was carrying a revolver in one hand and a shotgun in the other hand and they had been firing both weapons quite a bit during the past few minutes. Perhaps it was a little late to worry about the attracting attention thing.

Tay stopped at Linda's back door and put a hand on Claire's arm.

"You need to get out of here now. I have absolutely no idea how I could explain who you are or what you're doing here. Hell, I'm not even sure I *know* who you are or what you're doing here." Tay pointed to the park at the end of the alleyway. "Head out that way and cross the canal. I'm sure you can find a taxi—"

"I've got a motorcycle. That's where I left it. You don't think I walked here, do you?"

Claire smiled at Tay and an awkward silence followed.

Shouldn't they at least shake hands or something, Tay wondered? No, that would feel ridiculous.

Perhaps a more personal gesture might be appropriate considering what they had just been through together. A hug, maybe? Tay knew he was overthinking this. But he overthought everything, didn't he?

He decided he would just embarrass himself if he tried to hug Claire. He would probably embarrass her, too.

"Thanks for the backup," he said, and left it at that. "I don't know how this would have all come out without you."

"I only made noise. You did all the hard stuff."

"Tell August hello for me."

"I will."

"And then tell him to fuck off and stay the hell out of my life."

Off in the distance they heard the first faint *wal-wal-wal-wal* of sirens approaching.

Claire got tired of waiting for Tay to hug her so she stepped up, put her arms around him, and gave him a hard squeeze.

"I can't resist a heavily armed man," she laughed.

With the Mossberg in one hand and his .38 in the other, Tay didn't know what to do so he just stood there and let Claire hug him. He supposed the truth was he wouldn't have known what to do whether he had been holding the weapons or not, but having them gave him a way to laugh off his discomfort.

"So long, Sam," Claire said, stepping back.

"Goodbye, Claire."

She turned around and walked rapidly toward the park. She didn't look back, and Tay didn't watch her go.

Tay found a kitchen knife inside and cut Linda loose. As he sawed at the duct tape he told her quickly what had happened. He also told her how important it was that no one know Claire had been there.

When he got most of the duct tape off, Linda started ripping at the rest and in a moment she was standing up and rubbing her wrists.

"How are you going to explain it if someone looked out of a house and saw the two of you out there together?"

"The most they could have seen was a woman carrying a shotgun. They have no way of knowing that was Claire. So for all they—"

"I get it," Linda interrupted. "It wasn't Claire. It was me."

"Yes, it was, wasn't it?"

Tay handed Linda the shotgun. "Let's get back to the body and wait for the fast response cars."

"I just hope I have a minute or two to enjoy knowing the son of a bitch is dead before it gets crowded around here."

Tay and Linda leaned against the wall near Suparman's body to wait. Linda propped the shotgun next to her, and Tay laid his .38 down at his feet. It would be a very bad idea to be holding weapons in their hands when cars full of armed police arrived.

Tay fumbled in his pockets until he found his cigarettes. He shook one from the pack and automatically offered it to Linda. When she took it, he shook out another for himself and lit both of them.

"I didn't know you smoked," Tay said.

"I don't. But I figure this might be a good time to start."

Linda coughed slightly, just once, but then she leaned her head back against the wall and the two of them stood together smoking quietly and listening to the sirens coming closer.

"Maybe I shouldn't say this right now, sir, but I hope you'll consider me when the time comes for a new sergeant to be assigned to you."

"That time's not coming."

"I thought all inspectors in CID—"

"They want me out of CID, Linda."

"Out of CID? You, sir?"

"They've offered me a Deputy Superintendent's job. They're calling it a promotion, but it's an administrative position that has nothing to do with CID."

"Turn it down."

"They say I have to take it, or I have to retire."

Tay drew on his cigarette and exhaled a long stream of smoke.

"The time for people like me is over, Linda. This is no longer a world I understand, or one that understands me."

Linda cleared her throat.

"I'm not sure how to say this, sir, so I'm just going to say it. You saved my life. Thank you. It took a brave man to come in there all by himself and face down Suparman."

"I'm not a brave man."

"How can you—"

"I came in because I'm afraid of my mother. Can you imagine what she would say if I hadn't gotten you out of there in one piece?"

"I thought your mother passed away."

"Yes, she did."

Linda waited in puzzled silence for Tay to explain what he was talking about, but he said nothing else. He just stood there, smoking and listening to the sirens.

The fast response cars were coming closer. Tay and Linda both took out their warrant cards and got ready to hold them up when the first car arrived.

"Do you mind if I ask you just one more thing, sir? Before they get here?"

"No, I don't mind."

"It's that woman. Who is she? I mean, who is she *really*?"

Tay finished his cigarette and thought about how to answer that. When he had taken the last puff, he dropped the butt on the ground and rubbed it out with the toe of his shoe.

At exactly that moment, two fast response cars turned into the top of the street. The melancholy *wal-wal-wal-wal* of their sirens sounded doleful to Tay, like French horns playing the last notes of an elegy. Whether it was an elegy for Suparman's passage to the other side or one for the end of his own times, he couldn't say.

"I honestly don't know who she is, Linda." Tay raised his voice a little so she could hear him over the sirens. "Can we just say she's a girl I saw in a window and leave it at that?"

Then he tilted his head toward Sergeant Lee and gave her a look that was almost, but not exactly, a smile.

THE END

THE AUTHOR

Jake Needham is an American screen and television writer who began writing crime novels when he realized he didn't really like movies and television very much.

Mr. Needham has lived and worked in Hong Kong, Singapore, and Thailand for nearly thirty years. He is a lawyer by education and has held a number of significant positions in both the public and private sectors where he took part in a lengthy list of international operations he has no intention of telling you about. He, his wife, and their two sons now divide their time between homes in Thailand and the United States.

Please visit www.JakeNeedham.com to learn more about Jake Needham's novels and read his 'Letters from Asia' in which he tells his readers about some of the real people, places, and things that appear in his novels.

Inspector Tay #1

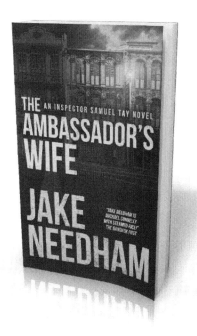

"*THE AMBASSADOR'S WIFE* is another terrific book from a terrific writer. In the genre of crime fiction set in Asia, Jake Needham is in a class of his own."
—*The Bangkok Post*

Inspector Tay #2

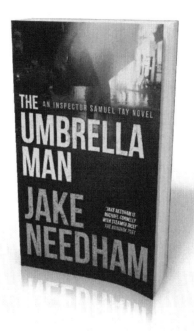

"Readers will empathize with the endearing flawed protagonist as his search for the truth forces him to come to terms with his past. The storyline – full of twists and turns – kept me up all night. This will not be the last time I read a book by Jake Needham."
– *Cosmopolitan Magazine*

Inspector Tay #3

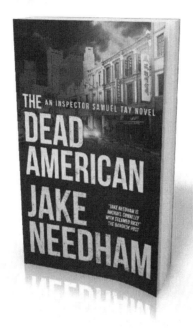

"For Mr. Needham, fiction is not just a good story, but an insight into a country's soul."
– *The New Paper, Singapore*

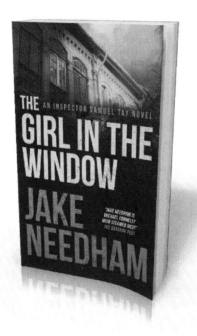

"Needham spins tales rooted in events you already know about, or think you know about, and reveals those events in ways you never even imagined. His prose has a kind of masculine lyricism that is almost quaint in an age of airport bookshelves brimming with the likes of Harold Coben and Robert Ludlum. It's clean, smooth and smart."

– The Bangkok Post

.

Made in the USA
Middletown, DE
05 August 2018